BEST DETECTIVE STORIES OF THE YEAR—1979

33rd Annual Collection

BEST DETECTIVE
STORIES
OF THE YEAR
—1979

33rd Annual Collection

Edited by
Edward D. Hoch

E. P. DUTTON / NEW YORK

For information contact: E.P. Dutton, 2 Park Avenue,
New York, N.Y. 10016

Library of Congress Catalog Card Number: 46-5872

ISBN: 0-525-06438-9

Published simultaneously in Canada by Clarke, Irwin & Company
Limited, Toronto and Vancouver

10 9 8 7 6 5 4 3 2 1

First Edition

For Marjorie and Jerry McMahon

Contents

    From *Alfred Hitchcock's Mystery Magazine*

PATRICIA L. SCHULZE—The Golden Circle   159
    From *Ellery Queen's Mystery Magazine*

EDWARD D. HOCH—Captain Leopold Incognito   167
    From *Ellery Queen's Mystery Magazine*

FRANK SISK—The Leech   185
    From *Fantasy & Science Fiction*

THE YEARBOOK OF THE DETECTIVE STORY   199

    Biography—FRANK SISK   199

    Bibliography   200

    Awards   204

    Necrology   205

    Honor Roll   207

Introduction

I wonder how many readers and collectors of mystery anthologies realize that there exists a growing number of books that may have escaped their attention—anthologies brimming with big names, classic stories, and thoughtful introductions. They aren't advertised or sold to the general public and chances are you won't find them on the shelves at your local library.

I'm speaking of textbooks designed for use in high school or college literature courses. Literature textbooks of forty years ago often included mysteries by Poe, Doyle, and Chesterton, along with the obligatory stories by Hawthorne, O. Henry, and Mark Twain, but the emergence of the textbook containing only detective stories is a recent development. The earliest I've been able to find is a Canadian volume for secondary schools published in 1965: *12 Detective Stories: Their History and Development*, edited by Grant Huffman (Toronto: McClelland and Stewart).

If we limit our definition of mystery textbooks to those that actually follow each story with a section of questions or assignments, at least four more appeared during the 1970s: *Detective Fiction: Crime and Compromise*, edited by Dick Allen and David Chacko (New York: Harcourt Brace Jovanovich, 1974); *Stories of Crime and Detection*, edited by Joan D. Berbrich (New York: McGraw-Hill, 1974); *The Detective Story*, edited by Saul Schwartz (Skokie, Ill.: National Textbook Company, 1975); and *Crimes and Clues*, edited by Stephen P. Clarke (Englewood Cliffs, N.J.: Prentice-Hall, 1978).

To these may be added five other mystery anthologies designed primarily—but not exclusively—for use in school reading programs or courses in the mystery: *Mystery Stories I*, edited by James Higgins (Boston: Houghton Mifflin, 1973); *Thirteen Classic Detective Stories* and *Classic Crime Stories*, both edited by Arthur Liebman (New York: Richards Rosen Press, 1974 and 1975); *Detection*, edited by James Gibson and Alan Ridout (London: John Murray, 1978); and *The World of Mystery Fiction*, edited by Elliot L.

Gilbert (Del Mar, Ca.: Publisher's Inc., 1978). This last is available with a separately bound study guide.

Looking over these ten volumes it's interesting to note that only Arthur Conan Doyle is reprinted in all of them. Edgar Allan Poe, Agatha Christie, and Dorothy L. Sayers appear in seven anthologies. G. K. Chesterton and Ellery Queen can be found in five books each, while Dashiell Hammett is reprinted in four. The most popular story is Doyle's "The Adventure of the Speckled Band," which appears five times. Poe's "The Purloined Letter" is in four books, while Jacques Futrelle's "The Problem of Cell 13" and Harry Kemelman's "The Nine-Mile Walk" are each reprinted three times.

It's not every year that detective stories as memorable as these are published. Yet we can't help feeling that the growing number of mystery texts, reflecting increased interest in the detective story on high school and college campuses, bodes well for the genre. The students reading those books today will, I hope, be the contributors to future volumes in this series.

During 1978 interest in the mystery short story continued to grow. Though there were still only three magazines in the field, a record number of anthologies appeared. Perhaps for the first time the number of stories reprinted in mystery anthologies during the year was greater than the number of new stories published.

The stories I've chosen for this year's volume reflect the wide range of today's mystery-suspense tale, from straight detection through crime to the borders of fantasy. I'm pleased to note that nearly half the selections are detective stories, and I hope this proportion can be maintained in future volumes. The Yearbook section at the back is as complete as possible, though to make the Honor Roll a bit more meaningful I've limited it to one hundred stories.

As always, special thanks are due my wife Patricia, who, along with me, read every one of the 426 new mystery-crime stories published in America during 1978. Thanks too to all who helped with the book, especially Fred Dannay, Eleanor Sullivan, Bill Pronzini, and Frank Sisk.

Edward D. Hoch

BEST DETECTIVE STORIES
OF THE YEAR—1979

33rd Annual Collection

Stephen King is the author of Carrie, Salem's Lot, The Shining, *and* The Stand, *four best-selling novels which have thrust him into the front rank of today's fantasy and horror writers. His frequent short stories are every bit as good, and have been reprinted in* The Year's Best Horror Stories *and* Year's Finest Fantasy. *This story, from his collection* Night Shift, *is one of King's rare non fantasies—a macabre crime tale about an organization that helps people quit smoking. It'll remind you of Roald Dahl at his best.*

STEPHEN KING
Quitters, Inc.

Morrison was waiting for someone who was hung up in the air traffic jam over Kennedy International when he saw a familiar face at the end of the bar and walked down.

"Jimmy? Jimmy McCann?"

It was. A little heavier than when Morrison had seen him at the Atlanta Exhibition the year before, but otherwise he looked awesomely fit. In college he had been a thin, pallid chain smoker buried behind huge horn-rimmed glasses. He had apparently switched to contact lenses.

"Dick Morrison?"

"Yeah. You look great." He extended his hand and they shook.

"So do you," McCann said, but Morrison knew it was a lie. He had been overworking, overeating, and smoking too much. "What are you drinking?"

"Bourbon and bitters," Morrison said. He hooked his feet around a bar stool and lighted a cigarette. "Meeting someone, Jimmy?"

"No. Going to Miami for a conference. A heavy client. Bills six million. I'm supposed to hold his hand because we lost out on a big special next spring."

"Are you still with Crager and Barton?"

"Executive veep now."

"Fantastic! Congratulations! When did all this happen?" He

tried to tell himself that the little worm of jealousy in his stomach was just acid indigestion. He pulled out a roll of antacid pills and crunched one in his mouth.

"Last August. Something happened that changed my life." He looked speculatively at Morrison and sipped his drink. "You might be interested."

My God, Morrison thought with an inner wince. Jimmy McCann's got religion.

"Sure," he said, and gulped at his drink when it came.

"I wasn't in very good shape," McCann said. "Personal problems with Sharon, my dad died—heart attack—and I'd developed this hacking cough. Bobby Crager dropped by my office one day and gave me a fatherly little pep talk. Do you remember what those are like?"

"Yeah." He had worked at Crager and Barton for eighteen months before joining the Morton Agency. "Get your butt in gear or get your butt out."

McCann laughed. "You know it. Well, to put the capper on it, the doc told me I had an incipient ulcer. He told me to quit smoking." McCann grimaced. "Might as well tell me to quit breathing."

Morrison nodded in perfect understanding. Nonsmokers could afford to be smug. He looked at his own cigarette with distaste and stubbed it out, knowing he would be lighting another in five minutes.

"Did you quit?" He asked.

"Yes, I did. At first I didn't think I'd be able to—I was cheating like hell. Then I met a guy who told me about an outfit over on Forty-sixth Street. Specialists. I said what do I have to lose and went over. I haven't smoked since."

Morrison's eyes widened. "What did they do? Fill you full of some drug?"

"No." He had taken out his wallet and was rummaging through it. "Here it is. I knew I had one kicking around." He laid a plain white business card on the bar between them.

QUITTERS, INC.
Stop Going Up in Smoke!
237 East 46th Street
Treatments by Appointment

"Keep it, if you want," McCann said. "They'll cure you. Guaranteed."

"How?"

"I can't tell you," McCann said.

"Huh? Why not?"

"It's part of the contract they make you sign. Anyway, they tell you how it works when they interview you."

"You signed a *contract*?"

McCann nodded.

"And on the basis of that—"

"Yep." He smiled at Morrison, who thought: Well, it's happened. Jim McCann has joined the smug bastards.

"Why the great secrecy if this outfit is so fantastic? How come I've never seen any spots on TV, billboards, magazine ads—"

"They get all the clients they can handle by word of mouth."

"You're an advertising man, Jimmy. You can't believe that."

"I do," McCann said. "They have a ninety-eight percent cure rate."

"Wait a second," Morrison said. He motioned for another drink and lit a cigarette. "Do these guys strap you down and make you smoke until you throw up?"

"No."

"Give you something so that you get sick every time you light—"

"No, it's nothing like that. Go and see for yourself." He gestured at Morrison's cigarette. "You don't really like that, do you?"

"Nooo, but—"

"Stopping really changed things for me," McCann said. "I don't suppose it's the same for everyone, but with me it was just like dominoes falling over. I felt better and my relationship with Sharon improved. I had more energy, and my job performance picked up."

"Look, you've got my curiosity aroused. Can't you just—"

"I'm sorry, Dick. I really can't talk about it." His voice was firm.

"Did you put on any weight?"

For a moment he thought Jimmy McCann looked almost grim.

"Yes. A little too much, in fact. But I took it off again. I'm about right now. I was skinny before."

"Flight 206 now boarding at Gate 9," the loudspeaker announced.

"That's me," McCann said, getting up. He tossed a five on the bar. "Have another, if you like. And think about what I said, Dick. Really." And then he was gone, making his way through the crowd to the escalators. Morrison picked up the card, looked at it thoughtfully, then tucked it away in his wallet and forgot it.

The card fell out of his wallet and onto another bar a month later. He had left the office early and had come here to drink the afternoon away. Things had not been going so well at the Morton Agency. In fact, things were bloody horrible.

He gave Henry a ten to pay for his drink, then picked up the small card and reread it—237 East Forty-sixth Street was only two blocks over; it was a cool, sunny October day outside, and maybe, just for chuckles—

When Henry brought his change, he finished his drink and then went for a walk.

Quitters, Inc., was in a new building where the monthly rent on office space was probably close to Morrison's yearly salary. From the directory in the lobby, it looked to him like their offices took up one whole floor, and that spelled money. Lots of it.

He took the elevator up and stepped off into a lushly carpeted foyer and from there into a gracefully appointed reception room with a wide window that looked out on the scurrying bugs below. Three men and one woman sat in the chairs along the walls, reading magazines. Business types, all of them. Morrison went to the desk.

"A friend gave me this," he said, passing the card to the receptionist. "I guess you'd say he's an alumnus."

She smiled and rolled a form into her typewriter. "What is your name, sir?"

"Richard Morrison."

Clack-clackety-clack. But very muted clacks; the typewriter was an IBM.

"Your address?"

"Twenty-nine Maple Lane, Clinton, New York."

"Married?"

"Yes."

"Children?"

"One." He thought of Alvin and frowned slightly. "One" was the wrong word. "A half" might be better. His son was mentally retarded and lived at a special school in New Jersey.

"Who recommended us to you, Mr. Morrison?"

"An old school friend. James McCann."

"Very good. Will you have a seat? It's been a very busy day."

"All right."

He sat between the woman, who was wearing a severe blue suit, and a young executive type wearing a herringbone jacket and modish sideburns. He took out his pack of cigarettes, looked around, and saw there were no ashtrays.

He put the pack away again. That was all right. He would see this little game through and then light up while he was leaving. He might even tap some ashes on their maroon shag rug if they made him wait long enough. He picked up a copy of *Time* and began to leaf through it.

He was called a quarter of an hour later, after the woman in the blue suit. His nicotine center was speaking quite loudly now. A man who had come in after him took out a cigarette case, snapped it open, saw there were no ashtrays, and put it away—looking a little guilty, Morrison thought. It made him feel better.

At last the receptionist gave him a sunny smile and said, "Go right in, Mr. Morrison."

Morrison walked through the door beyond her desk and found himself in an indirectly lit hallway. A heavyset man with white hair that looked phony shook his hand, smiled affably, and said, "Follow me, Mr. Morrison."

He led Morrison past a number of closed, unmarked doors and then opened one of them about halfway down the hall with a key. Beyond the door was an austere little room walled with drilled white cork panels. The only furnishings were a desk with a chair on either side. There was what appeared to be a small oblong window in the wall behind the desk, but it was covered with a short green curtain. There was a picture on the wall to Morrison's left—a tall man with iron-gray hair. He was holding a sheet of paper in one hand. He looked vaguely familiar.

"I'm Vic Donatti," the heavyset man said. "If you decide to go ahead with our program, I'll be in charge of your case."

"Pleased to know you," Morrison said. He wanted a cigarette very badly.

"Have a seat."

Donatti put the receptionist's form on the desk, and then drew another form from the desk drawer. He looked directly into Morrison's eyes. "Do you want to quit smoking?"

Morrison cleared his throat, crossed his legs, and tried to think of a way to equivocate. He couldn't. "Yes," he said.

"Will you sign this?" He gave Morrison the form. He scanned it quickly. The undersigned agrees not to divulge the methods or techniques or et cetera, et cetera.

"Sure," he said, and Donatti put a pen in his hand. He scratched his name, and Donatti signed below it. A moment later the paper disappeared back into the desk drawer. Well, he thought ironically, I've taken the pledge. He had taken it before. Once it had lasted for two whole days.

"Good," Donatti said. "We don't bother with propaganda here, Mr. Morrison. Questions of health or expense or social grace. We have no interest in why you want to stop smoking. We are pragmatists."

"Good," Morrison said blankly.

"We employ no drugs. We employ no Dale Carnegie people to sermonize you. We recommend no special diet. And we accept no payment until you have stopped smoking for one year."

"My God," Morrison said.

"Mr. McCann didn't tell you that?"

"No."

"How is Mr. McCann, by the way? Is he well?"

"He's fine."

"Wonderful. Excellent. Now . . . just a few questions, Mr. Morrison. These are somewhat personal, but I assure you that your answers will be held in strictest confidence."

"Yes?" Morrison asked noncommittally.

"What is your wife's name?"

"Lucinda Morrison. Her maiden name was Ramsey."

"Do you love her?"

Morrison looked up sharply, but Donatti was looking at him blandly, "Yes, of course," he said.

"Have you ever had marital problems? A separation, perhaps?"

"What has that got to do with kicking the habit?" Morrison asked. He sounded a little angrier than he had intended, but he wanted—hell, he *needed*—a cigarette.

"A great deal," Donatti said. "Just bear with me."

"No. Nothing like that." Although things *had* been a little tense just lately.

"You just have the one child?"

"Yes, Alvin. He's in a private school."

"And which school is it?"

"That," Morrison said grimly, "I'm not going to tell you."

"All right," Donatti said agreeably. He smiled disarmingly at Morrison. "All your questions will be answered tomorrow at your first treatment."

"How nice," Morrison said, and stood.

"One final question," Donatti said. "You haven't had a cigarette for over an hour. How do you feel?"

"Fine," Morrison lied. "Just fine."

"Good for you!" Donatti exclaimed. He stepped around the desk and opened the door. "Enjoy them tonight. After tomorrow, you'll never smoke again."

"Is that right?"

"Mr. Morrison," Donatti said solemnly, "we guarantee it."

He was sitting in the outer office of Quitters, Inc., the next day promptly at three. He had spent most of the day swinging between skipping the appointment the receptionist had made for him on the way out and going in a spirit of mulish cooperation— *Throw your best pitch at me, buster.*

In the end, something Jimmy McCann had said convinced him to keep the appointment—*It changed my whole life.* God knew his own life could do with some changing. And then there was his own curiosity. Before going up in the elevator, he smoked a cigarette down to the filter. Too damn bad if it's the last one, he thought. It tasted horrible.

The wait in the outer office was shorter this time. When the receptionist told him to go in, Donatti was waiting. He offered his hand and smiled, and to Morrison the smile looked almost predatory. He began to feel a little tense, and that made him want a cigarette.

"Come with me," Donatti said, and led the way down to the small room. He sat behind the desk again, and Morrison took the other chair.

"I'm very glad you came," Donatti said. "A great many prospective clients never show up again after the initial interview. They discover they don't want to quit as badly as they thought. It's going to be a pleasure to work with you on this."

"When does the treatment start?" Hypnosis, he was thinking. It must be hypnosis.

"Oh, it already has. It started when we shook hands in the hall. Do you have cigarettes with you, Mr. Morrison?"

"Yes."

"May I have them, please?"

Shrugging, Morrison handed Donatti his pack. There were only two or three left in it, anyway.

Donatti put the pack on the desk. Then, smiling into Morrison's eyes, he curled his right hand into a fist and began to hammer it down on the pack of cigarettes, which twisted and flattened. A broken cigarette end flew out. Tobacco crumbs spilled. The sound of Donatti's fist was very loud in the closed room. The smile remained on his face in spite of the force of the blows, and Morrison was chilled by it. *Probably just the effect they want to inspire,* he thought.

At last Donatti ceased pounding. He picked up the pack, a twisted and battered ruin. "You wouldn't believe the pleasure that gives me," he said, and dropped the pack into the wastebasket. "Even after three years in the business, it still pleases me."

"As a treatment, it leaves something to be desired," Morrison said mildly. "There's a newsstand in the lobby of this very building. And they sell all brands."

"As you say," Donatti said. He folded his hands. "Your son, Alvin Dawes Morrison, is in the Paterson School for Handicapped Children. Born with cranial brain damage. Tested IQ of 46. Not quite in the educable retarded category. Your wife—"

"How did you find that out?" Morrison barked. He was startled and angry. "You've got no goddamn right to go poking around my—"

"We know a lot about you," Donatti said smoothly. "But, as I said, it will all be held in strictest confidence."

"I'm getting out of here," Morrison said thinly. He stood up.

"Stay a bit longer."

Morrison looked at him closely. Donatti wasn't upset. In fact, he looked a little amused. The face of a man who has seen this reaction scores of times—maybe hundreds.

"All right. But it better be good."

"Oh, it is." Donatti leaned back. "I told you we were pragmatists here. As pragmatists, we have to start by realizing how difficult it is to cure an addiction to tobacco. The relapse rate is almost eighty-five percent. The relapse rate for heroin addicts is lower than that. It is an extraordinary problem. *Extraordinary.*"

Morrison glanced into the wastebasket. One of the cigarettes, although twisted, still looked smokable. Donatti laughed good-naturedly, reached into the wastebasket, and broke it between his fingers.

"State legislatures sometimes hear a request that the prison systems do away with the weekly cigarette ration. Such proposals are invariably defeated. In a few cases where they have passed, there have been fierce prison riots. *Riots,* Mr. Morrison. Imagine it."

"I," Morrison said, "am not surprised."

"But consider the implications. When you put a man in prison you take away any normal sex life, you take away his liquor, his politics, his freedom of movement. No riots—or few in comparison to the number of prisons. But when you take away his *cigarettes*—wham! bam!" He slammed his fist on the desk for emphasis.

"During World War I, when no one on the German home front could get cigarettes, the sight of German aristocrats picking butts out of the gutter was a common one. During World War II, many American women turned to pipes when they were unable to obtain cigarettes. A fascinating problem for the true pragmatist, Mr. Morrison."

"Could we get to the treatment?"

"Momentarily. Step over here, please." Donatti had risen and was standing by the green curtains Morrison had noticed yesterday. Donatti drew the curtains, discovering a rectangular window that looked into a bare room. No, not quite bare. There was a rabbit on the floor, eating pellets out of a dish.

"Pretty bunny," Morrison commented.

"Indeed. Watch him." Donatti pressed a button by the windowsill. The rabbit stopped eating and began to hop about crazily. It seemed to leap higher each time its feet struck the floor. Its fur stood out spikily in all directions. Its eyes were wild.

"Stop that! You're electrocuting him!"

Donatti released the button. "Far from it. There's a very low-yield charge in the floor. Watch the rabbit, Mr. Morrison!"

The rabbit was crouched about ten feet away from the dish of pellets. His nose wriggled. All at once he hopped away into a corner.

"If the rabbit gets a jolt often enough while he's eating," Donatti said, "he makes the association very quickly. Eating causes pain. Therefore, he won't eat. A few more shocks, and the rabbit will starve to death in front of his food. It's called aversion training."

Light dawned in Morrison's head.

"No, thanks." He started for the door.

"Wait, please, Mr. Morrison."

Morrison didn't pause. He grasped the doorknob . . . and felt it slip solidly through his hand. "Unlock this."

"Mr. Morrison, if you'll just sit down—"

"Unlock this door or I'll have the cops on you before you can say Marlboro Man."

"*Sit down.*" The voice was as cold as shaved ice.

Morrison looked at Donatti. His brown eyes were muddy and frightening. My God, he thought, I'm locked in here with a psycho. He licked his lips. He wanted a cigarette more than he ever had in his life.

"Let me explain the treatment in more detail," Donatti said.

"You don't understand," Morrison said with counterfeit patience. "I don't want the treatment. I've decided against it."

"No, Mr. Morrison. *You're* the one who doesn't understand. You don't have any choice. When I told you the treatment had already begun, I was speaking the literal truth. I would have thought you'd be tipped to that by now."

"You're crazy," Morrison said wonderingly.

"No. Only a pragmatist. Let me tell you all about the treatment."

"Sure," Morrison said. "As long as you understand that as soon as I get out of here I'm going to buy five packs of cigarettes and smoke them all on the way to the police station." He suddenly realized he was biting his thumbnail, sucking on it, and made himself stop.

"As you wish. But I think you'll change your mind when you see the whole picture."

Morrison said nothing. He sat down again and folded his hands.

"For the first month of the treatment, our operatives will have you under constant supervision," Donatti said. "You'll be able to spot some of them. Not all. But they'll always be with you. *Always.* If they see you smoke a cigarette, I get a call."

"And I suppose you bring me here and do the old rabbit trick," Morrison said. He tried to sound cold and sarcastic, but he suddenly felt horribly frightened. This was a nightmare.

"Oh, no," Donatti said. "Your wife gets the rabbit trick, not you."

Morrison looked at him dumbly.

Donatti smiled. "You," he said, "get to watch."

After Donatti let him out, Morrison walked for over two hours in a complete daze. It was another fine day, but he didn't notice. The monstrousness of Donatti's smiling face blotted out all else.

"You see," he had said, "a pragmatic problem demands pragmatic solutions. You must realize we have your best interests at heart."

Quitters, Inc., according to Donatti, was a sort of foundation—a nonprofit organization begun by the man in the wall portrait. The gentleman had been extremely successful in several family businesses—including slot machines, massage parlors, numbers, and a brisk (although clandestine) trade between New York and Turkey. Mort "Three-Fingers" Minelli had been a heavy smoker—up in the three-pack-a-day range. The paper he was holding in the picture was a doctor's diagnosis: lung cancer. Mort had died in 1970, after endowing Quitters, Inc., with family funds.

"We try to keep as close to breaking even as possible," Donatti had said, "But we're more interested in helping our fellow man. And of course, it's a great tax angle."

The teatment was chillingly simple. A first offense and Cindy would be brought to what Donatti called "the rabbit room." A second offense, and Morrison would get the dose. On a third offense, both of them would be brought in together. A fourth offense would show grave cooperation problems and would require sterner measures. An operative would be sent to Alvin's school to work the boy over.

"Imagine," Donatti said, smiling, "how horrible it will be for the boy. He wouldn't understand it even if someone explained. He'll only know someone is hurting him because Daddy was bad. He'll be very frightened."

"You bastard," Morrison said helplessly. He felt close to tears. "You dirty, filthy bastard."

"Don't misunderstand," Donatti said. He was smiling sympathetically. "I'm sure it won't happen. Forty percent of clients never have to be disciplined at all—and only ten percent have more than three falls from grace. Those are reassuring figures, aren't they?"

Morrison didn't find them reassuring. He found them terrifying.

"Of course, if you transgress a *fifth* time—"

"What do you mean?"

Donatti beamed. "The room for you and your wife, a second beating for your son, and a beating for your wife."

Morrison, driven beyond the point of rational consideration, lunged over the desk at Donatti. Donatti moved with amazing speed for a man who had apparently been completely relaxed. He shoved the chair backward and drove both of his feet over the desk and into Morrison's belly. Gagging and coughing, Morrison staggered backward.

"Sit down, Mr. Morrison," Donatti said benignly. "Let's talk this over like rational men."

When he could get his breath, Morrison did as he was told. Nightmares had to end sometime, didn't they?

Quitters, Inc., Donatti had explained further, operated on a ten-step punishment scale. Steps six, seven, and eight consisted of further trips to the rabbit room (and increased voltage) and more serious beatings. The ninth step would be the breaking of his son's arms.

"And the tenth?" Morrison asked, his mouth dry.

Donatti shook his head sadly. "Then we give up, Mr. Morrison. You become part of the unregenerate two percent."

"You really give up?"

"In a manner of speaking." He opened one of the desk drawers and laid a silenced .45 on the desk. He smiled into Morrison's eyes. "But even the unregenerate two percent never smoke again. We guarantee it."

The Friday Night Movie was *Bullitt,* one of Cindy's favorites, but after an hour of Morrison's mutterings and fidgetings, her concentration was broken.

"What's the matter with you?" she asked during station identification.

"Nothing . . . everything," he growled. "I'm giving up smoking."

She laughed. "Since when? Five minutes ago?"

"Since three o'clock this afternoon."

"You really haven't had a cigarette since then?"

"No," he said, and began to gnaw his thumbnail. It was ragged, down to the quick.

"That's wonderful! What ever made you decide to quit?"

"You," he said. "And . . . and Alvin."

Her eyes widened, and when the movie came back on, she didn't notice. Dick rarely mentioned their retarded son. She came over, looked at the empty ashtray by his right hand, and then into his eyes. "Are you really trying to quit, Dick?"

"Really." And if I go to the cops, he added mentally, the local goon squad will be around to rearrange your face, Cindy.

"I'm glad. Even if you don't make it, we both thank you for the thought, Dick."

"Oh, I think I'll make it," he said, thinking of the muddy, homicidal look that had come into Donatti's eyes when he kicked him in the stomach.

He slept badly that night, dozing in and out of sleep. Around three o'clock he woke up completely. His craving for a cigarette was like a low-grade fever. He went downstairs and to his study. The room was in the middle of the house. No windows. He slid open the top drawer of his desk and looked in, fascinated by the cigarette box. He looked around and licked his lips.

Constant supervision during the first month, Donatti had said. Eighteen hours a day during the next two—but he would never know *which* eighteen. During the fourth month, the month when most clients backslid, the "service" would return to twenty-four hours a day. Then twelve hours of broken surveillance each day for the rest of the year. After that? Random surveillance for the rest of the client's life.

For the rest of his life.

"We may audit you every other month," Donatti said. "Or every other day. Or constantly for one week two years from now. The point is, *you won't know.* If you smoke, you'll be gambling with loaded dice. Are they watching? Are they picking up my wife or sending a man after my son right now? Beautiful, isn't it? And if you do sneak a smoke, it'll taste awful. It will taste like your son's blood."

But they couldn't be watching now, in the dead of night, in his own study. The house was grave-quiet.

He looked at the cigarettes in the box for almost two minutes, unable to tear his gaze away. Then he went to the study door, peered out into the empty hall, and went back to look at the cigarettes some more. A horrible picture came: his life stretching before him and not a cigarette to be found. How in the name of God was he ever going to be able to make another tough presentation to a wary client, without that cigarette burning nonchalantly between his fingers as he approached the charts and layouts? How would he be able to endure Cindy's endless garden shows without a cigarette? How could he even get up in the morning and face the day without a cigarette to smoke as he drank his coffee and read the paper?

He cursed himself for getting into this. He cursed Donatti. And most of all, he cursed Jimmy McCann. How could he have done it? The son of a bitch had *known*. His hands trembled in their desire to get hold of Jimmy Judas McCann.

Stealthily, he glanced around the study again. He reached into the drawer and brought out a cigarette. He caressed it, fondled it. What was that old slogan? *So round, so firm, so fully packed.* Truer words had never been spoken. He put the cigarette in his mouth and then paused, cocking his head.

Had there been the slightest noise from the closet? A faint shifting? Surely not. But—

Another mental image—that rabbit hopping crazily in the grip of electricity. The thought of Cindy in that room—

He listened desperately and heard nothing. He told himself that all he had to do was go to the closet door and yank it open. But he was too afraid of what he might find. He went back to bed but didn't sleep for a long time.

In spite of how lousy he felt in the morning, breakfast tasted good. After a moment's hesitation, he followed his customary bowl of cornflakes with scrambled eggs. He was grumpily washing out the pan when Cindy came downstairs in her robe.

"Richard Morrison! You haven't eaten an egg for breakfast since Hector was a pup."

Morrison grunted. He considered *since Hector was a pup* to be one of Cindy's stupider sayings, on a par with *I should smile and kiss a pig.*

"Have you smoked yet?" she asked, pouring orange juice.

"No."

"You'll be back on them by noon," she proclaimed airily.

"Lot of goddamn help you are!" he rasped, rounding on her. "You and anyone else who doesn't smoke, you all think . . . ah, never mind."

He expected her to be angry, but she was looking at him with something like wonder. "You're really serious," she said. "You really are."

"You bet I am." *You'll never know how serious. I hope.*

"Poor baby," she said, going to him. "You look like death warmed over. But I'm very proud."

Morrison held her tightly.

Scenes from the life of Richard Morrison, October–November: Morrison and a crony from Larkin Studios at Jack Dempsey's bar. Crony offers a cigarette. Morrison grips his glass a little more tightly and says: *I'm quitting.* Crony laughs and says: *I give you a week.*

Morrison waiting for the morning train, looking over the top of the *Times* at a young man in a blue suit. He sees the young man almost every morning now, and sometimes at other places. At Onde's, where he is meeting a client. Looking at 45s in Sam Goody's, where Morrison is looking for a Sam Cooke album. Once in a foursome behind Morrison's group at the local golf course.

Morrison getting drunk at a party, wanting a cigarette—but not quite drunk enough to take one.

Morrison visiting his son, bringing him a large ball that squeaked when you squeezed it. His son's slobbering, delighted kiss. Somehow not as repulsive as before. Hugging his son tightly, realizing what Donatti and his colleagues had so cynically realized before him: love is the most pernicious drug of all. Let the romantics debate its existence. Pragmatists accept it and use it.

Morrison losing the physical compulsion to smoke little by little, but never quite losing the psychological craving, or the need to have something in his mouth—cough drops, Life Savers, a toothpick. Poor substitutes, all of them.

And finally, Morrison hung up in a colossal traffic jam in the Midtown Tunnel. Darkness. Horns blaring. Air stinking. Traffic hopelessly snarled. And suddenly, thumbing open the glove compartment and seeing the half-open pack of cigarettes in there. He looked at them for a moment, then snatched one and lit it with the dashboard lighter. If anything happens, it's Cindy's fault, he told himself defiantly. I told her to get rid of all the damn cigarettes.

The first drag made him cough smoke out furiously. The second made his eyes water. The third made him feel lightheaded and swoony. It tastes awful, he thought.

And on the heels of that: My God, what am I doing?

Horns blatted impatiently behind him. Ahead, the traffic had begun to move again. He stubbed the cigarette out in the ashtray, opened both front windows, opened the vents, and then fanned the air helplessly like a kid who has just flushed his first butt down the john.

He joined the traffic flow jerkily and drove home.

"Cindy?" he called. "I'm home."

No answer.

"Cindy? Where are you, hon?"

The phone rang, and he pounced on it. "Hello? Cindy?"

"Hello, Mr. Morrison," Donatti said. He sounded pleasantly brisk and businesslike. "It seems we have a small business matter to attend to. Would five o'clock be convenient?"

"Have you got my wife?"

"Yes, indeed." Donatti chuckled indulgently.

"Look, let her go," Morrison babbled. "It won't happen again. It was a slip, just a slip, that's all. I only had three drags and for God's sake *it didn't even taste good!*"

"That's a shame. I'll count on you for five then, shall I?"

"Please," Morrison said, close to tears. "Please—"

He was speaking to a dead line.

At 5 P.M. the reception room was empty except for the secretary, who gave him a twinkly smile that ignored Morrison's pallor and disheveled appearance. "Mr. Donatti?" she said into the intercom. "Mr. Morrison to see you." She nodded to Morrison. "Go right in."

Donatti was waiting outside the unmarked room with a man who was wearing a SMILE sweatshirt and carying a .38. He was built like an ape.

"Listen," Morrison said to Donatti. "We can work something out, can't we? I'll pay you. I'll—"

"Shaddap," the man in the SMILE sweatshirt said.

"It's good to see you," Donatti said. "Sorry it has to be under such adverse circumstances. Will you come with me? We'll make this as brief as possible. I can assure you your wife won't be hurt . . . this time."

Morrison tensed himself to leap at Donatti.

"Come, come," Donatti said, looking annoyed. "If you do that, Junk here is going to pistol-whip you and your wife is still going to get it. Now where's the percentage in that?"

"I hope you rot in hell," he told Donatti.

Donatti sighed. "If I had a nickel for every time someone expressed a similar sentiment, I could retire. Let it be a lesson to you, Mr. Morrison. When a romantic tries to do a good thing and fails, they give him a medal. When a pragmatist succeeds, they wish him in hell. Shall we go?"

Junk motioned with the pistol.

Morrison preceded them into the room. He felt numb. The small green curtain had been pulled. Junk prodded him with the gun. This is what being a witness at the gas chamber must have been like, he thought.

He looked in. Cindy was there, looking around bewilderedly.

"Cindy!" Morrison called miserably. "Cindy, they—"

"She can't hear or see you," Donatti said. "One-way glass. Well, let's get it over with. It really was a very small slip. I believe thirty seconds should be enough. Junk?"

Junk pressed the button with one hand and kept the pistol jammed firmly into Morrison's back with the other.

It was the longest thirty seconds of his life.

When it was over, Donatti put a hand on Morrison's shoulder and said, "Are you going to throw up?"

"No," Morrison said weakly. His forehead was against the glass. His legs were jelly. "I don't think so." He turned around and saw that Junk was gone.

"Come with me," Donatti said.

"Where?" Morrison asked apathetically.

"I think you have a few things to explain, don't you?"

"How can I face her? How can I tell her that I . . . I . . ."

"I think you're going to be surprised," Donatti said.

The room was empty except for a sofa. Cindy was on it, sobbing helplessly.

"Cindy?" he said gently.

She looked up, her eyes magnified by tears. "Dick?" she whispered. "Dick? Oh . . . Oh God . . ." He held her tightly. "Two men," she said against his chest. "In the house and at first I thought they were burglars and then I thought they were going to rape me and then they took me someplace with a blindfold over my eyes and . . . and . . . oh it was *h-horrible*—"

"Shhh," he said. "Shhh."

"But why?" she asked, looking up at him. "Why would they—"

"Because of me," he said. "I have to tell you a story, Cindy—"

When he had finished he was silent a moment and then said, "I suppose you hate me. I wouldn't blame you."

He was looking at the floor, and she took his face in both hands and turned it to hers. "No," she said. "I don't hate you."

He looked at her in mute surprise.

"It was worth it," she said. "God bless these people. They've let you out of prison."

"Do you mean that?"

"Yes," she said, and kissed him. "Can we go home now? I feel much better. Ever so much."

The phone rang one evening a week later, and when Morrison recognized Donatti's voice, he said, "Your boys have got it wrong. I haven't even been near a cigarette."

"We know that. We have a final matter to talk over. Can you stop by tomorrow afternoon?"

"Is it—"

"No, nothing serious. Bookkeeping really. By the way, congratulations on your promotion."

"How did you know about that?"

"We're keeping tabs," Donatti said noncommittally, and hung up.

When they entered the small room, Donatti said, "Don't look so nervous. No one's going to bite you. Step over here, please."

Morrison saw an ordinary bathroom scale. "Listen, I've gained a little weight, but—"

"Yes, seventy-three percent of our clients do. Step up, please."

Morrison did, and tipped the scales at one-seventy-four.

"Okay, fine. You can step off. How tall are you, Mr. Morrison?"

"Five-eleven."

"Okay, let's see." He pulled a small card laminated in plastic from his breast pocket. "Well, that's not too bad. I'm going to write you a prescription for some highly illegal diet pills. Use them sparingly and according to directions. And I'm going to set your maximum weight at . . . let's see . . ." He consulted the card again. "One-eighty-two, how does that sound? And since this is December first, I'll expect you the first of every month for a weigh-in. No problem if you can't make it, as long as you call in advance."

"And what happens if I go over one-eighty-two?"

Donatti smiled. "We'll send someone out to your house to cut off your wife's little finger," he said. "You can leave through this door, Mr. Morrison. Have a nice day."

Eight months later:

Morrison runs into the crony from the Larkin Studios at Dempsey's bar. Morrison is down to what Cindy proudly calls his fighting weight: one sixty-seven. He works out three times a week and looks as fit as a whipcord. The crony from Larkin, by comparison, looks like something the cat dragged in.

Crony: Lord, how'd you ever stop? I'm locked into this damn habit tighter than Tillie. The crony stubs his cigarette out with real revulsion and drains his scotch.

Morrison looks at him speculatively and then takes a small white business card out of his wallet. He puts it on the bar between them. You know, he says, these guys changed my life.

Twelve months later:
Morrison receives a bill in the mail. The bill says:

QUITTERS, INC.
237 East 46th Street
New York, N.Y. 10017

1 Treatment	$2500.00
Counselor (Victor Donatti)	$2500.00
Electricity	$ .50
TOTAL (Please pay this amount)	$5000.50

Those sons of bitches! he explodes. They charged me for the electricity they used to . . . to . . .

Just pay it, she says, and kisses him.

Twenty months later:
Quite by accident, Morrison and his wife meet the Jimmy McCanns at the Helen Hayes Theatre. Introductions are made all around. Jimmy looks as good, if not better than he did on that day in the airport terminal so long ago. Morrison has never met his wife. She is pretty in the radiant way plain girls sometimes have when they are very, very happy.

She offers her hand and Morrison shakes it. There is something odd about her grip, and halfway through the second act, he realizes what it was. The little finger on her right hand is missing.

A recent phenomenon of magazine publishing is the appearance of municipal periodicals, devoted to the life-style of a particular urban area and not usually sold on a national basis. Such magazines generally use little fiction, but the quarterly Buffalo Spree *is the exception, publishing several short stories in each issue. The subject matter is not confined to the Buffalo, N.Y., area, as can be seen in this fine suspenseful tale of a paradise gone wrong. Zena Collier has published juvenile books and a number of excellent short stories in magazines like* The Literary Review *and* Southwest Review. *Her appearances in the suspense field are all too rare, though she has been published in* Alfred Hitchcock's Mystery Magazine *and in a Hitchcock anthology.*

ZENA COLLIER
Little Paradise

There was no longer any doubt about it; they were lost. This was their first time on the creek from which this maze of narrow waterways derived, winding around in convoluted curves, dotted at frequent intervals with tiny uninhabited islands, all of which looked alike. A friend had recommended the area. "Great for canoeing. Pleasing prospects at every turn. None of those damn speedboats and water-skiers." For the past hour, in fact, they had seen no other boats at all: no canoes or dinghies, no cabin cruisers with their seemingly mandatory quota of bluff types wearing commodore hats, holding martini glasses or beer. (Earlier that day, one such, at sight of their canoe, had leaned over the rail, hollering at them, flapping a hand back and forth against his mouth to produce what was meant to be an Indian war whoop. "Hey, you Tarzan, she Jane, huh?" Laughter.)

"What time is it getting to be?" Peter asked.

"Just gone five." Frances rested her paddle for a moment.

They had been out since ten. All day the sun had shone from a cloudless sky, dappling the leaves of the branches that dipped over the water, stippling the water with shade. Insects with gossamer wings hummed past. Occasionally the *ts, ts, ts* of a cedar waxwing, the dry rattle of a kingfisher, broke the silence. Otherwise all was still.

It was the kind of day on which they congratulated themselves on their acquisition of the canoe. For people of their tastes and principles, the canoe had proved an ideal choice. It offered no disturbance, by noise or pollution, to its passengers or to nature; it required no particular skill, maintenance, or expensive berthing. Best of all, it made easily possible days of escape from the tensions of their everyday lives. Peter, a thin dark man with a face all angles, was a graphics designer who had recently left his agency job to free-lance. Frances, redhaired, with a pleasant down-to-earth manner, was a social worker attached to one of the great metropolitan hospitals. For both of them, a Saturday spent this way brought a necessary renewal of the spirit.

It was with regret that they'd decided at four o'clock to start for home. They were due at a party at seven; it was going to take them a while to paddle back to the point of starting, then the drive home would take the better part of an hour. So they had turned around and headed back, stroking steadily. Until they'd become aware, suddenly, that they had passed the same spot twice; they recognized it because of an uprooted tree which lay in the water, its exposed roots forming a natural driftwood sculpture upon which someone had tossed, or placed, a beer can. ("Look at that," Frances had said earlier, shaking her head. The trappings of *their* mid-day meal—paper plates, napkins, the bottle emptied of wine—had been carefully stowed in a paper bag and replaced in the canoe, to be properly disposed of on their arrival home.)

"We must have gone in a circle," Frances said.

"Keep going left. We'll hit the creek further on."

They resumed paddling.

"Are you tired?" Peter asked, after a while.

"No." In fact, she had begun to ache between the shoulder-blades, but she knew that if she said so, Peter would suggest putting on the motor and she didn't want that.

When he had first bought the motor, she had been very much against it. An outboard on a canoe was surely a contradiction? But there was a point to it, Peter maintained. "We'll use it just to reach the outskirts of more remote areas, then take it off." Still, the sound of the engine starting up always jarred her unpleasantly, and ruined, she felt, the peace; she disapproved, too, of the trail of blue smoke it occasionally emitted, though Peter said that was just a matter of some needed adjustment.

"That island over there, with the willows, did we pass it before?"

"I don't know. They all look alike. Can't you tell from the sun?"

"I *thought* I could." He sounded exasperated.

"We're never going to make the Robsons' by seven."

Minutes later, the sound of the engine cut the still air, and they were moving along at a steady rate. But with little success. "We passed this before. I remember those sumacs . . ."

"Yes," Peter said wearily. "Now what?"

"Let's try over there." Frances pointed. "There was an inlet. Perhaps it leads somewhere."

The inlet narrowed after the first few yards, the banks growing gradually higher and closer. Soon the trees met overhead in a solid archway, the foliage forming a verdant tunnel as the passage between grew narrower and narrower.

Frances shivered. How dark it seemed, and cold. . . . Had the sun gone permanently, or was it just—

"We're coming out!"

Abruptly they were out of the dimness, out of the tunnel, finding themselves on a sunlit lake, a pond, really, perhaps a hundred yards across, with shallow sloping banks covered with woodland.

"Look!"

Across the pond was a house set almost at the water's edge, and beside it a redwood table where people sat, adults and children.

"Thank heaven! We can ask directions."

The people watched as the canoe put-putted across the pond toward them. In the still and sunlit scene, the motor sounded terribly loud. A desecration, Frances thought, regretting it, sorry not only to be invading these people's privacy but to be disturbing the peace of this serene spot.

But the adults—two women and two men—smiled at them as the canoe approached. Peter idled the motor, then reached out and kept his hand on the bank, steadying the canoe as he talked.

"Sorry to disturb you, but we're lost. How do we get back to the start of Forked Creek?"

One of the men stood up and approached. "You're a long way off. It'll take you quite a while."

"Not with this." Peter nodded at the motor. But just then, as though on cue, the motor died. "Damn! Out of gas, I'm afraid. Can you by any chance let me have some fuel?"

"Sorry, we haven't any. We've no cars or powerboats or any such thing."

The others came over. The men admired the canoe and asked questions about the motor; they said they hadn't seen a motor on a canoe before. The children—a boy and girl in their early teens, and a little girl who seemed about five—stood watching and listening. The little girl said shyly, "I'm glad you're going to stay."

One of the women rumpled the child's blond curly hair. "This is my daughter Cassandra—Cassie."

Frances smiled at Cassie, an engaging child with sturdy, golden-brown baby-fat limbs. The whole group, in fact, was glowing with health, tanned by sun and wind; the women's dimpling smiles showed white even teeth; the men were tall, broad-shouldered, muscular, friendly.

"Would you care to join us for something to eat?" the other woman asked. "We're just starting dinner."

"Please do," Cassie's mother urged. "Just family style. I'm Amy Carner, by the way, and this is my husband Robert, and his brother Martin and Martin's wife, Lorraine. And their twins, Andy and Jennifer."

"Do stay," Lorraine said. "Food'll give you energy for the return trip home. We'd love to have you."

"Yes, we would," Martin said.

Peter glanced at Frances. "We wouldn't want to impose—"

"No imposition at all," Robert said. "We don't get many visitors. Just, occasionally, people like yourselves, who end up here lost."

"Thtay, thtay," Cassie pleaded, finger in her mouth.

Frances's eyes met Peter's. The smell of meat cooking on the outdoor fireplace wafted over enticingly. They had eaten nothing at all for hours. And the Robsons were a lost cause by now.

"That's awfully kind of you. If you're sure—"

For answer, Robert bent down and pulled the canoe in to the bank. Martin put out a hand and helped Frances alight. Lorraine took them into the house to wash up.

Outside again, at the table, Frances realized just how hungry she was. She and Peter ate with enormous appetite. All the food was delicious: the salads and corn were homegrown; the steaks and hots were the best she'd ever tasted, Frances thought, and said so.

"This is a beautiful spot . . ." She glanced at the pond lying still as glass beneath the sun, at the greenness of the trees reflected in the water. No sign, besides themselves, of human habitation;

nothing to spoil or disturb the scene's tranquility. "It must be lovely here in winter, too. Do you live here all year round?" she asked.

Amy nodded. It was like a Christmas card scene in winter, she said, when the pond froze and snow lay on the woods and the hills beyond.

"Though lately some rackety snowmobiles have come through." Martin sliced more meat and proffered the platter. "A couple of 'em came to a sticky end near here. Ever ridden one?"

"Not I." Peter took a bite of steak.

"Hate them," Frances said. "Fouling up the countryside."

Robert gave her a glance. "Yet you put on a motor—"

"That," Peter said, "was my idea. Fran was against it. But we only use it for certain contingencies."

"We've a rowboat, ourselves." Martin speared another sausage. Lorraine passed potato salad.

"We do what we can, in our way, to preserve—"

"In our small way," Amy said. "Meat? Tomatoes, Peter? Frances?"

Not another thing, they protested, smiling, not another morsel of steak or succulent sausage, sun-warm tomato or butter-clad corn.

For dessert there was cherry pie with iced tea.

"Delicious." Peter sipped the cool amber liquid. "Different."

Yes, it was an herbal tea, Amy said, her own recipe.

Frances drank hers slowly, leaving half—she'd never liked any kind of tea.

The sun lay low on the horizon now. Frances and Peter helped carry things into the house.

Andy and Jennifer appeared with fishing rods. "Where's the boat?"

"Being caulked," Robert said. "You can't take it."

"Oh." Andy turned to Peter. "Would it be O.K. if we use your canoe? They bite better out in the middle of the pond."

Peter hesitated. "We have to be getting along pretty soon."

Very soon, Frances thought; the canoe had no light, and being out on the water at night was not an inviting prospect.

"Is twenty minutes any good to you?"

"Great," Andy said. "Thanks a lot."

Cassie slipped her hand into Frances's. "Come and play with me."

"What shall we play?"

"I'll show you."

Cassie led her outdoors, round to the other side of the house. On a small patch of flagstone, she demonstrated a game played with coins, using the coins as play objects—a kind of Pitch Penny. She had a large stock of coins, of all denominations, kept in what was obviously an old purse of her mother's.

Once, as they played, a quarter pitched clumsily by Frances ended up in the grass. They searched but to no avail. "I'm sorry, Cassie."

"It doesn't matter. It's only game money."

"But—"

"I'll get more," Cassie said. "There's more when I want it. Daddy gives it to me."

They played several games. By now the house glimmered palely through the dusk; the shadows of evening were thickening everywhere.

Frances straightened. "That's it, Cassie. I have to go home now."

Cassie did not argue, just stood silent, finger in her mouth, as Frances turned and went in search of Peter.

She found him on the bank, with the others, looking out over the water. "Peter, shouldn't we—"

"Yes, we have to be getting along." He turned to the others. "We're very grateful for all your hospitality."

"You've been so kind," Frances said. "That marvelous din-ner . . . this idyllic setting. Thank you for letting us share your little paradise."

"Must you rush off?"

"How about a drink? One for the road, as it were?"

They really had to get going, Peter said. "But thank you again, for everything."

Martin cupped his hands around his mouth. "Andy! Jennifer!" His voice rang across the dark mass of water. "Come along! Our guests are leaving!"

By now the youngsters were almost completely invisible. Andy's voice, floating back, seemed disembodied. "Just a min-ute—something's biting!"

Frances glanced at Peter, who shrugged. Clearly they would have to wait; they could hardly spoil the children's fun after accepting their parents' gracious hospitality.

"You see, you'll just have to come in for a nightcap." Martin's hand descended on Peter's shoulder.

They sat around the living room, sipping a liqueur that Robert had poured. Not the sort of thing Frances liked usually—and Peter, she knew, didn't care for it at all—an elderberry wine, or something like that, that Robert had made.

It must be the wine, combined with the rigors of the day, that was making her feel so sleepy now, she thought; it took a huge effort to keep her eyelids open. Seconds later, in fact, she saw with dismay that Peter, slumped on the sofa flanked by Robert and Martin, had yielded; his eyes were closed, his head tilted forward.

Dreadful! She began to stammer some kind of apology for their drowsiness. But where, oh where, were Andy and Jennifer? How could they go on fishing in the darkness like that, especially when they knew the canoe was needed?

As though the thought had given birth to the event, they appeared, carrying fishing gear. She tried to stand, to speak, but her legs were suddenly weak, her vision blurred, her thoughts addled.

Now her head sank irresistibly forward. But though her eyes closed she was not quite asleep, for she heard voices. Or was she in fact asleep and dreaming; were the voices part of the dream?

Not the woman. It wasn't her idea. That was Lorraine.

She's in it just as deeply as him.

Only a canoe . . .

But the motor . . . That was Robert.

On and on it went, a kind of debate. Parts of it she missed, as consciousness seemed to ebb and flow, the line lost between dream and reality.

Look. That was Andy. *We found these.*

Silence.

You see? Lorraine again. *They could have tossed that bottle, that trash, overboard. I vote we let them go. Anyway*—Someone walked across the room, drowning out the voice—*hardly worth it . . . not particularly large . . .*

Large . . . The canoe? "Let them go?"

Fear began at the edge of awareness, working inward like a worm in an apple.

Hush, she's stirring!

Someone approached, touched her, spoke her name. She let her head slump further forward.

Not she. They're out, both of them.

I want the money. That was Cassie, whining. *She lost one of my quarters.*

Goodness, child, you ought to be in bed! Amy, take her upstairs, it's long past her bedtime.

Be a good girl, Cassie, someone else said. *You'll get the money. You always do, don't you?*

Thieves, then? Common robbers, lying in wait for unwary boaters? But—

Complimented me on the way I cooked the steaks . . .

Laughter.

That was funny? The steaks?

A memory: the sight of the meat invitingly singed by the fire. The sausages. "We make them, ourselves," Amy had said.

Her thoughts spun like a Catherine wheel. Her heart pounded harder and harder—surely it would burst the flesh that housed it. Flesh.

Oh God, she must be sick to be thinking this way, as sick as the rest of them, every one of them, the whole picturebook family with the bloom of health, the radiance of summer, upon them. Summer . . . And what of winter, the hapless snowmobile riders? Thought stopped at the unthinkable, ran screaming in the other direction. A dream, yes, a nightmare. Any moment now she would awake to see sunlight coming in the bedroom window, would get up, start breakfast, make plans with Peter for their day on the water.

All right. We've talked long enough. Robert cleared his throat.

No denying that sound—the reality of it. The reality of their situation, hers and Peter's, here and now. Oh God, Peter, wake up! Though what could they do, even then, the two of them, trapped here? A diversion? What could take their attention, if only for a moment? But they would need, she and Peter, more than a moment to reach the canoe, then get away, paddling, across the water. Unless they left the canoe and tried through the woods. But—

A door slammed. A voice said excitedly, "Dad! Andy! Everybody, come out here!" The girl, Jennifer.

There was a rush of movement, footsteps, the door slammed again, then silence.

A hiss: "Fran!"

She opened her eyes, to meet Peter's. The room was empty except for themselves.

"Did you hear—?"

"Yes! What shall we do?"

They're coming back! Play dead!"

The door opened again. There were hurrying footsteps, whispers. Robert's voice said, "Shake them, get them up! Hurry!"

A hand on her shoulder shook her, hard.

"Wake up, Frances! Peter! Time to go home. It's getting late." The tone was friendly, just the least bit urgent. "Sleepy? You'll be all right once you're outside."

What was this? For now, dazed, they were being led outside, urged along, hastened down to the canoe in the moonless night. Thick darkness . . . "You'll want to hurry . . . It's getting late. The long day must have been too much for you . . . sleeping like babies. . . ."

Was that all it really was, after all? They had fallen asleep after the meal; it had all been a product of too much food and drink and fatigue?

They were in the canoe now, in the water, helped in by Martin and Lorraine. The canoe rocked. Robert steadied it carefully, placed paddles in their trembling hands. "Owe you an apology . . . motor's gone, I'm afraid. Andy and Jenny were fooling around . . . sank like a stone."

"Never mind!" Peter's voice was almost a croak. "Doesn't matter!"

They were off, paddling like demons, shivering, shivering in the sharp night air.

"To the left . . ." Martin's voice floated after them. "After you're through Scylla and Charybdis, go right three times, then left at the uprooted tree. You'll see it."

They would, for now a moon emerged from the clouds, painting the scene with a frozen light.

"What happened?" Frances whispered.

"God knows! Keep going!"

The canoe cut swiftly across the water. But as the darkness of the tunnel yawned before them, Frances hesitated, turned, and saw a cabin cruiser pulling close to shore, several figures on deck. A voice floated across the water. " . . . don't know how we could have missed our way like that . . ."

"We must warn them, Peter! We have to warn them!"

He pushed her around. "Keep going. There's nothing we can do."

In the blackness of the tunnel, the only sound was the soft *slap* of the paddles dipping in the water, while from somewhere far away came the high, screeching giggle of a loon.

When an author writes a story about a private eye and titles it "The Man in the Lake," after Chandler's classic The Lady in the Lake, *it had better be good! Happily, Ernest Savage's stories about private detective Sam Train are very good indeed. They've begun to appear regularly in* Ellery Queen's Mystery Magazine *and* Alfred Hitchcock's Mystery Magazine, *and they're always a treat. This is one of the best.*

ERNEST SAVAGE
The Man in the Lake

I have always thought the lake dwarfs the mountains around it. It is such a noble water it should have a more noble frame, more Alpine—a Matterhorn on one side, an Eiger on the other, as accent points. But God listens when you quibble over Tahoe's beauty. . . .

It does not invite man's rapacious participation. Its waters are frigid all year round, its beach is of hard-edged stone. An empty beer can within a mile of it is a special abomination, and there must be ten million of them by now. It's 1,600 feet deep, but it's already filling with the detritus of man's passing parade, his offal, his stink. Twelve million years in the making, we'll have it beat dead in another century. It cannot take us. Tahoe.

They lived in a 7,000-square-foot house—the two of them, plus a maid. You probably live in 1,400 square feet, you and the wife and four kids. And cat and dog. She had something made of white fur on her lap, but she didn't tell me what it was and I didn't ask. It breathed, but it neither purred nor barked. She was seated on a couch a quarter mile long in front of the windows overlooking the lake. Mrs. Wilson. The maid had put me down in a chair that gave me a view of her against the spread of the lake and its low embracing hills. I'd just spent four hours getting there from San Francisco and I was in one of those moods where the customer is always wrong; but mine generally are, anyway.

A lawyer named Marcus had hired me yesterday morning, Thursday, to come up and help Mrs. Wilson find her missing husband, Bill. The lawyer had asked me to meet him in a dimly lit bar around the corner from my place on Van Ness Avenue and he'd handed me a thousand dollars in a plain unmarked envelope. Two five-hundred-dollar bills.

When he told me I'd have to come up to Lake Tahoe to do the job, I almost handed it back. I'd caught Mackinaw trout and Kokanee salmon in Tahoe up until fifteen years ago, but I hadn't been back since because there's no way to get there anymore without driving through miles of what looks like the condemned side of downtown Reno, and that makes me sick. Tahoe should have been fenced off at the turn of the century.

"Marcus told me Mr. Wilson's been missing since Monday night," I said after the rote preliminaries. Marcus hadn't told me much of anything else except that he was Wilson's lawyer and had been for thirty tears.

"Yes," she said. "He left here around seven that evening and hasn't been back since." She was a contralto. In half-silhouette against the window, she looked to be about my age, 45. Maybe in pure sun she'd look older, but she didn't sound it.

"How old is Mr. Wilson?" I said.

Her brows lifted. "Is that germane?"

"Please, Mrs. Wilson." I flipped a hand. "I'll ask a lot of stuff and maybe only ten percent'll be germane—a word I'm not fond of."

"That seems like a low average, Mr. Train. Bill is sixty-seven. Would you prefer 'pertinent'?"

"Where'd he go when he left here?"

"To South Tahoe. He took his boat. Or perhaps 'impertinent.'"

"*His* boat?"

"Yes, Mr. Train, *his* boat, his fifty-thousand-dollar cruiser. We're rich, Mr. Train, which I can see offends you. We have *two* boats and four cars, and apartments in San Francisco and at Cap d'Ail on the Côte d' Azur in France, and these spacey little shoes I have on cost ninety-five dollars."

I stared at her. The rich amaze me—they're so damned uncomfortable, even with each other. We don't have the tradition in this country yet; it takes generations to be at ease with ill-gotten gains. "Is that germane, Mrs. Wilson?"

Something twitched across her lips. She put the fur thing on the

couch beside her and stood up."Would you like a drink, Mr.
Train?" she said, and began walking toward a bar against the left
wall of the big room.

"Yes, scotch," I said. It was only two in the afternoon, but I'm
less a clock-watcher than I used to be. She was tall and slender and
she moved swiftly and well, and who says I don't like the rich? I
just don't like how they get it or what they do with it.

It was better after that. Her husband was a leader of the
environmentalists around Tahoe, she told me, the antigrowth
people, and they'd been at war with the developers for years now,
an increasingly bloody war. She appreciated the irony of his
position, she said early on, since his fortune was based on development around the lake, but as you approach the grave, she
added in an interesting touch, different lights illuminate your
path.

The already complex issues in the dispute were further tangled
by the fact that Tahoe is divided almost equally between Nevada
and California, as well as split up between five different counties
in the two states. There was no clear way out of the mess, she said,
but Monday night leaders of the various factions had gathered
together in South Tahoe to search for one. The meeting had
failed, as they all had, and broken up around 11:30. A cabbie had
taken Wilson back to the marina where he'd moored the boat, and
he hadn't been seen since.

"What do the cops think?" I said.

"They suspect foul play, Mr. Train."

"And you don't?"

"I don't *want* to."

"When did you call the cops?"

"Wednesday morning."

"Why so late?"

"I wanted to give him time."

"He's done this before—disappeared?"

"Not for so long."

"When was the last time, and where'd he go?"

"Three or four months ago. He went down to San Francisco."

"The apartment?"

"Yes."

"Have you checked there?"

"Yes, of course. Daily. But there's been no answer. He's not
there."

"Do you love him, Mrs. Wilson?"

"Is that germane?"

"You bet."

"If you suspect me of some sort of hugger-mugger in this thing, Mr. Train, don't waste your time. I love him. I love him very much." It rang true.

"How long have you been married?"

"Twenty years."

"Kids?"

"No."

"Do you inherit?"

"Yes, of course."

"A bundle?"

"A bundle, Mr. Train."

"That was an interesting line, Mrs. Wilson, about 'as you approach the grave.'"

She shrugged.

"*Is* he approaching the grave—assuming he's not there already?"

"We all are."

"Is he ill, doddering?"

"He could take you, I think. He's got ten, fifteen good years left."

"At which time you'll be what? Fifty-five?"

"I'll be ten or fifteen years older than I am now."

I smiled. She was a good contestant. "Have they found the boat?" I said.

"No."

"Have they looked?"

"Of course they have, and so have I—all day Wednesday and Thursday. I mentioned we have two boats. I toured the whole lake."

"And—?"

"Nothing, of course, or I would have said so."

"Have you looked anywhere else?"

"Like where, for instance? When we find the boat, Mr. Train, we'll know where to look for Bill." She got up from the couch again and took my half-full glass from my hand. Hers was empty. Forty, I thought, having gotten a better look at her face.

"How do *you* feel about growth, or no growth?" I said to her back.

She turned. "I don't want one more bad thing to happen to the lake." Her eyes narrowed. "I'm entirely on Bill's side."

"Who isn't?" I said.

"Hundreds aren't."

"Name one."

"Well, Marcus, for starters. The jolly fat man who hired you."

"Why isn't he?" I said.

"Ask him when you see him next."

"What'll he tell me?"

"He'll tell you that Bill's quixotic stand is costing him thousands. Bill owns property that is blocking a lot of development. He's costing a lot of people thousands. He's breaking a lot of people."

"Would Marcus make those thousands if Mr. Wilson were dead?" I didn't want a hundred suspects, I wanted one.

She started to answer, then thought about it for a moment. "I'm not sure what the arrangements are between them," she said, her voice shaking a little. She turned back to the bar, her hands momentarily up to her eyes.

I heard the big front door open and shut and heard sharp steps clack across the slate-floored entry hall before dying in the thick wool carpeting of the living room. A man entered to my right and walked toward Mrs. Wilson.

"It's in," he said, and then he saw me, half turned, and stared.

"What's in?" I said.

"You are," Mrs. Wilson answered, her voice clear again. The man had a folded newspaper in his hand and Mrs. Wilson took it from him and opened it. "Where?" she said to him.

"Second page, first column on the left."

She scanned a moment before reciting as follows: " 'Mrs. William Wilson, wife of the missing Lake Tahoe civic leader, announced late Thursday that she'd hired the distinguished San Francisco private investigator, Sam Train, to assist local authorities in the search for her husband, missing since Monday night.' "

" 'Distinguished'?" I said.

"You'd prefer something else?"

"Almost anything. Look, Mrs. Wilson, Marcus hired me. How come you take the credit?"

"Marcus's secretary phoned yesterday and told Millie he'd hired you and that you'd be up today."

"Millie the maid?"

"Yes. Harley and I"—she indicated the man—"were out on the lake looking for Bill."

"Did you call Marcus back?"

"No. His secretary also said he'd just flown to Hawaii on vacation."

"Did Marcus's secretary suggest that you take the credit—if that's the word?"

"No, but Harley and I thought it would look better coming from us."

"Appearances mean that much to you, Mrs. Wilson?"

"Not normally. But this isn't a normal situation."

I stood up and Mrs. Wilson went through the formality of introductions. Harley Wilson was Bill's nephew. He had one of those porcelain-perfect faces that are half teeth and outrageously handsome, but almost nothing else. His handshake was a carefully calibrated macho squeeze. He probably played a lot of tennis. "A pleasure," he said, lying.

"How come you waited for Marcus to hire a P.I.," I said to her, "if appearances are so important to you in this case?"

"I didn't intend to hire anyone," she said. "I still believe Bill will come back when he's ready."

"On what evidence?"

"Intuition. I have a feeling."

"Yeah," I said. "I've got one too."

It was three o'clock. I took Route 28 to the south end of the lake, where Wilson had last been seen. Without too much trouble I found the local Sheriff's Office and was steered to a plainclothesman named Hanley. I introduced and identified myself and watched his eyes turn cold. A newspaper was open on his desk.

"We don't need help on this thing, Train," he said.

"You mean you've found him?"

"Don't get smart. I mean we will find him."

"Dead or alive?"

"Dead, probably. But we still don't need help."

"Do you mind if I express a thought, Hanley?"

"As long as it's distinguished."

"So you read that, huh? A bad choice of words, as I told the author."

"What's your thought, Train?"

"This: have you found a car that's been lying around here since Monday night?"

"We find two or three a week."

"This would be new, Hanley, and probably a rental. An Impala, maybe. And probably in the marina lot where Wilson moored his boat."

Hanley was silent a moment before he said, "So—?"

"You found one?"

"We found one this morning. An LTD. What made you think we would?"

"Look," I said. "Wilson got aboard his boat Monday night and neither he nor it have been seen since. Do I have that right?"

"Yes."

"O.K., so what are the possibilities? He was either alone, or he wasn't alone. If he was alone, he would have gotten home as expected, unless the boat blew up or something."

"Not likely," Hanley said. "Somebody would have seen it or heard it, or both."

"O.K., so let's assume he wasn't alone. Let's assume somebody was on the boat when Wilson boarded, and if we assume that, we can assume he probably drove to the marina beforehand, since nobody walks anymore. And since the boat disappeared and he was on it, he couldn't come back for his car. What about the LTD?"

"A rental from Sacramento. It was in the marina lot. The contract in the glove compartment said the renter's name was Frank Smith."

"Good ole Frank Smith," I said softly.

"You think that's an alias?"

"I think it's a *nom de guerre*, Hanley."

"Are you being distinguished now?"

"Half of them call themselves Frank Smith for some reason. He's a hired killer, Hanley. Or *was*, as the case may be."

"You think they—what? Killed each other on the boat? And then what? Sank it?"

I didn't answer. I spent a half minute sorting through the possibilities, and there seemed to be a lot of them. "Wilson," I said finally, "is head of the no-growth forces, right? Who's his opposite number?"

"There are lots of 'em."

"Who's the meanest?"

"Well, Phil Enderby maybe. He's a big construction man."

"Has he been questioned about this?"

"No. Why should he be?"

"Who *have* you questioned?"

"Well, nobody yet. We don't have anything to go on yet."

I stared at him. "Do you assume Wilson's dead, Hanley?"

"Well, yes. Probably."

"Do you assume he was murdered?"

"Well, all right. Probably."

"Do you assume he was murdered by a friend, or an enemy?"

"All right, Train, an enemy!"

"Enderby's a friend?"

"No!"

"A friend of yours maybe—"

You say something like that and then watch what happens. County cops are almost always hooked up with the local power factions, one side or the other. It's not necessarily bad, it's just a fact of life, but Hanley was making it look bad. He got red around the eyes and white around the lips. It took him thirty seconds to decide not to spit in my eye, but I spoke first. I said, "Was Enderby at the meeting Monday night?"

"He was there."

"And he's all busted up over Wilson's disappearance, I suppose."

"He's loving it."

"You've talked to him about it?"

"Every day."

"You're on his side, right?"

"And you're on Wilson's."

"It's my Indian blood," I said, giving myself antecedents I neither have nor deserve. "Me no like the trashing of the Big-Jewel-in-the-Sky, which is what my forefathers called this lake, Hanley. You guys want to line it with neon-lit gunk and fill it with your sewage. You're damn right I'm on Wilson's side!"

"Get out of the county, Train!"

"Spoken in the true Western tradition, Sheriff. It'll be a pleasure."

"And stay out," he added, and I almost laughed.

"You bet," I said.

It was six when I got back to Mrs. Wilson's house on the lakeshore road. The sun was just below the Sierra crest in the west, the sugar pines along that serrated ridge haloed in its dying rays. The lake was cobalt blue and serene in the quiet twilight air, and if you squinted you could think long thoughts about the way it once was around there.

Harley opened the door after I'd rung the bell. "Well, Train!" he said genially. "Back so soon?" He was drunk, his eyes luminous with booze. "Come in, sir, come in!" He swept the door wide.

I stayed where I was. "Marcus," I said. "Just how fat is he, Harley?"

"Sir?"

"Mrs. Wilson said Marcus is a jolly fat man."

"He is."

"How fat?"

"Well, fat," Harley said. "Fat." The drink in his hand spilled a little on the slate floor as he illustrated.

"And how jolly, Harley?"

"Less jolly than fat, my dear sir, but he laughs a lot, often at nothing. Such odd questions. I thought you'd met the man."

"It was dark. What's the address of Wilson's apartment in San Francisco?"

"My, such odd questions."

"You don't know it?"

"Of course I know it. It's in Blenheim Towers on Kearny Street."

"Where's Mrs. Wilson?"

"She's on the patio preparing steaks to grill, while Millie prepares the salad—a Caesar, *naturellement.* Perhaps you'd care to join us, *mon vieux.*" His arm swept wide again and there was a touch of mine host in the pose I thought premature. He was hard to take on an empty stomach.

"No thanks," I said. "But *bon appétit* anyway."

He gave me a dazzling smile as I turned and walked back up the driveway to my aging Dart.

Blenheim Towers adorns a rise of land near the Bay, an enclave of inscrutable wealth, w/vu. Penile towers, tumescent in their rape of space. I live on Van Ness, which can be described as nowhere, minus one. My view is of bodies in the street.

I must move, I keep telling myself, but I probably won't. There's no running from it.

I brood a lot when I'm home. While moving, I can maintain the illusion of progress, the hope of change. But squatting here in my

Laz-E-Boy, watching the eleven o'clock body count, rage rises in my gorge like bad food.

Poor Tahoe, I was thinking. I'd chickened out on that one. Fifteen years ago, while fishing on its crystal-clear waters, I'd seen, forty feet down, a beer can sharply enough to read the label and I'd rowed back to shore for the last time. I should have stayed and fought somehow, but I'd gone away and stayed away. Wilson, at least, was fighting them—or had been.

I got up and turned off the news. It was 11:15.

I took a cab and was there in fifteen minutes. The top of the building was lost in the night air, but the entrance, done in Renaissance style, was well lit and a pleasure to the eye. I told the cabbie to wait and walked through the ornate bronze doors of Blenheim Towers as though it weren't for the first time.

A night porter looked up from a book on his desk, shoved his glasses higher on the bridge of his nose, and said, "Sir?" A gun in a holster was three inches from his right hand and he closed that gap by half, instinctively. Everybody's armed in this town. Behind him was a wall of mailboxes.

I veered over and stopped in front of his desk and said, "Marcus."

"I'm sorry, sir, " he said, "But we don't have a Marcus here." He was a big man, about my age and size, and he looked competent in his natty blue uniform. But he had subornable eyes—a natural-born doorman.

"Of course," I said, as though it had slipped my mind. "I meant to say 'Wilson.' "

"The Wilsons are at their place on Lake Tahoe," he said. "In fact, they're seldom here, sir."

His eyes looked like a minimum of ten dollars, so I pulled twice that much from my wallet and laid it on his desk. "For a pencil and paper," I said.

"Certainly, sir," he said, and produced them from a drawer, the twenty disappearing before my very eyes.

I wrote: "Please call Sam Train as soon as possible," and put down my number. I shoved the paper across to him and he folded it without reading it. "Give it to whoever's there," I said, and he assured me with a winning smile he would. In fact, I thought, he'd probably run it up right now.

The call wakened me at seven the next morning, Saturday. I

don't come out of sleep quick as a dog, but I clearly heard this voice say, "Train? This is Marcus. I got your note."

"Marcus," I said, clearing my throat. "You're supposed to be on vacation."

"How do you know I'm not?"

"O.K.," I said, "I don't. I'll be over in an hour."

"Have you had breakfast?"

"A civilized man wouldn't ask that question."

"Are there any? Look, Train, ham, eggs, juice, toast, and coffee. They'll be ready for you when you get here. I told the gunslinger downstairs to pass you through."

"O.K., Mr. Wilson," I said. "But make it an hour and a half. We've got time now."

He'd started out in life as a short-order cook in Denver, he told me over breakfast, and nobody, he said, could fry eggs the way he could. I told him I'd never considered that one of the higher culinary arts, but they were good, over easy with the yolks done just right.

The protocol was no business talk while eating and that was O.K. with me. From my seat at the table I had a nice view of the Ferry Building and the Bay Bridge beyond, and I don't often get to see the world from this height. He didn't argue when I called him Wilson.

With coffee he lit a cigarette and asked me how I'd worked it out. "And don't tell me it was simple," he said.

"But it was," I said. "Smith parked his car in the marina lot and waited for you on the boat—that's pretty obvious."

"Smith?"

"That's what he called himself—Frank Smith—but it's a popular name amongst hit men. You mean you didn't know his name?"

"No. After I killed him, I just took the money from his wallet because I didn't have much with me and I knew I'd need it. I didn't look for an I.D."

"O.K.," I said. "So yesterday morning the cops found his car in the marina lot, which meant he hadn't been able to get back to it. And the boat had disappeared, which meant, probably, that somebody had sunk it, and since there were only two of you aboard and he was in no shape to pick up his car, it must have been you. Which meant you were alive and well.

"Also, you're neither fat nor particularly jolly, which is how your wife described Marcus."

"Well, I knew I couldn't get away with it for long, Train. I just wanted it to hold up long enough for you to find out who set me up." His eyes darkened. "Who did? A guy named Enderby?"

"Later on that," I said. "How'd you kill him?"

"With these." He held up two meaty, tough-looking hands.

"Tell me how it went."

"Well, I'd just moved out from the marina, maybe a hundred feet into the lake, when I looked behind me for some reason— maybe I didn't like the feel of the boat with the extra weight—and there he was, ten feet away in the bright moonlight, with a gun in his hand."

"And then?"

"I gave it hard left wheel just as he fired and it threw him off his feet. His shot nicked me in the arm, but I didn't even know it until later. I jumped him and grabbed his neck and banged his head against the deck until he was damn well dead." He pushed to his feet in the anger of recall. "To *bushwhack* a man," he said, as though it were the ultimate sin. He'd led a sheltered life.

"Let me see the wound," I said. He'd been favoring that left arm all morning.

"It's nothing."

"Let me see it," I said, and he took off the robe he was wearing and showed me a nasty-looking rip through the upper bicep of his left arm. It was infected. "I'll get a doctor for that," I said.

"No, he'll report it."

"Not this one." I got up and went over to the desk where the phone was and made a call and came back. "O.K., after you killed him, what? The doctor will be over in twenty minutes. His name's Quinlan and he's qualified. So what happened next?"

"Well, I took the boat out onto the lake and over to the east shore where I own this big stretch of land and I know nobody lives. It's one of the pieces they want me to open for development, but when I die it's going to become a state park. It's in my will.

"Anyway, I took ten five-hundred-dollar bills—can you imagine that?—from this rat's wallet and opened the sea cocks over this spot about a hundred fifty feet deep and let her go. It's about sixty yards to shore from there and I swam it. Then I walked back down the lakeshore road to where there's a phone booth and I called this limousine operator I know and offered him a five-hundred-dollar bill—a little wet, maybe—to drive me down here and keep his mouth shut about it."

"That was Monday night?"

"Yes. And I was beat and sore, and mad and confused. I knew what he was, of course, and that somebody'd hired him, but I couldn't figure out who. Anyway, Thursday I got hold of you, and you know the rest. In fact, you know more than I do probably."

"I think I do."

"In fact, you might even think you know who did it, right?"

"I think I do," I said. "But I could be wrong."

"Who is it? Enderby? Phil Enderby?"

"Well, who are the possibilities?" I asked. "You should know that better than I."

"Come on, Train, damn it!"

"Wait. We may have a way to prove it. Did Smith say anything to you before he shot?"

"No, why should he? Wait a minute!" He reconsidered, his brow furrowed. Without knowing it, he began to rub his left elbow. Pain from the infection would be accumulating there.

"What did he say?"

"Well, let me see— He said, 'Are you Mister Bill Wilson?' Yeah, he said, 'Are you Mister Bill Wilson?' "

"What kind of voice? High? Low?"

"Well, kind of high, thin and high. Like this." He tried it and then tried it again, a little higher.

"How about this?" I said, and tried it, and then tried it again and again until he said I was close. "Are you Mister Bill Wilson?" I said finally, and he said, "That's it! Right on the money."

"Now let's call this Enderby," I said.

"Is he the one, Train?"

"Somebody described him as being delighted at your continued absence, Wilson. Have you got his number?"

"Yes." He got up and led me to the desk where I'd phoned the doctor and he showed me Enderby's number.

I got him at his office in a couple of minutes and said, right off, "Enderby, I want more money."

"Who doesn't?" he said. "Who is this?" He had a big direct voice.

"Wilson's dead," I said, "and I want more money for the job. Five grand more."

"What makes you think Wilson's dead?" His voice had dropped an octave, a growl.

"Come on," I said. "You hired me to do it and I did it. I want another five thou."

There was a long silence on the line and I looked at Wilson and shook my head. "Who is this?" Enderby said quietly, and I hung up.

"Not Enderby," I said.

"All right, who?"

"You know, don't you?"

"It's Marcus, isn't it, Train? It's just that I didn't want to think so. It's been building a long time."

"Does he win or lose with you dead?"

"He wins—big. I'm blocking him from a lot of fat fees and it's hurting him bad."

"Where is he?"

"In Hawaii. There's some kind of a lawyers' conference he's attending there. That's why I used his name when I hired you. I knew he'd be out of town."

"Who'd you hire to call your wife?"

"A public stenographer told her what to say."

"Why did you want her to know?"

"I thought it might ease her worry, Train. I love her and she loves me."

"She's got company, you know."

"You mean Harley?" he grinned. "Dear Harley. Some company. If my brother knew, he'd twirl in his grave."

I let it go. "What time is it," I said, "in Hawaii?"

He glanced at his watch. "Three hours' difference, I think. So wake him up. And when you're through with him, let me have him. To bushwhack a man, for Chrissakes!"

The phone rang and Wilson jumped nervously before answering. It was the man downstairs announcing the arrival of Doc Quinlan. Wilson said to send him up.

"Has that phone rung before?" I asked. "I mean since Tuesday morning?"

"No. Why should it have? Nobody knows I'm here. Look, Train, I'm just uptight, that's all."

I let Quinlan in at the door and made terse introductions before they both went off to the bedroom. I told Wilson I'd call Marcus while he was gone, but I didn't. Why waste the money? Even a fool's money.

I was glad for the time alone. I stood at the window and looked down at the morning traffic in the Bay. It all looked proper and orderly and clean from this expensive height, but there are places in that Bay where if you dip your hand your nails'll fall off. I turned away. You can't just let your mind drift anymore; it'll snag on something ugly.

Quinlan looked flushed and happy as he followed Wilson back into the room. He'd cleaned and dressed Wilson's wound, he told me, and had given him a shot and a bottle of pills to take. He was smiling broadly, well pleased with himself.

"How much did you give him?" I asked Wilson acidly. "One of Smith's bills?"

Wilson shrugged. "So?"

"Damn it! That's too much."

"Hell, Train, it's not mine."

"No? It was to begin with."

I took Quinlan by the arm and led him to the door. "You owe me at least two free ones," I said savagely. "Who the hell do you think you are, DeBakey?"

His shifty, part-time-drunk's eyes glanced around the big elegant room at my back. "No, but he isn't exactly a charity case either, Sam."

"Two free ones," I said as I shoved him out the door.

I was mad at Wilson. I was mad at Wilson for several reasons, but mostly for not knowing how to dispense money with a sense of its value. "How much," I said, "did you give the alligator downstairs last Tuesday morning for not recognizing who you were? Another five C's?"

"I *had* only five-hundred-dollar bills. But, hell—"

"Yeah, I know, you think they're not yours, but you're wrong, Wilson. A week ago they were."

"Do you know what you're saying, Train?"

"Yeah, I'm saying your wife hired the hit man."

"No. Sheila couldn't—"

"She did."

"You can't prove it."

"In a court of law, maybe not, but I can prove it to you, Bill."

He went over and slumped down in a big leather chair and looked every one of his sixty-seven years. The front part of his mind didn't want the truth, but the back part did, or he wouldn't have hired me. "How can you prove it?" he said. He didn't look up.

"You got here early Tuesday morning and you haven't been out of the place since, except to go hire me. Is that right?"

"Yes."

"And the phone hasn't rung since then."

"No," he said, and looked up now.

"That tells it to you, doesn't it, Bill?"

"No! That doesn't tell me a damn thing." He was still fighting it.

"She told me," I said, "that you'd disappear now and again for a day or two. Where would you come —here?"

"If we were up at the lake, yes."

"And she would phone to check?"

"Yes, usually." He straightened in his chair and rubbed his face with the palms of his hands, around the eyes mostly, where the ache had probably begun. He saw it now; he'd probably seen it all along, but those eyes were also staring across the widening gap between his years and hers, between old age and youth.

"You've been here almost five days now," I said, "and she hasn't called. She told me she had for the sake of form, Bill, but she hasn't. She hasn't because she thinks you're at the bottom of the lake. She hired somebody to put you there, so she hasn't called anywhere for you. She figured one of your many enemies would get blamed."

He was silent for a long time.

"Do you want me to phone her," I said, "and make like Frank Smith?"

"No."

"Do you want me to do anything?"

"No, you've earned your money."

"*Nobody* earns a thousand bucks in a day and a half, Wilson."

He didn't answer. He didn't believe that; he'd done it himself countless times probably. But he had a problem: he had a body in a boat to account for, a technical homicide to explain. I thought he could use my help and told him so, but he turned me down. He said he'd take care of it; he said he'd take care of everything. He looked at me. "She gave me twenty good years," he said.

Two weeks later I read in the Saturday morning issue of the *Chronicle* that Wilson, his wife, and nephew had been killed in an automobile crash between Tahoe and Carson City. The road serpentines down a few thousand feet of slope between the lake and the city below and it's a hazardous run. There are a lot of places in its twenty miles where a car can go over the edge and drop a couple of hundred feet into rocks, and that's what the Wilson car had done.

Wilson had been at the wheel, and they said it was accidental.

Maybe they'll name that park after him, I thought. And I hoped so.

A lunatic killer prowls the countryside, and three strangers come together at a freshly dug grave. This Mystery Writers of America Edgar nominee by the prolific and versatile Bill Pronzini conjures up the sort of suspense that was popular in the golden days of radio drama. One can almost hear the sound of that shovel in the earth, with the waves breaking against the beach in the background.

BILL PRONZINI
Strangers in the Fog

Hannigan had just finished digging the grave, down in the tule marsh where the little saltwater creek flowed toward the Pacific, when the dark shape of a man came out of the fog.

Startled, Hannigan brought the shovel up and cocked it weaponlike at his shoulder. The other man had materialized less than 20 yards away, from the direction of the beach, and had stopped the moment he saw Hannigan. The diffused light from Hannigan's lantern did not quite reach the man; he was a black silhouette against the swirling billows of mist. Beyond him the breakers lashed at the hidden shore in a steady pulse.

Hannigan said, "Who the hell are you?"

The man stood staring down at the roll of canvas near Hannigan's feet, at the hole scooped out of the sandy earth. He seemed to poise himself on the balls of his feet, body turned slightly, as though he might bolt at any second. "I'll ask you the same question," he said, and his voice was tense, low-pitched.

"I happen to live here." Hannigan made a gesture to his left with the shovel, where a suggestion of shimmery light shone high up through the fog. "This is a private beach."

"Private graveyard, too?"

"My dog died earlier this evening. I didn't want to leave him lying around the house."

"Must have been a pretty big dog."

"He was a Great Dane," Hannigan said. He wiped moisture

47

from his face with his free hand. "You want something, or do you just like to take strolls in the fog?"

The man came forward a few steps, warily. Hannigan could see him more clearly than in the pale lantern glow: big, heavy-shouldered, damp hair flattened across his forehead, wearing a plaid lumberman's jacket, brown slacks, and loafers.

"You got a telephone I can use?"

"That would depend on why you need to use it."

"I could give you a story about my car breaking down," the big man said, "but then you'd just wonder what I'm doing down here instead of up on the Coast Highway."

"I'm wondering that anyway."

"It's safe down here, the way I figured it."

"I don't follow," Hannigan said.

"Don't you listen to your radio or TV?"

"Not if I can avoid it."

"So you don't know about the lunatic who escaped from the state asylum at Tescadero."

The back of Hannigan's neck prickled. "No," he said.

"Happened late this afternoon," the big man said. "He killed an attendant at the hospital—stabbed him with a kitchen knife. He was in there for the same kind of thing. Killed three people with a kitchen knife."

Hannigan did not say anything.

The big man said, "They think he may have headed north, because he came from a town up near the Oregon border. But they're not sure. He may have come south instead—and Tescadero is only twelve miles from here."

Hannigan gripped the handle of the shovel more tightly. "You still haven't said what *you're* doing down here in the fog."

"I came up from San Francisco with a girl for the weekend," the big man said. "Her husband was supposed to be in Los Angeles, on business, only I guess he decided to come home early. When he found her gone he must have figured she'd come up to this summer place they've got and so he drove up without calling first. We had just enough warning for her to throw me out."

"You let this woman throw you out?"

"That's right. Her husband is worth a million or so, and he's generous. You understand?"

"Maybe," Hannigan said. "What's the woman's name?"

"That's my business."

"Then how do I know you're telling me the truth?"

"Why wouldn't I be?"

"You might have reasons for lying."

"Like if I was the escaped lunatic, maybe?"

"Like that."

The big man shifted his feet. "If I was, would I have told you about him?"

Again Hannigan was silent.

"For all I know," the big man said, "*you* could be the lunatic. Hell, you're out here digging a grave in the middle of the night—"

"I told you, my dog died. Besides, would a lunatic dig a grave for somebody he killed? Did he dig one for that attendant you said he stabbed?"

"Okay, neither one of us is the lunatic." The big man paused and ran his hands along the side of his coat. "Look, I've had enough of this damned fog; it's starting to get to me. Can I use your phone or not?"

"Just who is it you want to call?"

"Friend of mine in San Francisco who owes me a favor. He'll drive up and get me. That is, if you wouldn't mind my hanging around your place until he shows up."

Hannigan thought things over and made up his mind. "All right. You stand over there while I finish putting Nick away. Then we'll go up."

The big man nodded and stood without moving. Hannigan knelt, still grasping the shovel, and rolled the canvas-wrapped body carefully into the grave. Then he straightened, began to scoop in sandy earth from the pile to one side. He did all of that without taking his eyes off the other man.

When he was finished he picked up the lantern, then gestured with the shovel, and the big man came around the grave. They went up along the edge of the creek, Hannigan four or five steps to the left. The big man kept his hands up and in close to his chest, and he walked with the tense springy stride of an animal prepared to attack or flee at any sudden movement. His gaze hung on Hannigan's face; Hannigan made it reciprocal.

"You have a name?" Hannigan asked him.

"Doesn't everybody?"

"Very funny. I'm asking your name."

"Art Vickery, if it matters."

"It doesn't, except that I like to know who I'm letting inside my house."

"I like to know whose house I'm going into," Vickery said.

Hannigan told him. After that neither of them had anything more to say.

The creek wound away to the right after 50 yards, into a tangle of scrub brush, sage, and tule grass; to the left and straight ahead were low rolling sand dunes, and behind them the earth became hard-packed and rose sharply into the bluff on which the house had been built. Hannigan took Vickery onto the worn path between two of the dunes. Fog massed around them in wet gray swirls, shredding as they passed through it, reknitting again at their backs. Even with the lantern, visibility was less than 30 yards in any direction, although as they neared the bluff the house lights threw a progressively brighter illumination against the screen of mist.

They were halfway up the winding path before the house itself loomed into view—a huge redwood-and-glass structure with a wide balcony facing the sea. The path ended at a terraced patio, and there were wooden steps at the far end that led up alongside the house.

When they reached the steps Hannigan gestured for Vickery to go up first. The big man did not argue; but he ascended sideways, looking back down at Hannigan, neither of his hands touching the railing. Hannigan followed by four of the wood runners.

At the top, in front of the house, was a parking area and a small garden. The access road that came in from the Coast Highway and the highway itself were invisible in the misty darkness. The light over the door burned dully, and as Vickery moved toward it Hannigan shut off the lantern and put it and the shovel down against the wall. Then he started after the big man.

He was just about to tell Vickery that the door was unlocked and to go on in when another man came out of the fog.

Hannigan saw him immediately, over on the access road, and stopped with the back of his neck prickling again. This newcomer was about the same size as Vickery, and Hannigan himself; thick through the body, dressed in a rumpled suit but without a tie. He had wildly unkempt hair and an air of either agitation or harried intent. He hesitated briefly when he saw Hannigan and Vickery, then he came toward them holding his right hand against his hip at a spot covered by his suit jacket.

Vickery had seen him by this time and he was up on the balls of his feet again, nervously watchful. The third man halted opposite the door and looked back and forth between Hannigan and Vickery. He said, "One of you the owner of this house?"

"I am," Hannigan said. He gave his name. "Who are you?"

"Lieutenant McLain, Highway Patrol. You been here all evening, Mr. Hannigan?"

"Yes."

"No trouble of any kind?"

"No. Why?"

"We're looking for a man who escaped from the hospital at Tescadero this afternoon," McLain said. "Maybe you've heard about that?"

Hannigan nodded.

"Well, I don't want to alarm you, but we've had word that he may be in this vicinity."

Hannigan wet his lips and glanced at Vickery.

"If you're with the Highway Patrol," Vickery said to McLain, "how come you're not in uniform?"

"I'm in Investigation. Plain clothes."

"Why would you be on foot? And alone? I thought the police always traveled in pairs."

McLain frowned and studied Vickery for a long moment, penetratingly. His eyes were wide and dark and did not blink much. At length he said, "I'm alone because we've had to spread ourselves thin in order to cover this whole area, and I'm on foot because my damned car came up with a broken fanbelt. I radioed for assistance, and then I came down here because I didn't see any sense in sitting around waiting and doing nothing."

Hannigan remembered Vickery's words on the beach: *I could give you a story about my car breaking down.* He wiped again at the dampness on his face.

Vickery said, "You mind if we see some identification?"

McLain took his hand away from his hip and produced a leather folder from his inside jacket pocket. He held it out so Hannigan and Vickery could read it. "That satisfy you?"

The folder corroborated what McLain had told them about himself; but it did not contain a picture of him. Vickery said nothing.

Hannigan asked, "Have you got a photo of this lunatic?"

"None that will do us any good. He destroyed his file before he escaped from the asylum, and he's been in there sixteen years. The only pictures we could dig up are so old, and he's apparently changed so much, the people at Tescadero tell us there's almost no likeness anymore."

"What about a description?"

"Big, dark-haired, regular features, no deformities or identifying marks. That could fit any one of a hundred thousand men or more in Northern California."

"It could fit any of the three of us," Vickery said.

McLain studied him again. "That's right, it could."

"Is there anything else about him?" Hannigan asked. "I mean, could he pretend to be sane and get away with it?"

"The people at the hospital say yes."

"That makes it even worse, doesn't it?"

"You bet it does," McLain said. He rubbed his hands together briskly. "Look, why don't we talk inside? It's pretty cold out here."

Hannigan hesitated. He wondered if McLain had some other reason for wanting to go inside, and when he looked at Vickery it seemed to him the other man was wondering the same thing. But he could see no way to refuse without making trouble.

He said, "All right. The door's open."

For a moment all three of them stood motionless, McLain still watching Vickery intently. Vickery had begun to fidget under the scrutiny. Finally, since he was closest to the door, he jerked his head away, opened it, and went in sideways, the same way he had climbed the steps from the patio. McLain kept on waiting, which left Hannigan no choice except to follow Vickery. When they were both inside, McLain entered and shut the door.

The three of them went down the short hallway into the big beam-ceilinged family room. McLain glanced around at the fieldstone fireplace, the good reproductions on the walls, the tasteful modern furnishings. "Nice place," he said. "You live here alone, Mr. Hannigan?"

"No, with my wife."

"Is she here now?"

"She's in Vegas. She likes to gamble and I don't."

"I see."

"Can I get you something? A drink?"

"Thanks, no. Nothing while I'm on duty."

"I wouldn't mind having one," Vickery said. He was still fidgeting because McLain was still watching him and had been the entire time he was talking to Hannigan.

Near the picture window that took up the entire wall facing the ocean was a leather-topped standing bar; Hannigan crossed to it. The drapes were open and wisps of the gray fog outside pressed against the glass like skeletal fingers. He put his back to the window and lifted a bottle of bourbon from one of the shelves inside the bar.

"I didn't get your name," McLain said to Vickery.

"Art Vickery. Look, why do you keep staring at me?"

McLain ignored that. "You a friend of Mr. Hannigan's?"

"No," Hannigan said from the bar. "I just met him tonight, a few minutes ago. He wanted to use my phone."

McLain's eyes glittered slightly. "Is that right?" he said. "Then you don't live around here, Mr. Vickery?"

"No, I don't live around here."

"Your car happened to break down too, is that it?"

"Not exactly."

"What then—exactly?"

"I was with a woman, a married woman, and her husband showed up unexpectedly." There was sweat on Vickery's face now. "You know how that is."

"No," McLain said, "I don't. Who was this woman?"

"Listen, if you're with the Highway Patrol as you say, I don't want to give you a name."

"What do you mean, *if* I'm with the Highway Patrol as I say? I told you I was, didn't I? I showed you my identification, didn't I?"

"Just because you're carrying it doesn't make it yours."

McLain's lips thinned and his eyes did not blink at all now. "You trying to get at something, mister? If so, maybe you'd better just spit it out all at once."

"I'm not trying to get at anything," Vickery said. "There's an unidentified lunatic running around loose in this damned fog."

"So you're not even trustful of a law officer."

"I'm just being careful."

"That's a good way to be," McLain said. "I'm that way myself. Where do you live, Vickery?"

"In San Francisco."

"How were you planning to get home tonight?"

"I'm going to call a friend to come pick me up."

"Another lady friend?"

"No."

"All right. Tell you what. You come with me up to where my car is, and when the tow truck shows up with a new fanbelt I'll drive you down to Bodega. You can make your call from the Patrol station there."

A muscle throbbed in Vickery's temple. He tried to match McLain's stare, but it was only seconds before he averted his eyes.

"What's the matter?" McLain said. "Something you don't like about my suggestion?"

"I can make my call from right here."

"Sure, but then you'd be inconveniencing Mr. Hannigan. You wouldn't want to do that to a total stranger, would you?"

"*You're* a total stranger," Vickery said. "I'm not going out in that fog with you, not alone and on foot."

"I think maybe you are."

"No. I don't like those eyes of yours, the way you keep staring at me."

"And I don't like the way you're acting, or your story, or the way *you* look," McLain said. His voice had got very soft, but there was a hardness underneath that made Hannigan—standing immobile now at the bar—feel ripples of cold along his back. "We'll just be going, Vickery. Right now."

Vickery took a step toward him, and Hannigan could not tell if it was involuntary or menacing. Immediately McLain swept the tail of his suit jacket back and slid a gun out of a holster on his hip, centered it on Vickery's chest. The coldness on Hannigan's back deepened; he found himself holding his breath.

"Outside, mister," McLain said.

Vickery had gone pale and the sweat had begun to run on his face. He shook his head and kept on shaking it as McLain advanced on him, as he himself started to back away. "Don't let him do it," Vickery said desperately. He was talking to Hannigan but looking at the gun. "Don't let him take me out of here!"

Hannigan spread his hands. "There's nothing I can do."

"That's right, Mr. Hannigan," McLain said, "you just let me handle things. Either way it goes with this one, I'll be in touch."

A little dazedly, Hannigan watched McLain prod Vickery into the hall, to the door; heard Vickery shout something. Then they were gone and the door slammed shut behind them.

Hannigan got a handkerchief out of his pocket and mopped his forehead. He poured himself a drink, swallowed it, poured and drank a second. Then he went quickly to the door.

Outside, the night was silent except for the rhythmic hammering of the breakers in the distance. There was no sign of Vickery or McLain. Hannigan picked up the shovel and the lantern from where he had put them at the house wall and made his way down the steps to the patio, down the fogbound path toward the tule marsh.

He thought about the two men as he went. Was Vickery the lunatic? Or could it be McLain? Well, it didn't really matter; all that mattered now was that Vickery might say something to somebody about the grave. Which meant that Hannigan had to dig up the body and bury it again in some other place.

He hadn't intended the marsh to be a permanent burial spot anyway; he would find a better means of disposal later on. Once that task was finally taken care of, he could relax and make a few definite plans for the future. Money was made to be spent, particularly if you had a lot of it. It was too bad he had never been able to convince Karen of that.

At the gravesite Hannigan set the lantern down and began to unearth the strangled body of his wife.

And that was when the third man, a stranger carrying a long sharp kitchen knife, crept stealthily out of the fog. . . .

The most frequent contributor to this annual series, Jack Ritchie, produced a number of excellent stories last year, including detective stories in Ellery Queen's Mystery Magazine *and some fine fantasies in* Alfred Hitchcock's Mystery Magazine. *I've chosen this typically Ritchie-esque crime caper from* The Elks Magazine *because it deserves a wider audience among mystery readers. It's short and sweet, managing to deliver both style and substance in a mere 1,500 words.*

JACK RITCHIE
Delayed Mail

It was clearly a case of mistaken identity.

They thought they'd kidnapped Harvey Pendleton. We do look a bit alike, I suppose, but he is the owner of the Pendleton Snowmobile Company and I am not. I am merely one of his clerks.

It had been near noon on Monday when Mr. Pendleton opened his office door, looked out, and discovered that I was the nearest human being.

He tossed me his car keys. "Wilbur, gas up my car and have the oil and tires checked. I'll be driving to Madison this afternoon and I won't have time to do it myself."

"Yes, sir," I said. I put on my topcoat and went downstairs to the parking lot behind the plant. I approached the Lincoln in the parking space clearly labeled *Pendleton*.

Just as I inserted the key into the car lock, a green and white sedan drew up behind me and two large men leaped out. They seized me and shoved me onto the rear floor of their automobile.

One of them planted his feet firmly on my back so that I could not rise and the other jumped behind the wheel of the car and we sped off, tires squealing.

"Now look here," I demanded. "What is this all about?"

The man with his feet on my back said, "What does it look like?"

I tried an intelligent guess. "A kidnapping?"

"That's right, mister."

I allowed myself to chuckle. "You have the wrong person. My name is Crawford. Wilbur Crawford. I suspect that you are really after Mr. Pendleton."

The man above me was not buying. "Shut up."

I tried several more times to tell them that they had the wrong man, but all it got me were some kicks in the ribs, so I resigned myself to giving up for the time being.

It was a rather long drive, especially for me on the floor of the car. According to my wristwatch, it was nearly two hours before the car finally pulled onto a crunching driveway and came to a stop.

From the little conversation the two of them exchanged en route, I learned that the man driving was Max, and the individual with the feet, Clarence.

He removed them from my back now. "All right, get out."

I saw that we were in a rather dreary countryside and parked in the driveway next to a farmhouse. My first thought was to make a run for it, but Clarence had a firm grip on my arm and pushed me toward the house.

Once inside, I spoke up again. "My name is Wilbur Crawford. Not Pendleton. And I do not own the Pendleton Snowmobile Company. I am merely a clerk in his employ."

"Sure," Clarence said. "Sure." Nevertheless, they led me to the second floor and a small bedroom.

Clarence shoved me inside and locked the door, leaving me alone. I went immediately to the single small window. I found that it was throughly covered with a heavy wire grill bolted to the window frame. Clearly preparations had been made for someone's confinement.

I looked down at their car still in the driveway. Perhaps it had been stolen, but on the other hand, would they risk driving a stolen car for nearly two hours with a kidnap victim inside? Perhaps the car really did belong to one of them. I decided that there might be some point in memorizing the license plate number.

I noticed a small ventilation grating in the floor and got down on my hands and knees. Below me I saw Clarence and Max watching TV.

Eventually the TV programing reached the five o'clock news.

A Wilbur Crawford had been kidnapped this afternoon from

the parking lot behind the Pendleton Snowmobile factory. A witness had seen him being hustled into a car by two men. The witness had been too far away to get the license plate number, but he described the auto as being a late model green and white sedan.

The police theorized that the kidnappers might have abducted the victim in the mistaken belief that he was Harvey Pendleton, president of the Pendleton Snowmobile Company.

Below me, Clarence swore, and got out of his easy chair. I heard him coming up the stairs.

He unlocked the door and stared at me. "So you really aren't Harvey Pendleton?"

"That is what I have been trying to tell you."

He glared. "You're worth nothing to me. Absolutely nothing."

I smiled. "In that case, you might as well let me go."

There was a silence and then he said, "What makes you think that we have any idea of letting you go? No matter who you are?"

I cleared my throat. Clearly this was a moment to buy time. "On the other hand, I may not be worthless to you after all. You should still be able to get your money. Send the ransom note to Mr. Pendleton himself."

"What good would that do? Why would Pendleton give us $200,000 for your hide? You said yourself that you're only one of his clerks."

"Yes, but do you think that Mr. Pendleton would dare *not* pay my ransom?"

"Why wouldn't he?"

"Because of the publicity involved. What would the newspapers say about him if he flatly decided not to ransom me and left me to my fate? Whatever that might be. People would be upset by his lack of humanity. They would stop buying his snowmobiles. His factory would have to close. Do you think he would want that to happen just because of a measly $200,000? But if he came up with the money, he would be hailed by the entire nation."

Clarence rubbed his jaw. "You might have something there at that."

I nodded eagerly. "The entire country would begin buying snowmobiles. He'd have to expand his factory. Money would come pouring in."

"All right," Clarence said. "Don't oversell it."

He took me downstairs and handed me a ball-point pen and some paper. "Start writing what I tell you."

He dictated. They wanted $200,000 in small unmarked bills for my return. They would give Pendleton a week to get the money together and then they would get in touch with him again.

When I finished the letter, I addressed an envelope and affixed a stamp Clarence handed me.

He shoved the envelope into his pocket, took me upstairs, and locked me in again.

I suspected that now Clarence was keeping me alive just in case he needed me once more—to write another note, or to prove to someone that I was still alive and therefore worth the ransom.

Monday passed. Tuesday. Wednesday.

By Thursday morning, I began to wonder if the letter had ever gotten to Mr. Pendleton at all.

At two o'clock that afternoon I was at the small window when I saw the cars parking about a half a mile down the country road. Men began getting out of the vehicles and fanning across the fields, sneaking up on the house.

I was at the floor grating watching Clarence and Max before their television set when the state troopers stormed into the living room. Clarence and Max were caught completely by surprise and they surrendered meekly.

When I got downstairs, Clarence was still blinking at the suddenness of events. "How did you find us?" he asked the captain of the state troopers.

The captain smiled. "It was the envelope you used to send the ransom note. The zip code was wrong so it was delayed. In fact the zip code was *so* wrong that we wondered if maybe Mr. Crawford wasn't trying to tell us something—like an automobile license plate number. We ran it through the Motor Vehicle Department and came up with your green and white sedan."

Max looked at Clarence reproachfully. "How could you mail a letter with my license plate number on it?"

Clarence shrugged. "Why am I supposed to remember the license number of *your* car?"

When I returned to my job, I was something of a hero. But only until the next Monday morning when Mr. Pendleton opened his office door, looked out, and discovered I was nearest.

He tossed me his car keys. "Wilbur, gas up my car and have the oil and tires checked. I'll be driving to Madison this afternoon and I won't have time to do it myself."

This time I was not kidnapped.

Finding a mystery which combines a good puzzle with an unusual back-
ground seems to be a lot more difficult than it once was, but occasionally
one still turns up. Francis M. Nevins, Jr., who won a Mystery Writers of
America Edgar award for his 1974 study of Ellery Queen, Royal
Bloodline, *combines careers as a law professor and a mystery writer with*
a nostalgia for old movies that led to this story. In it con man Milo Turner
turns detective to solve a mystery at a convention of Western film buffs.

FRANCIS M. NEVINS, JR.
Filmflam

The old man brought back a flood of memories. He reclined
against a pile of cushions on my davenport, breathing raggedly,
gnarled fingers twisting the heavy cane across his lap. His hair was
gray and thin now, his gaze vacant, but that wrinkled and liver-
spotted face with the frozen-looking expression on its left profile
was still unmistakably the evil phiz of Buster Domke, villain in
dozens of the B Western movies of my Saturday matinee boy-
hood. The young woman who had accompanied him to my L.A.
hideaway called herself Tina Noel and claimed to be both Buster's
niece and his nurse. She was tall and honey-tan, wore her hair
long and loose, and was lushly endowed with the attributes of
cinematic success.

"We don't want to prosecute him, Mr. Turner," she insisted.
"We don't even want the six thousand back, just the tapes. God,
hours of inside Hollywood history and it'll all be lost if that—" She
groped for the proper word, remembering that I was a member
of the same profession.

"Con man," I filled in helpfully.

"If he tapes over Uncle Bus's material before you can reach
him," she finished. Buster Domke just sat there on the davenport,
nodding mechanically.

In a screwy way the job made sense. Five months ago a bright
redbearded young man had called on the retired but not yet
disabled Domke and introduced himself as Ronald Stephenson.

He had said he was a free-lance writer and an old-movie freak, working on a definitive history of the B Western. Could he have the privilege of taping an interview with Buster about his years as one of the foremost villains of that genre?

Over the next few days he had bought the old man gourmet dinners, lubricated him with choice blends of liquor, lavished flattery and nostalgia on him, and soon had him opened up like a sardine can. Anecdotes and reminiscences of all the top cowboys of the thirties and forties—Buck Jones, Tex Ritter, Brett Kane, Roy Rogers—had poured out of the old-timer in a torrent, and Stephenson had captured them all on his portable cassette recorder.

Domke had worn the black hat in dozens of B Westerns and was a living storehouse for the kind of unsanitized reportage that the studios had paid fortunes to hush up during Hollywood's golden age. All the stories about who was sleeping with whom and who hated whom were squirreled away in Domke's prodigious memory—and stayed there until this Stephenson had come into his life, and driven out of it with ten or twelve cassettefuls of those stories plus $6,000 of the old man's savings, which was supposed to finance the conversion of the tapes into an autobiography.

About a month after Stephenson's scam, Domke had suffered a stroke and Tina Noel had come west to care for her uncle. It was she who wanted the tapes back. "I have a boyfriend in publishing who says Uncle Bus can clear thirty or maybe forty thousand on his life story if it's marketed right." On the reasonable hypothesis that it takes one to catch one, she had used another boyfriend who had underworld contacts to get in touch with me and hire me to find Stephenson and buy or steal those tapes. "After all, they're worthless to him now that he's gotten Uncle Bus's money."

Her persuasiveness, not to mention her other endowments, finally won me. "All right. I'm not a licensed detective but business has been slow lately and for a two-thousand-dollar fee plus expenses I'll stretch a point. Now describe this Stephenson to me again."

"I'm sorry I can't do better," she said, bending forward gorgeously, "but I didn't come out here till after Uncle Bus's stroke and by then the man was long gone. All I could get from Uncle is that he was tall, thin, about twenty-five, had a red beard and a lot of freckles, knew an incredible lot about B Westerns, and was a genius at getting people to talk freely."

"Rings no bells," I told her. "But maybe I can find him anyway. If he's working this scam on other old movie people he may be using the same tapes over and over, or maybe he really is a movie freak and saves the cassettes for their historical value."

I stood politely as Tina helped her uncle to his feet, and with her certified check for my advance of $1,000 tucked snugly in my breast pocket I escorted them out of my apartment and down the long white corridor to the elevator. "I'll keep in touch," I promised. "Mr. Domke, I wish we could have met sooner. I've admired you for thirty-five years."

"Any time, any time," Buster mumbled hollowly. "Always a pleasure." As the cage door slid shut between us I recalled how malevolently noble he had looked in his prime, like Milton's Satan astride a midnight black stallion, and almost had to blink back a tear. But then, I always was a sentimentalist.

I went back to my hideyhole, set the deadbolt and the chain lock, cleared away my guests' glasses, poured myself a fresh jolt of Southern Comfort on the rocks, and thought a bit. Two sips later I gave up and reached for the easy way out. I plunked down on the carpet near the phone and dialed the genial proprietor of the world's only human supermarket, Jock Schultz.

" . . . You read me right, Jocko, I couldn't turn the chick down. Thanks for steering her to me. Now maybe you can help me help her."

The Jock didn't seem all that eager to lend a hand. "I—ah— received the impression, when her boyfriend talked to me, that she wanted to find some fellow who had cut himself a chunk of her uncle's bankroll. Now, Milo, we can't betray another member of the profession."

"I know the union rules," I sighed. "All she wants is for me to buy some worthless tapes from this other guy. But, Jocko, I never heard of anyone with the description she gave who worked that kind of scam." I repeated Tina's word picture of Stephenson and then popped the big question. "Who is this new man in the game, Jock? What do you know about him?"

He waited a minute as if debating how much he should spill. "All right," he agreed at last, "as long as you guarantee it's ethical. Have you ever heard of the brave new hobby of film collecting?"

"Film collecting? You mean to tell me some people collect movies the way others go after stamps or coins or old beer bottles?"

"Thousands of people, in all walks of life, all over the land. It if sounds strange to you, think how a medieval monk would have reacted to the notion of people owning copies of the books they read. It's the wave of the future, my boy. A few collectors restrict themselves to 35mm prints but that requires a complete theater in the home and a monstrous lot of storage space, so most of 'em stick to the 16mm prints which are lighter and much cheaper. A fair number of collectors specialize in one type of movie—old horror films or comedies or cartoons—or Westerns. May I suggest that you research the subject in rapid order."

"Why the hurry?" I asked him.

"The Western film collectors throw festivals every year," the Jock explained patiently. "A big one opens in Nashville next week. The collectors who organize these affairs pay the expenses of six or eight old cowboy movie people who fly down and chat with the fans and share memories. If young carrot-top is still working the same game he may well go to Nashville to line up more marks."

Which, translated from Jockian into English, meant that he had reliable word Stephenson was indeed on the same scam and was definitely going to Nashville. "Sounds logical," I murmured smoothly. "Worth a try anyway. Thanks a mil, Jock, I'll talk to you soon."

Early the next morning I put in a long-distance call to the Nashville Chamber of Commerce and quickly convinced a magnolia-kissed voice on the other end that I was an L.A. *Times* reporter doing a piece on the old cowboy stars who were coming to the festival. Miss Cornpone cooperated bounteously with dates, times, places, the names of the festival organizers and of the invited guests. Russell Hayden! Peggy Stewart! I. Stanford Jolley! Ah, those memories of Saturday afternoons in the front row at the Odeon, bouncing in my seat to the rhythm of the action. The chase music, the gorgeous running inserts, the flying leaps, the dancelike fistfights. Almost 30 years had drained off my life since I'd last seen a B Western, and I relished the prospect of looking at some again.

But first I paid a visit to the L.A. Public Library and checked out every book they had on the life and times of that fabulous genre. I lugged the books back to my pad, curled up on my davenport where Buster Domke had sat, and glutted myself on nostalgia.

At 8:17 P.M. five evenings later the jumbo jet from L.A. touched down at Nashville's pocket-sized airport. I collected my gear from the onboard storage bin and grabbed a cab to the Talltree Inn where the festival was to open next morning. The hotel was in the heart of the city, a high steel-and-glass finger surrounded by new buildings that the country-western music boom had brought to the sleepy old community. Standing in the broad spacious lobby you could look straight up 24 stories to the top. The rooms were on the east and west walls, all of them facing waist-high balconies and the huge central well, and on the south side four glass-walled elevators studded with electric bulbs rose and dropped continually in a dizzying light show.

I took my place in the line near the registration desk, surrounded by paunchy middle-aged men in ten-gallon hats and vaguely Western leisure suits, chatting in heavily Southern accents on one topic and one only. "I surely wish pore ole Johnny Mack Brown coulda made one of these here conventions before he passed away." "Got two mint original Ken Maynards I'm lookin' to trade for some Tim McCoys." "Haven't seen Russ or Peggy yet but Wild Bill Wentworth was in the cocktail lounge a while ago."

I tested my newly acquired expertise by trying to identify every allusion to a B Western personality, scored passably high, and snagged myself a room on 16 West under the name of Grover P. York, accountant, of Tatamy, Pennsylvania, which is one of several nondescript identities I keep, so to speak, in my hip pocket. The bellgirl led me through knots of fans and collectors swapping hobbytalk into the science-fictional elevator and up to the sixteenth floor.

Gear stowed away, I stretched on the queen-size bed, balanced the phone on my chest, and dialed the hotel operator. "Could I have Mr. Ronald Stephenson's room number, please?...Well, could you tell me if he has a reservation?...Thanks just the same." Which established that if redbeard was among the sagebrush brigade he was using another name. But freckled as he was, I didn't think I could mistake what he used for a face. I freshened up, changed into chinos and a cactus-print sports shirt, and buzzed down to the lobby to get oriented.

Once every few years I feel the presence of a guardian angel watching over me. As the elevator dropped me toward ground level I faced the glass rear wall and looked down at the panorama of lights and open space and chandeliers hanging on mile-long chains, and people the size of midgets, and suddenly there he was. Riding the Up escalator from the lobby to the mezzanine, growing big as life as he rose and I descended. A tall thin young man, beardless but with neatly trimmed hair the color of a freshly painted fire engine and enough freckles for a one-man St. Patrick's Day parade.

I stabbed the button for Mezzanine, dashed out, scanned the visible area on all sides, and damn it, in the few seconds the elevator had taken to reach that floor, he'd dematerialized. At first I thought he'd gone into one of the eight or ten meeting rooms but then I realized that the festival didn't begin till tomorrow morning, so the rooms must be locked for the night. That left only one likely destination for him on this floor, and I trotted down the corridor till I passed the swinging cedar door labeled MEN. I parked myself behind a pillar and waited for him to show.

Three minutes later, when he poked through the swing door and headed back for the escalator, I glanced around, saw we had the area to ourselves, and took a long chance. I tiptoed behind him till I was almost close enough to touch his freckled neck, then I called out, "Ron Stephenson! How's life, old buddy?"

He froze like Lot's wife, the backs of his ears turned red, and very cautiously, so as to gain time to recover his cool, he pivoted to face me. "Sorry, friend," he smiled thinly, pointing to the convention name-tag pinned to his beige T-shirt. "You got the wrong guy. My name's Bob Saunders."

I mumbled a sheepish apology and ducked into the john till he'd vacated the area. Then I headed for the house phone on the mezzanine and spoke to another hotel operator. "Could I have the room number of Mr. Robert Saunders, please?"

Jotting down 1407 on a scrap of paper, I reflected that being a detective seemed an easier way to make a living than being a con man. I'd give him a few hours to socialize with the marks, then around midnight I'd pay him a visit and make my pitch about the tapes. I boarded the Down escalator to the lobby, aiming to patronize the bar.

And all of a sudden my guardian angel gave me another nudge. Whom did I spot standing in the line before the registration desk but a certain young woman, tall and honey-tan and with hair worn long and loose, who was supposed to be 3,000 miles due

west of Nashville playing nurse to dear old Uncle Bus! It looked as
if I was playing in a deeper game that I'd been told.

I set my traveling alarm clock for midnight, doused the lights,
snatched a snooze, and at 20 minutes into the new day I took the
fire stairs down two flights, crossed to the east wing, and knocked
on 1407. There was a crawling kind of noise from behind the
door, and some groans. The sounds came nearer and the door
inched open just enough so I could see someone sprawled in the
darkness of the entrance foyer.

I wedged myself in and stared down at a young carrot-top who
looked like he'd been bounced around the inside of a laundry
dryer. His lips were puffy, his T-shirt ripped, his freckles overlaid
with ripe bruises. The room was a mess, as if a wild ape had been
pawing through its contents. I kicked the door shut and helped
him to the bed, then soaked bathtowels in cold water to bring him
around.

"Who mistook you for a tackling dummy?" I asked when he was
more or less coherent again.

He muttered, "No one. It's private, I can handle it myself."

"You look it," I told him. "Come on, Stephenson, this is business. In case you don't recognize me through that shiner, I'm the
guy who stopped you on the mezzanine. I want to buy those tapes
you made with Buster Domke five months ago if you haven't
erased them yet. I'll go as high as five hundred." Actually my limit
was considerably higher, but that didn't concern him. "They're
worthless to you but Domke can make a tidy sum if they're turned
into his life story."

He lay there thinking, the wheels turning almost visibly behind
his blackening eyes. "Mister, either you're a damn fool or someone's conned you. My God, you can't sell your autobiography to a
publisher these days unless you were a superstar, and except for
these old-time Western nuts who the hell ever heard of Buster
Domke?" Then his eyes got shrewd and cautious and he rolled
out of bed, groped among the spare blankets in the bottom
dresser drawer, and came up with a .45 automatic in his fist.

"You think I didn't recognize you downstairs? You think I'm
dumb enough to believe Milo Turner was scammed by a half-
paralyzed old man? Look, you know why those tapes are worth a
mint, and I know, and I know you know, but it was me he told how
Kane was killed, not you, so you can just go dig a hole for yourself,

get me?" So high was his dudgeon his voice had climbed to almost a screech.

"Stephenson, you overestimate me drastically," I protested in all modesty, hands duly raised. "But okay, it's your ball game. May I leave the room?"

He waved me out with the barrel of his .45. I toyed with the notion of politely instructing him that you had to cock the hammer before you could fire that weapon, but chose to leave the damn fool in his ignorant bliss. I backed into the corridor and headed for the fire stairs and the rest of my night's sleep.

Next morning I checked in at the festival desk on the mezzanine and in return for my twenty bucks was given a plastic-covered badge in the name of Grover P. York, a convention program, a guide to eating out in Nashville, and a floor plan of the hotel. A bulletin board behind the registration tables was jammed with typed and handwritten offers to buy, sell, or swap B Westerns, and a wall poster listed the special guest stars of this year's festival. Russell Hayden, famous as Hopalong Cassidy's sidekick Lucky. Peggy Stewart, queen of the B Westerns. I. Stanford Jolley, notorious Western-film badman. James Mandell, Brett Kane's young pal Buddy in the Arizona Rider series. William Wentworth, director of dozens of classic B Westerns.

I studied my program, analyzed the titles of the six features that were playing simultaneously in the six screening rooms at this hour, took a gamble on something called *Rawhide Mail* starring Jack Perrin, whoever he was, and walked out after ten truly ghastly minutes. Down the hall another screening room was showing a Hoppy feature called *Lumberjack.* I sampled it, liked what I saw enormously, and stayed to the end. People kept drifting in and out of the rooms, watching a snatch of action, going to grab a smoke or a cup of coffee or just to chat with other fans or tour the dealers' room where 50 or 60 merchants of nostalgia had set up shop on folding tables covered with green cloth and were offering films, movie books, posters, publicity stills, and every other known variety of cowboy memorabilia.

Rich and poor, young and old, male and female, everyone wore just a shirt and slacks or jeans at these festivals. There were no social distinctions: if you loved those great old low-budget all-but-interchangeable flicks, you belonged. Before the afternoon break I had caught a Lash LaRue, a Sunset Carson, a Don Barry, and pieces of two Gene Autrys. But not once did I catch a glimpse of Tina Noel or Mr. Carrot Thatch, and I began to wonder if they were off somewhere together.

Around 4:00 P.M., the screening rooms emptied and everyone trooped down to the hotel's Grand Ballroom for the daily event known as the Panel of Stars. Three or four of the invited guests sat on the dais and fielded questions from the throng of collectors and fans. "Mr. Hayden, how did you like playing Lucky in the Hoppy pictures?" "Would Miss Stewart tell us about working with Sunset Carson?" The answers were all cut to the same measure: everyone was a gentleman and a scholar, a prince of a fellow, and a joy to work with. That was what the fans had come to hear. To be told that one of their old idols had been a rummy, or beat his horse, or pawed every woman in sight, would be like going to church and hearing the preacher say that God was a stupid myth.

Somehow, in the middle of the ritual q-and-a, my brain sprang out of neutral and I understood what that cryptic reference of Stephenson's to Kane being killed must mean. I raised an eager hand and in due course was recognized from the dais.

"Mr. Mandell," I boomed out, "could you tell us about Brett Kane?"

With his steel-gray hair and his big burly frame James Mandell looked like a veteran truck driver, except that he wore leather gloves as if his hands were cold in that excessively air-conditioned room—or as if they'd been bruised in a fistfight. Coming into the ballroom during the introduction of the guests, I'd heard the master of ceremonies say that Kane had retired from the movies 20 years ago and gone into the chemical business.

"Brett Kane," he repeated in a whiskey baritone, the name carrying him back to the simpler days when he'd played the Arizona Rider's teenage pal, Buddy. "Brett Kane was a tough, feisty, hard-working, loving man. I rode beside him in, oh, sixteen Arizona pictures—that was 1938 to 1940. Spence Bennet directed half and ole Wild Bill there did the rest." He swung his head to the medium-sized middle-aged man at the end of the dais. "Buster Domke was the bad guy in most of them. Regular little old stock company we had." As if on cue the fans gave a round of loud applause for good old Buster.

I took my head in my hands and asked what I thought might be an unpopular question but from my point of view a necessary one. "Could you tell us how Brett Kane died?" I called out.

The man at the end of the dais reached for the microphone. William Wentworth, the Alfred Hitchcock of the low-budget action directors as I'd heard someone call him. His craggy face looked long and deeply lived in, and his eyes gleamed half with delight and half with grief. "I directed the last Arizona Rider picture," he said into the mike, "oh, hell, what was its name, *Across the Badlands* or something. It was the last few scenes, we were shooting Brett chasing Buster Domke on horseback, and Buster had emptied his .45 at Brett, then tossed it away. The gun was supposed to be important evidence in the story, so I told Brett to sort of swoop over in the saddle when he rode past the gun and skim it up at full gallop.

"Well, I've always been a bug about getting the action scenes to look right, so we took our time and shot that chase and pickup from a bunch of different camera angles, something we almost never did on those B pictures. Finally about the seventh time poor Brett just sort of keeled over in the saddle and hit the dirt. Well, we called Linda, that was his wife, loveliest girl on God's earth, and we rushed him to the hospital, but it was too late. Turned out the poor guy had known for a month that his heart had gone bad but he was too damn proud to tell anyone but his best friend, Buster Domke. That's how Brett Kane died—in the saddle."

There was an uncomfortable silence in the huge room, then someone started clapping and within seconds the whole room was applauding the memory of a cowboy who had died with his boots on.

I made this my cue to slip quietly out of the ballroom. I'd been scanning the room every few minutes during the questions and answers and still saw no sign of Stephenson or Tina. I decided to run up to 1407, and if it seemed vacant, to use my skeleton keys to do a quickie search. As I left the room a chubby teenager was asking Russ Hayden whether he thought Gabby Hayes or Andy Clyde was the funnier cowboy comedian.

I stepped out of the elevator and sighted across the central well on a diagonal line. At the far end of the east wing, three or four rooms beyond Stephenson's, a wheeled housekeeping cart stood at an open door. It was late in the day for the maids still to be cleaning, but with the festival the hotel was fuller than usual. The door to 1407 was shut tight.

But not for long. After I had kept watch for three or four minutes the door eased open a few inches, then all the way, and

my elusive client Tina Noel came flying out into the hallway
toward me without even bothering to close the door behind her. I
ran to intercept her at the junction of the south and east cor-
ridors, grabbed her from behind with a hand over her mouth as
she raced past me. I pulled her through the door to the fire stairs
and sat her down on the chilly concrete floor. "Okay," I said
gently, fingers still against her mouth. "Easy now, no screams, just
take a deep breath and start talking."

"He's dead oh God he's dead," she kept repeating like a stuck
record. "I knocked on his door and it was a little bit open and I
walked in and he was on the floor with blood all over his head and
a gun with a bloody butt in the bathroom doorway and then I
realized the maid was a couple of doors away so I had to stay there
with oh my God his body until she was out of sight and then I ran."

"Did you take anything?"

"N-n-no!" In that tight blouse and slacks there didn't seem
room to conceal anything, so this once I believed her.

"Touch anything?"

"No. I don't know. Yes. Maybe. Oh God, how can I remember?"
Her voice rose to the edge of hysteria and I made a move to cover
her mouth again but she seemed to get over it then. "What are we
going to do, call the police or—"

A sharp loud screech, muffled by the walls, cut off her question. I peeped through the square pane of glass set into the fire
door at eye level and saw the maid rocketing down the corridor
toward the elevators.

"It's being done," I reported confidently. "Come on now, on
your feet and up two flights to my room. I'll give you a stiff drink
and hold your dainty little hand, and you will spill your soul out."

And after downing most of my Southern Comfort, she did.

"I have this boyfriend on the L.A. bunco squad, and after Uncle
Bus and I spoke to you, well, I thought I'd ask this boyfriend if the
police knew anything about Ronald Stephenson, so I described
him the way I did for you."

"You have a boyfriend for every occasion," I remarked.

"He came up with this young con man who's used a lot of
different names," she went on as if she hadn't heard me, "and
taken several old-timers in the entertainment business for a few
thousand apiece. He even gave me a copy of a police artist's sketch
of what the man looked like, and then he checked with some

informants and found out the man was about to leave for Nashville. Well, a month ago Uncle Bus got an invitation to be a guest at this festival, so I figured Stephenson was coming here to work his con on more old-timers. That's why I left Uncle Bus with the housekeeper for a few days and came here too."

"Without bothering to contact me before or after you arrived," I added in an injured tone. "What were you going to do, use your charms to get the tapes from him?"

"If I had to," she said. "I just circulated around the hotel last night till I spotted someone who resembled that artist's sketch, and then I casually bumped into him and, well, didn't discourage him."

"Fast work," I commented admiringly. "When I saw him about 12:30 this morning he mentioned Buster's stroke, which didn't happen till a month after he'd conned your uncle, so I knew you and he had gotten together. What time did you leave him last night?"

"Ten thirty or so. He invited me to come back today for a drink before dinner," she explained euphemistically. "I thought I could search his room and maybe find the tapes while he was asleep."

"Did you see him or talk to him between eleven last night and just now?"

"No!" She half choked on the word. "I spent the day shopping, just got back an hour ago. My God, you don't think *I* killed him!"

"For what those tapes are worth you might have," I said wisely. Milo's Maxim #37: When you know nothing, pretend you know everything.

It worked. She bit down troubledly on her luscious lower lip and gazed up at me. "Then you know about Brett Kane's heart attack."

"And the horse and gun stunt and the whole works," I lied brilliantly. "Stephenson spilled the beans last night."

"Then you know there's enough in it for both of us." She treated me to a suggestive smile and wriggled a bit in her chair. "Let's be partners, Milo, okay? Uncle Bus has money, I'll take him and a fifth of what you collect elsewhere, and the rest's all yours."

This woman would have been a survivor even in Machiavelli's Italy. There was something about her cold-bloodedness that sent a needle spray of fear down my backbone. "I'll think about it," I told her noncommittally. "Later. Right now I've got an espionage mission. You stay where you're sitting, I'll be back."

Being two stories above and almost directly across the central well from the corpse's room, I was ideally located for rubbernecking. The panel had broken up downstairs and the fans and collectors were streaming back to their rooms to get cleaned up before dinner. Those who had sharp eyes and were well situated as I was could tell something unusual was happening in Room 1407. The more curious among them stood or crouched at various strategic points along the balconies, making me much less conspicuous as I watched.

The plainclothesmen and evidence technicians seemed to be well into their routine. My guess was that at first they'd treat it casually as the work of a sneak thief surprised by an unexpectedly returning guest. Then when they checked the registration on the .45 and learned from the medical examiner's report that the corpse had been in another brawl 16 hours or so before his death, and ran into blank walls trying to notify the so-called Robert Saunders's relatives, they'd get serious about investigating and forget about the sensitivities of the hotel management. I figured I had until tomorrow morning at most to make my move. I came in from my balcony observation post, shut the door, went over to Tina on the bed, and issued my marching orders.

"You go back downstairs and mingle. Find James Mandell, the guest star who wears the gloves." I tore out of my convention booklet the page with the photo of Brett Kane's teenage sidekick as he looked today. "Don't attract his attention but watch him. If anyone looking like a cop approaches him, exit gracefully, go to your room, and wait. Report back here at ten tonight."

I hustled her out, checked my billfold, rode downstairs to get a five changed into quarters at the front desk, and cabbed to the local Greyhound terminal where I used a pay phone to call L.A.

"Yeah, Jock, it's me. In Nashville. Is the supermarket still open? Good, because I need to convince some people that I'm a detective on whatever they call the homicide squad in this burg. Who can fix me up with ID? . . .Thanks a ton, Jocko, I'll tell you why later." I hung up, dialed the number of the friendly local document forger Jock had given me, made arrangements to pick up my police credentials at 9:30, and killed the intervening time over bourbon and rare sirloin at a charcoal grill.

By 10:25 I was back in my room, listening to Tina report that no one who smelled official had come near Mandell. "Beautiful," I said. "Where was he when you left him?"

"Down in Screening Room Two. They're running an Arizona Rider film."

I told her to go back to her room and hang loose, rode down to the mezzanine, and sauntered into the screening room. It was dark, lit only by the projector lamp and cigarette glows, but filled with the noise of gunshots and hoofbeats. I spotted Mandell in the back row, still wearing those gloves, watching his forty-years-younger image in the time-mirror of the film. I let him commune with his memories until the final action scene was over, then I gave him a gentle tap on the shoulder.

"Lupton, hotel security," I introduced myself softly in the Southern accent I had picked up by osmosis from the evening newscasts since the last election. "Mr. Mandell, we have a guest named Robert Saunders who claims you assaulted him last night. I'd like to speak to you privately about it, if you don't mind, sir."

He stared at me through truckdriver-tough eyes as if I were a talking fruitcake and slapped his gloved hands together in the chilly room. "Me? Assault someone? With these?" he whispered over the strains of the dialogue on the screen. "Mr. Lupton, there was a time when I scrapped quite a bit, and generally came out on top. But not since '72. Not since the chemical explosion in my plant that winter." He hesitated, then slid his hands between his thighs and shucked both of his gloves off. "Go ahead, feel them before they turn the lights up."

I ran my fingers over his. They felt cold and lifeless, like the hands of a department-store mannequin magically endowed with mobility. Flexible hands, made of some kind of plastic, good for eating and other simple operations, but no good at all for a fistfight. Or for beating a man to death with the butt end of a .45 automatic.

"I was lucky that explosion didn't take more than my hands." Mandell whispered. "That's why I wear gloves whenever I can. Now will you believe me that this Saunders, whoever he is, is full of hooey?"

I apologized with all the Southern courtesy at my command and slipped out of the room as Mandell tugged his gloves back on and Brett Kane's wonder horse White Falcon nudged him into the heroine's arms for the fadeout.

So my first hunch about the identity of Stephenson's assailant had been a ripe juicy lemon. But if it wasn't Mandell that the redhead had been trying to blackmail over Kane's death, there was only one person left in the hotel who fitted.

I found him alone in a booth at the far end of the dimly lit lounge on the basement level, his eyes misted enough to show he'd been lapping the sauce for at least a couple of hours. Now that I saw his hands close up for the first time, I noticed that the knuckles were raw and bruised as if they'd been in a recent fight. I squeezed in beside him and flashed my shiny new ID.

"Lieutenant Winningham," I identified myself in what I hoped was a soothing Southern monotone. "We know pretty much what happened up in Room 1407, sir, if you'd like to tell us about it."

For the second time that day Milo's Maxim #37 proved its value. William Wentworth needed to unburden himself to someone and he was just lit enough not to question my official status. "Yeah," he said heavily. "Sure, I'll tell you. Buy you a drink?"

"Sorry, sir, I'm on duty," I replied virtuously. "Don't let it stop you, though."

He signaled the redcoated barman for another double Johnnie Walker. "I don't suppose you know much about B Westerns, Lieutenant, or the people that made them. We were a bunch of wild roughnecks, but we were a real community. Actors, directors, stuntmen, photographers—most of us anyway. We worked our butts off out in the boonies every day and got drunk as skunks every night and were back on the set at eight the next morning like nothing had happened. I was about twenty-five, and getting the contract to direct half the Arizona Riders was my first big break. I started to work with Buster Domke and Jimmy Mandell and Brett Kane.

"Some guy at the panel today asked what Kane was like." I modestly forbore to reveal that the guy was me. "Jimmy said Kane was the finest man on God's green earth, because that's what the fans came to hear. It was a damn lie. Brett Kane was a sick sadistic animal. He liked to make people hurt, women especially. He beat that lovely wife of his so bad she couldn't wear a bathing suit for all the marks he left on her. I was involved with Linda for a while before she married Kane, but I knew if I tried to do anything he'd get me blackballed as a director and ruin me. He enjoyed doing stuff like that.

"Well, they shot half the Rider pictures in Utah and half on the back lot in L.A. When Kane was in Utah with the other director and the crew, Linda, well, she'd come stay with me. I tried to talk her into leaving him but she was afraid. He'd told her he'd throw acid in her face if she ever tried to leave. Listening to her and seeing what he'd turned her into was like a chain saw tearing me up inside.

"To cut it short, Buster Domke and I went out drinking one night about a month before it happened. Buster got drunk and let it slip that he'd driven Kane to the doctor's the day before and that the doc had told Kane he had a bum ticker and if he didn't quit action pictures he'd die. Kane made Domke swear he'd never tell a soul, but Buster never could keep a secret when he was smashed.

"Well, sometime during that spree with Domke I got my idea. I went home that night and looked at the script of the next Rider picture I was going to shoot, and I rewrote it to play up a scene about Domke's gun being important evidence. Then I added a bit where Kane is chasing Domke and swoops down in the saddle and scoops up the gun Domke had dropped. When we went out to do the picture a week later I whizzed through the other scenes so fast it made the cameraman's eyes pop, so I'd have time to shoot that scoop-up sequence over and over.

"I had a rep for taking trouble over my action so it didn't look fishy. We worked out there under that broiling sun and I made Kane ride into camera range and bend way over in the saddle at a full gallop and pick up that gun over and over and over till finally he fell off his horse and died, just the way I wanted him to.

"No one suspected a thing, except Buster, of course, but he was sweet on Linda too and for her sake he kept his mouth shut. That is, until that redheaded con man got him drunk five months ago and squeezed the story out of him, and then paid a call on me for a contribution. When he learned I was coming to this Nashville wingding he told me he was coming too, to line up more suckers, and that I could buy the tapes down here for ten thousand dollars.

"Well, I visited him last night, knocked him around a little, searched his room, took what tapes I found, and thought that was the end of it. He called me again this morning, said that he had duplicates of all the tapes hidden back in L.A. and that anyway I'd missed the tape where Buster talks about Kane's death. He played me a piece of it over the phone to show he wasn't lying, and told me he was upping the price to twenty thousand down and ten thousand a year for the rest of my life.

"Well, I didn't care about myself, I'm a tired old man and no

one's going to prosecute for something that happened back in
1940. But I still cared about Linda, who's alive and happily
married and just as lovely as ever and still a dear friend of mine,
and I didn't want to see her name in a scandal. So I said I'd see him
in his room at 3:30, half an hour before the panel. When I got
there he pulled an automatic on me, said he was going to bust my
nose with it for the licking I gave him the night before.

"Well, the damn fool hadn't even cocked the hammer, so I
rushed him and yanked the gun away and kept smacking him on
the head with it till he wasn't moving anymore. Guess I smacked
him too hard, huh? Then I found that last cassette, took it to my
room, cut the tape into little strips, flushed them down the john,
and washed up and went down to the panel and listened to Jimmy
Mandell tell everyone what a prince Brett Kane was. It was only
two hours ago I heard someone in the lobby say there was a guy
dead in 1407, and I've been drinking steadily ever since. I'd have
gone down to headquarters and confessed before morning."

"I'm glad I found you first," I said, improvising with wild
abandon. "You see, sir, our independent investigation bears out
your contention that you killed the man in self-defense, and
anyway he was a blackmailer and a menace to decent folks from
way back. We understand things like that down heah, Mr. Wentworth. So why don't you just forget all about it and trust us to close
the case in some civilized manner?"

Wentworth stared across at me with a look of incomprehen-
sion, as if he'd never dreamed of a homicide cop proposing such
an arrangement. He straightened up, pressed his temples between his palms, and gave all the symptoms of a man who's been
shocked sober. But my cerebrum was in gear now and roaring like
a race car at Le Mans, and nothing was going to keep me from
finishing first.

"You know, sir, I've been thinking about that story of yours," I
went on. "For almost forty years you've believed that you and you
alone were responsible for Brett Kane's death, is that right?"

"Well, of course I was!" The director sounded almost indignant
that I would think of denying him the credit.

"As an experienced investigator," I said, "I see the picture
differently. Think back on the way it happened, sir. The way that
suggestion of how to take advantage of Kane's bad heart seemed
to generate spontaneously that night. Now, isn't it much more
likely that the real power behind that suggestion was—what was
his name again? Buster Dobkins."

"Domke," he corrected mechanically.

"Whatever. Isn't it much more plausible that this Domke fellow deliberately told you about Kane's heart ailment, and that it was Domke who subtly planted the suggestion during that drinking bout as to how Kane could safely be disposed of? After all, sir, you said yourself that he was sweet on Linda too."

I could tell by his eyes that he was straining to relive that scene, in another dimly lit bar, straining to recapture the nuances of that long-ago night. One minute I thought he'd bought my version, the next his eyes seemed to reject it. Of course, I had a reason to support my version, a reason I was keeping close to my chest. Only if Buster Domke had been implicated in Kane's death in a blackmailable way, and had drunkenly said something incriminating during those taped talks with Stephenson, could Tina Noel have hoped to use the tape to squeeze her uncle dry, as she'd stated to me. Even though Tina herself had never heard the tape, Domke must have let something slip that had tipped her off to what he had done back in 1940, and it stood to reason that during her tête-à-tête with Stephenson last night she had offered him pretty much the same deal she'd made me, with her taking exclusive rights to bleed Uncle Bus and twenty percent of whatever Stephenson got elsewhere.

Wentworth's rough-hewn face suddenly seemed to relax, as if an impossible burden had unexpectedly been lifted from his shoulders. "Why, damn it all, you have to be right!" he exploded in a sort of perverse joy. "That Domke, that wily sneaky calculating—oh, hell, if it wasn't for that damn stroke he had I could call him right now and put it to him point-blank and know for sure. But no, I don't need to do that, I see how it was now, and you're right, Lieutenant. My God, I'm not a killer!"

"Well, Mr. Wentworth," I replied smoothly, "that makes us even. Because I'm no lieutenant." And leaving the Hitchcock of the action film with the world's biggest gape of stupefaction across his craggy kisser, I slid out of the red plush booth and jogged briskly to the nearest exit.

I had no reason to stay in Nashville any longer so I packed my bags that night and checked out and caught a postmidnight flight to Chicago that connected with a nonstop to L.A. I didn't bother to say goodbye to Tina, who was probably still in her room waiting for me to tell her what had happened. Her thousand-buck advance hadn't even covered my expenses thanks to the cost of the fake detective ID, but I decided it was safer to take a loss than go partners with that guileful sexpot. At the first opportunity she'd have slit my throat. She must suspect, of course, that it was Wentworth who'd clubbed the redhead into the hereafter, but she couldn't open her mouth without choking herself in the stew, and most assuredly she couldn't prove a thing.

As the 747 sailed west across the black velvet sky I debated trying to locate Stephenson's pad in L.A. when I landed and glomming those duplicate tapes of his so no one else could hold them over Buster's or Wentworth's head. I'd enjoyed so many of their movies in my formative years that I figured I owed them that much.

But then, I always was a sentimentalist.

Considering the fact that arson has become one of the most frequent and serious of urban crimes, there's surprisingly little fiction devoted to it. Stewart Sterling's nine novels about Fire Marshall Ben Pedley have been out of print for years, and among short stories only Stanley Ellin's fine arson tale "The Nine-to-Five Man" comes immediately to mind. The powerful story that follows is set just a few years in the future, and appeared in Dark Sins, Dark Dreams, *an anthology of science fiction crime stories edited by Barry Malzberg and Bill Pronzini. Its author is a young San Francisco writer whose novels and stories, mainly in the science fiction field, are receiving increasing critical acclaim.*

ELIZABETH A. LYNN
The Fire Man

TONY:

He knew that he was being watched.

In the middle of a torching, nothing disturbed him. He went about his work with a specialist's precision. Firemen in their asbestos rigs, sweating in the sun, were a familiar annoyance; the presence of a stranger in civvies an ignorable one—but sharper. He distrusted observers in suits.

He poured a gasoline trail down the Victorian hallway, and sight-checked the windows. No glass. Once they had stopped him halfway through because some marshal had missed a stained-glass window. This was the last house—the trigger house. Soon the block would erupt, a small nova, to flare inward and burn to ash. Up on Parnassus Heights, the poured-concrete buildings of the hospital leered at him. *We're safe*, they said. *We're not wood.* Lording it over a valley of wreckage. *Devastation Row.*

One of us will get you, he thought. *Wind, water, fire, or the earthquake. You won't stand.*

He tucked an end of soft rope into a crack of the wooden oil-soaked floor, and began to back up, unrolling it. His arms and legs were aching with tension, and the gasoline smell was making his throat catch. With painful self-discipline Dellara forced himself to slow down, to pace the yards out. *If they would only let him work at night—the sight, the sound of flames against the night sky!*

Far enough. He took a box of kitchen matches from his pocket, and fumbled one out. The sizzle and flare as it caught calmed him rock-steady. He touched the flame to the end of the cord, and watched it travel across the bare earth up to the door of the house. Kneeling, he laid his head on his knee, cloth rough on his face, and rocked, back, forth, back, forth. . . .

It caught. Air bellowed as it rushed into the house, drawn through windows and door frames by the sucking fire. The firemen moved back a little. The visitor went with them. Tony Dellara knelt, watching the conflagration.

When he was sure that no power short of the hand of God could put the fire out, he stood up. Home now, to an old rooming house on Buena Vista, a firebug's gingerbread dream. From its windows he could see the rubbish that was downtown San Francisco. The quake had ripped the city like rotten cloth, toppling its towers: Coit Tower, Transamerica, the Hilton, and leaving the wreck of the Bay Bridge scattered over Treasure Island like the bones of a beached whale. The Golden Gate stood still; the city's symbol. No one used it now. Its approaches were down.

It gleamed orange in the sunlight like his fire.

Now there was time to check out the stranger. The man's head was cocked back; he was watching the fire. Tony strolled over to Lee Harris, the chief marshal. Mostly the firemen ignored him: some of them, Tony guessed, feared or despised or envied him. Lee Harris, for reasons he never needed to voice, hated the arsonist's guts. "Nice day," he said. "No wind." Lee nodded. "Department being investigated?"

"Not that I know of. Why?"

"The dude in a suit. He's been watching pretty close."

Lee grinned tightly. "He's watching *you*, Dellara. He's some big shot from Recon, name of Susman. Think they're going to take you off the job?"

"Maybe," Tony said softly. *You'd like that, wouldn't you, you bastard.* He repeated to himself, as he walked away: "*Susman. From Recon.*"

JAKE:
"Claudia, is she in?" he demanded.

The secretary looked at him coldly. She did not like him. She knew he wanted Marta's job. "She's in, Mr. Susman. She wanted an hour free to get some work done, and she's getting it."

Jake sighed. "Please call me when the hour's up." He went back to his desk. He shuffled papers, emptied the overflowing ashtray, put a file away. He read the top paper on the pile on his desk, buried it under six reports, and then fished it out again. He could take it to Marta. "We, the undersigned, respectfully petition the Department of Urban Reconstruction to exempt from its program blah-blah, blah-blah." A house on Duboce, near Noe, built in 1886, still standing. He knew what she would say. *No.*

When Claudia called him, he walked in holding the petition before him like a shield. "What d'ya think?"

She took it, looked at it, and laid it down on the desk. "Why waste my time with this crap?" she said.

"I know the area—I live there. It's right near Franklin Hospital. That block's in pretty good shape."

"You want me to approve it? Okay, Jake. Now—what do you really want to talk about?"

She had short black hair and classic Irish skin, like cream. The jade pendant the office staff had given her for her thirtieth birthday matched the green of her eyes.

"Come to dinner with me tonight?"

"No, Jake."

"You'll have to say yes sometime."

She shrugged. He gave it up, slapped his pockets for his cigarettes, and then ostentatiously folded his hands on his lap. "It's about your pyrotechnics experiment—Tony Dellara." She raised her eyebrows. "I watched him Friday morning." He wished Marta allowed smoking in her office. He suddenly needed something to do with his hands.

"Odd occupation for a day off."

"He burned a block of the old Haight. Just like that—gone."

"That's his job."

"I thought we were hired to build the city up, not burn it down," he said.

Marta tapped a pencil on the desk. "Burning takes less time than the bulldozers, cranes, and trucks, and uses less gasoline than they do. Those old blocks are mostly deathtraps. You know that. We can build over them after we clear them out."

"Burning's dangerous."

"So far there hasn't been an accident."

"It doesn't employ as many people as the bulldozers."

"It frees them to work on the building project."

"It pollutes the air."

"True."

She did not want to fight with him. "And Dellara?" he said. "What made you pick him for the job?"

"He applied for it. And I knew him casually, ten years ago in New York. He was a fire insurance investigator for twelve years. He knows his work."

"You ought to see his face, when he lights that fuse," Jake said. "It's just not normal, Marta. Have you thought—he's got to be obsessive?"

"You're not a psychiatrist. Have you talked with him, Jake? He's a sensitive man."

"I looked up his file. I was curious. Did you know he was twice questioned in cases of suspected arson?"

"Along with every volunteer fireman in the Bronx!" she said. "He told me about it when I interviewed him."

Jake's fingers itched for a cigarette. "What he does is essentially destructive."

"At the moment it's helping us rebuild San Francisco. What's eating you, Jake? Show me something wrong. Show me where Dellara's made a mistake—I'll drop the experiment like that!" Her palm cracked the desk. "But till the experiment proves valueless, your suspicions sound as irrational to me as those of a businessman who won't hire kikes."

Jake flushed. "Okay," he capitulated. "Let's drop it." He grinned. "It isn't that important. Are you sure you can't make dinner tonight?"

"Goodbye, Jake," she said.

He went back to his cubicle, and reached for his smokes, savoring the harsh taste. *What the hell does she care about Tony Dellara?* he wondered. He saw in his mind the figure kneeling—*like a goddam sun-worshiper*—in the dust. *I'll go again. Today's Tuesday. Friday— I'll go again.*

Friday he followed Dellara home.

I don't understand what makes a man like that tick. He doesn't look crazy—but neither do men who molest little girls. . . . Nice place he lives. I wonder what we're paying him. I think Marta liked him. Cool, so cool, green eyes, jade eyes—she doesn't go out at all. Executive women . . . Do

*his neighbors know? Hello, Mr. Jones, I'm your next-door neighbor, I'm a
pyromaniac. . . . Slander, that's slander, I'm only guessing—maybe I'm
wrong and Marta's right. . . .*

He stopped by the mailbox to light a cigarette, careful to keep
his face turned away from the windows of the house.

TONY:
Dellara watched Susman strike the match.

*Did he think I wouldn't notice someone following me home? Shucks his
suit for a denim jacket and he thinks it's a disguise.* He wanted to go
down and grab Susman by his clean, pressed collar, shake him,
scream at him. *Why are you following me?* Recklessly he went down
the street. Susman was still there, smoking. Tony tapped him on
the shoulder. "Got a spare?" he said. Automatically Susman slapped his pocket for his pack, and shook out a cigarette. "Thanks."
Tony pulled out his matches and lit it. The flame burned between
them. "You live around here?"

"Uh—no," Susman said. "See you around."

Dellara waited until he turned the corner of Roosevelt, heading
down. Then, slowly, he started to walk in the same direction.

From the pay phone at the corner of Henry Street, he made his
call, grinning at the thought of Susman. *Wouldn't you like to
know* . . . "May I tell her who's calling?" the secretary said.

"Tell her it's Tony Dellara."

In a moment he heard her voice. "Tony? You *swore* you
wouldn't call me here."

"It's important. About a guy who works for you. Name of
Susman."

"Jake? What—"

"He watched me last Friday. And this morning. He even followed me home. It's getting me nervous. Pull him off, Marta.
You're his boss."

"Friday's his day off, Tony; he can go where he likes."

"I don't like being watched."

"Yes," she said, "I remember." He saw her for a moment as he
had first seen her, back in the Bronx, ten years ago: thin white
face, black curls, green eyes, trembling against the brick wall in
the light of the flames. He recalled his own unholy burst of fear
and rage.

"He doesn't know, does he?"

"No. Nobody knows."

But Me. "Tell him to lay off," he said again, trying to be gentle. "Suggest it to him, Marta. It's bad luck to rattle a torch."

"Tony!"

He hung up. Then he stood with his forehead pressed to the cold plastic of the phone booth, forcing himself under control. *Get cool. Get cool.*

JAKE:

Bitch. Charlie had gotten the blanket spread out under the tree, and the girl was making him wait. Jake sympathized. *There she was. Nice.* She came quickly across the yard and into the shadows, screened by the tall grass. Almost immediately they were in each other's arms, clothes off and pushed to one side. Jake could feel himself getting hot.

He left the window. *What are you, a voyeur? Getting into teenagers?* The air in the cottage smelled suddenly stale, poisoned with the reek of a thousand dead cigarettes. *Marta's right, I should stop smoking.*

He was sure, positive, that Marta had once had something going with Dellara. She jumped so quickly to his defense. . . . "He's a sensitive man." He went to the window again, and opened it. They were still at it.

It was not enough to tell himself that there were a lot of other women, that all cats were gray in the dark, and that if he waited long enough, asked often enough, she would say yes, or *he* would lose interest.

Monday, he thought. *Monday I'll get in there again, talk to her about Dellara. Suggest that she have an impartial observer evaluate the success of the burning program. The Army? She's so damn sure of herself, always. I need to shake her up a little.*

Despite himself, he looked out the window. Charlie and the girl were still joined, but clearly finished. The tension in his own groin was turning into an ache. *Ah, damn.* He went to the bed. *Marta,* he thought. *So cool—so beautiful and so cool—bitch . . .*

TONY:

Monday night. There were lights on in the second-floor apartment of the Victorian. He eased open the basement door. The passageway to the yard was cluttered with garbage cans. He went through. A dark shape in the back of the yard, the cottage seemed very small. *Nice yard; well kept. A lemon tree. A concrete barbecue pit.* He went to look at it. *Perfect.*

It was stuffed with papers and old rags. He dropped the laundry bag he was carrying to the ground. In it were more rags, stained with paint and turpentine. A coil of dirty clothesline, a can of paint thinner. A half-used, untraceable book of matches.

Party noise blared from the house in front. Tony took a pair of cheap gardener's gloves from the bag and stooped to rub them in the dirt. Then he put them on and unrolled the clothesline. He uncapped the paint thinner and began to dip the line in the can at random. When it was spotted completely with liquid, he laid one end of it in the barbecue pit and snaked it through the yard to the steps of the cottage, letting it fall in haphazard circles. He peered in curiously through the front window, but could see nothing except the shadowy fronds of a hanging fern.

Get moving. There are people in that front house. He went back to the barbecue pit and stuffed the rags he had brought on top of the debris already there. Then he poured some paint thinner around, not very much, and lodged the partially full can in the pit.

You can't stay to watch this one. You'll have to imagine it. The adrenaline rush was beginning to race his heartbeat. He took out a cigarette and lit it, savoring the blue flare of the little flame in the darkness. He took a few puffs. Then he stuck the cigarette against the inside of the matchbook, almost touching the cardboard but not quite. He folded the flap over, compressing the cigarette a little, and tucked the end in.

He cleared a space in the pit and laid the matchbook in it. Then he picked up the laundry bag, and, with one quick backward longing look, left.

He threw the laundry bag into an alley a block away, after scuffing his feet on it a few times. He threw the gloves over a fence. Then he went to the pay phone.

She answered at once, as if she'd been expecting it. *It's been a long time.* "A gift for you," he said. "The one hundred block of Henry Street."

She said nothing. He hung up. He began to run slowly, a man out jogging on a summer's night. *She would come.* He was sure of it. *She would come.*

JAKE:

Jake Susman saw the fire trucks halfway down the street. *Hell. Hope it's not too close.* A few steps more he realized how close it was, and ran.

They had snaked a hose through the basement steps of the Victorian. A fireman blocked his way. "Can't get in there, buddy."

"But that's my house back there!" They had another hose going up the front steps. Charlie was standing on the sidewalk. "Charlie, what happened?"

"Dunno, man. We were partying, and all of a sudden—whoosh! Fire. These folks sure messing up our house."

"How bad—"

"Couldn't see. Looked like it started in the yard, but it spread fast." He spoke with unconscious relish. "You got insurance?"

"Are you kidding?" Jake grabbed at one of the firemen. There seemed to be fifty of them around the house. "Can I go in there—" He pointed to the first floor of the Victorian. "All I want to do is look. That's my cottage back there."

"Yeah, okay." Jake ran down the hall, jumping over the hose. Obscenely stiff with water, it went through the hall, into the kitchen, and out the back door into the yard. A fireman grabbed him before he got to the kitchen.

"But that's my *house!*" Jake said. He looked over the man's shoulder. All he could see was flame.

"We've got to wet this place down; get outside! There's enough alcohol upstairs to fly a plane. You want the rest of the block to go, too? Get out of here!"

He went back into the street. A crowd had gathered. *They always do at fires. Goddam ghouls. Disaster's a spectator sport.* Smoke stung his eyes. A red glow came through the windows of the Victorian. The firemen were still inside. They came out, running, dragging the hose, and began to back into the street, playing a stream of water on the front of the house. "Back, get back." The police were there. Helplessly, Jake moved back. *This isn't real,* he thought. *It's a movie by Sam Peckinpah.*

Fire shot out of the second-floor window of the Victorian.

Jake suddenly saw Marta.

She was backed against the streetlight, her eyes on the fire-men—no, on the flames. He shoved his way over to her. "Marta!" he yelled. "What are you doing here?"

For an instant he thought she had not heard him, and he took a breath to yell again. Then she turned to stare at him. She seemed to be looking at him from very far away.

She nodded, once, and then, as if pulled by a magnet, she turned back to the flames. *Christ. Oh, Christ.* His mouth was suddenly dry. He wet his lips to talk to her. Another tongue of flame shot out the window of the house. Her whole body shook.

He understood, then. But there was nothing he could say to her that she would hear. *Dellara,* he thought. But it barely seemed important.

He slumped against the streetlight pole. "Ahh," said the crowd, moving restlessly. The fire made a hungry sound. Then it began to eat out the front of the house.

Edward Wellen's frequent short stories in mystery and science fiction magazines are always a treat. Here he manages a considerable feat in just two pages, producing one of the year's best short shorts.

EDWARD WELLEN
The Adventure of the Blind Alley

Feeling his way through the pea-soup fog, Police Constable Cooper paused at the noise of a struggle. He stared hard to hear. At the first outcry and the noise of scuffling his hand had whisked to his whistle. But before he could blow a blast to frighten off the attacker, he heard the sickening sound of a cosh on a skull, then the thump of a falling body.

He withheld the blast and with heavy caution, in order to catch the assailant red-handed, he lifted his boots toward the rough breathing and the tearing of cloth.

P.C. Cooper smiled tightly to himself. He knew this to be a narrow cul-de-sac and himself to be between the attacker and escape. He had the culprit all but in his arms.

He winged out his cape and moved slowly but steadily into the blindness of the alley. But a curb leaped out of nowhere. P.C. Cooper's stumble and his muffled oath warned the attacker. The constable blew a savage blast. "In the name of the law, stand fast!"

P.C. Cooper heard fleeing footsteps, the ring of a hobnailed boot striking an iron mudscraper, then the creak of a door and the snick of a latch. The culprit, then, was a denizen of this unsavory alley.

The constable swore under his breath. He had his man—and yet he did not have him. He knew there were a half-dozen doors on either hand. Unless the constable located the right door straightway, the culprit would have time to change from his wet outer clothes and to hide what he had stolen from the victim.

The victim. A dozen paces deeper into the alley, and the constable saw the shape of the victim on the cobblestones.

Feeling sudden clamminess and chill, P.C. Cooper stood over the fallen man. He eyed a familiar hawklike profile, a bloodied deerstalker cap, a still-clutched violin case. Rents showed in the victim's clothes where hurried hands had torn away a watch chain and snatched a wallet. That the mighty manhunter should have fallen prey to a common robber!

The victim stirred. A word came forth. "Constable . . ."

P.C. Cooper knelt, careless that his knee touched the wet stones. The blood-blinded face had not turned toward him. How had the man known to call him constable?

The whistle, of course. The habits and skills of a lifetime would not have failed him even in the direst of moments. Though stunned, the great detective would have taken note of some clue, and most likely clung to consciousness now solely to impart that clue.

"Sir, did you see your assailant? Can you describe him?"

A painful shake of the head.

"Do you know where he ran to?"

A painful nod.

P.C. Cooper's heart surged, but the man had only consciousness enough to point vaguely and gasp, "A flat . . ."

The constable grimaced in disappointment. The great detective had told P.C. Cooper only what P.C. Cooper already knew.

A flat, indeed! This was an alley of rooming houses—nothing but flats.

P.C. Cooper removed his cape and wadded it under the great detective's head as a cushion. Then the constable rose and duty took over. His whistle guided answering whistles.

Each blast, each echo, ached. It hurt him to think that his colleagues would find him simply standing there, waiting, while the culprit was safe behind one of those unseen doors.

A flat . . .

P.C. Cooper shook his head. Why should those words keep ringing in his mind? They had originated in the poor stricken mind of the great detective.

A flat . . .

Pounding boots pulled up. P.C. Cooper recognized the figure of P.C. Lloyd.

Lloyd was a Welshman, and Welshmen are famous for having perfect pitch.

Swelling with authority, Cooper seized Lloyd's arm and pointed him.

"Man, hurry and kick the mudscrapers with your great hobnailed boots and find the one that sounds A flat."

Barbara Owens, a Californian, published this first story in Ellery Queen's Mystery Magazine *last year. A powerful, poignant tale of a farm girl in the big city, "The Cloud Beneath the Eaves" won the Mystery Writers of America Edgar award as the best short story of 1978—the second time in three years the honor has gone to an* Ellery Queen's Mystery Magazine *"first story."*

BARBARA OWENS
The Cloud Beneath the Eaves

May 10: I begin. At last. Freshborn, dating only from the first of May. New. A satisfying little word, that "new." A proper word to start a journal. It bears repeating: I am new. What passed before never was. That unspeakable accident and the little problem with my nerves are faded leaves, forgotten. I will record them here only once and then discard them. Now—it's done.

I have never kept a journal before and am not sure why I feel compelled to do so now. Perhaps it's because I need the proof of new life in something I can touch and see. I have come far and I am filled with hope.

May 11: This morning I gazed long at myself in the bathroom mirror. My appearance is different, new. I can never credit myself with beauty, but my face is alive and has lost that indoor pallor. I was not afraid to look at myself. That's a good sign.

I've just tidied up my breakfast things and am sitting at my little kitchen table with a steaming cup of coffee. The morning sun streams through my kitchen curtains, creating lacy, flowing patterns on the cloth. Outside it's still quiet. I'm up too early, of course—difficult to break years of rigid farm habits. I miss the sound of birds, but there are several large trees in the yard, so perhaps there are some. Even a city must have some birds.

I must describe my apartment. Another "new"—my own apartment. I was lucky to find it. I didn't know how to find a place, but a waitress in the YWCA coffee shop told me about it, and when I saw it, I knew I had to have it.

It's in a neighborhood of spacious old homes and small unobtrusive apartment houses; quiet, dignified, and comfortably frayed around the edges. This house is quite old and weathered with funny cupolas and old-fashioned bay windows. The front and side yards are small, but the back is large, pleasantly treed and flowered, and boasts a quaint goldfish pond.

My landlady is a widow who has lived here for over 40 years, and she's converted every available space into an apartment. She lives on the first floor with several cats, and another elderly lady lives in the second apartment on that floor. Two young men of foreign extraction live in one apartment on the second floor, and I have yet to see the occupant of the other. I understand there's also a young male student living in part of the basement.

That leaves only the attic—the best for the last. It's perfect; I even have my own outside steps for private entry and exit. Because of the odd construction of the house, my walls and ceilings play tricks on me. My living room and kitchen are one large area and the ceiling, being under the steepest slope of the roof, is high. In the bedroom and bath the roof takes a suicidal plunge; as a result, the bedroom windows on one wall are scant inches off the floor and I must stoop to see out under the eaves, for the ceiling at that point is only four feet high. In the bath it is the same; one must enter and leave the tub in a bent position. Perhaps that's why I like it so much; it's funny and cozy, with a personality all its own.

The furnishings are old but comfortable. Everything in my living-room area is overstuffed, and although the pieces don't match, they get along well together. The entire apartment is clean and freshly painted a soft green throughout. It's going to be a delight to live here.

I spent most of yesterday getting settled. Now I must close this and be off to the neighborhood market to stock my kitchen. I've even been giving some thought to a small television set. I've never had the pleasure of a television set. Maybe I'll use part of my first paycheck for that. Everything is going to be all right.

May 12: Today I had a visitor! The unseen occupant from the apartment below climbed my steps and knocked on my kitchen (and only) door just as I was finishing breakfast. I'm afraid I was awkward and ill-at-ease at first, but I invited her in and the visit ended pleasantly.

Her name is Sarah Cooley. She's a widow, small and stout, with gray hair and kind blue eyes. She'd noticed I don't have a car and offered the use of hers if I ever need it. She also invited me to attend church with her this morning. I handled it well, I think, thanking her politely for both offers, but declining. Of course I can never enter a car again, and she could not begin to understand my feelings toward the church. However, it was a grand experience, entertaining in my own home. I left her coffee cup sitting on the table all day just to remind myself she'd been there and that all had gone well. It's a good omen.

I must say a few words about starting my new job tomorrow. I try to be confident; everything else has worked out well. I'm the first to admit my getting a job at all is a bit of a miracle. I was not well prepared for that when I came here, but one trip to an employment agency convinced me that was pointless.

Something must have guided me to that particular street and that particular store with its little yellow sign in the window. Mr. Mazek was so kind. He was surprised that anyone could reach the age of 32 without ever having been employed, but I told him just enough of my life on the farm to satisfy him. He even explained how to get a Social Security card, the necessity of which I was not aware. He was so nice I regretted telling him I had a high-school diploma, but I'm sure he would never have considered someone with a mere eighth-grade education. Now my many years of surreptitious reading come to my rescue. I actually have a normal job.

May 13: It went well. In fact, I'm so elated I'm unable to sleep.

I managed the bus complications and arrived exactly on time. Mr. Mazek seemed pleased to see me and started right off addressing me as Alice instead of Miss Whitehead. The day was over before I realized it.

The store is small and dark, a little neighborhood drugstore with two cramped aisles and comfortable clutter. Mr. Mazek is old-fashioned and won't have lunch counters or magazine displays to encourage loitering; he wants his customers to come in, conduct their business, and leave. He's been on that same corner for many years, so almost everyone who enters has a familiar face. I'm going to like being a part of that.

Most of the day I just watched Mr. Mazek and Gloria, the other clerk, but I'm convinced I can handle it. Toward the end of the day he let me ring up several sales on the cash register, and I didn't make one mistake. I'm sure I'll never know the names and positions of each item in the store, but Mr. Mazek says I'll have them memorized in no time and Gloria says if she can do it, I can.

I will do it! I feel safer as each day passes.

May 16: Three days have elapsed and I've neglected my journal. Time goes so quickly! How do I describe my feelings? I wake each morning in my own quiet apartment; I go to a pleasant job where I am needed and appreciated; and I come home to a peaceful evening of doing exactly as I wish. There are no restrictions and no watchful eyes. It's as I always dreamed it would be.

I'm learning the work quickly and am surprised it comes so easily. Gloria complains of boredom, but I find the days too short to savor.

Let me describe Gloria: she's a divorced woman near my own age, languid, slow-moving, with dyed red hair and thick black eyebrows. She's not fat, but gives the appearance of being so because she looks soft and pliable, like an old rubber doll. She has enormous long red fingernails that she fusses with constantly. She wears an abundance of pale makeup, giving her a somewhat startling appearance, but she's been quite nice to me and has worked for Mr. Mazek for several years, so she must be reliable.

I feel cowlike beside her with my great raw bones and awkward hands and feet. We're certainly not alike, but I'm hoping she becomes my first real friend. Yesterday we took our coffee break together, and during our conversation she stopped fiddling with her nails and said, "Gee, Alice, you know you talk just like a book?" At first I was taken aback, but she was smiling so I smiled too. I must listen more to other people and learn. Casual conversation does not come easily to me.

Mr. Mazek continues to be kind and patient, assuring me I am learning well. In many ways he reminds me of Daddy.

I've already made an impression of sorts. Today something was wrong with the pharmaceutical scales, so I asked to look at them and had them right again in no time. Mr. Mazek was amazed. I hadn't realized it was a unique achievement. Being Daddy's right hand on the farm for so many years, there's nothing about machinery I don't know. But I promised I wouldn't think about Daddy.

May 17: Today I received my first paycheck. Not a very exciting piece of paper, but it means everything to me. I hadn't done my figures before, but it's apparent now I won't be rich. And there'll be no television set for me. I can manage rent, food, and a few extras. Fortunately I wear uniforms to work, so I won't need clothes soon.

Immediately after work I went to the bank and opened an

account with my check and what remains of the other. I did that
too without a mistake. And now it's safe. It looks as though I've
really won; they would have come for me by now if she had found
me. I'm too far away and too well hidden. Bless her for mistrust-
ing banks; better I should have taken it than some itinerant thief.
She's probably praying for my soul. Now, no more looking back.

May 18: I don't work on weekends; Mr. Mazek employs a
part-time student. I would rather work since it disturbs me to
have much leisure. It's then I think too much.

This morning I allowed myself the luxury of a few extra minutes in bed, and as I watched the sun rise I noticed an odd
phenomenon beneath the eaves outside my window. Because of
their extension and perhaps some quirk of temperature, the
eaves must trap moisture. A definite mist was swirling softly
against the top of the window all the while the sun shone brightly
through the bottom. It was so interesting I went to the kitchen
window to see if it was there, but it wasn't. It continued for several
minutes before melting away, and nestled up here in my attic I
felt almost as though I were inside a cloud.

This morning I cleaned and shopped. As I was carrying gro-
ceries up the steps, Sarah Cooley called me to come sit with her in
the backyard. She introduced me to the other widow from the
first floor, Mrs. Harmon. Once again Sarah offered her car for
marketing, but I said I like the exercise.

It was unusually soft and warm for May, and quite pleasant
sitting idly in the sun. A light breeze was sending tiny ripples
across the fishpond, and although the fish are not yet back in it I
became aware that some trick of light made it appear as though
something were down there, a shadowy shape just below the
surface. Neither of the ladies seemed to notice it, but I could not
make myself look away. It became so obvious to me something
was down there under the water that I became ill, having no
choice but to excuse myself from pleasant company.

All day I was restless and apprehensive and finally went to bed
early, but in the dark it came, my mind playing forbidden scenes.
Over and over I heard the creaking pulleys and saw the placid
surface of Jordan's pond splintered by the rising roof of Daddy's
rusty old car. I heard tortured screams and saw her wild crazy
eyes. I must not sit by the fishpond again.

May 19: I was strong again this morning. I lay and watched the
little cloud. There is something strangely soothing about its silent
drifting; I was almost sorry to see it go.

I ate well and tried to read the paper, but I kept being drawn to the kitchen window and its clear view of the fishpond. At last I gave up and went out for some fresh air. Sarah and Mrs. Harmon were preparing for a drive in the country as I went down my steps and Sarah invited me, but I declined.

Mr. Mazek was surprised to see me in the store on Sunday. They were quite busy and I offered to stay, but he said I should go and enjoy myself while I'm young. Gloria waggled her fingernails at me. I lingered a while, but finally just bought some shampoo and left.

A bus was sitting at the corner, and not even noticing where it was going I got on. Eventually it deposited me downtown and I spent the day wandering and watching people. I find the city has a vigorous pulse. Everyone seems to know exactly where he's going.

I must have left the shampoo somewhere. It doesn't matter. I already have plenty.

May 20: Today I arrived at the store early. Last week I noticed that the insides of the glass display cases were dirty, so I cleaned them. Mr. Mazek was delighted; he said Gloria never sees when things need cleaning.

Gloria suggested I should have my hair cut and styled, instead of letting it just hang straight; she told me where she had hers done. I'm sure she was trying to be friendly and I thanked her, but I have to laugh when I think of me wearing something like her dyed red frizz.

Mr. Mazek talked to me today about joining some sort of group to meet new people. He suggested a church group as a promising place to start. A church group, of all things! Perhaps he thought I came into the store yesterday because I was lonely and had nothing better to do.

Tonight my landlady, Mrs. Wright, inquired if I had made proper arrangements for mail delivery. Since I've received none, she thought there might have been an error. Again I regretted having to lie. Only the white coats and she would be interested in my whereabouts, and I have worked too hard to evade them.

I am restless and somewhat tense this evening.

May 24: My second week and second paycheck in the bank, and it still goes well.

I've realized with some regret that Gloria and I are not going to be friends. I try, but I'm not fond of her. For one thing, she's lazy; I find myself finishing half of her duties. She makes numerous errors in transactions, and although I've pointed them out to her,

she doesn't do any better. I'm undecided whether to bring this to
Mr. Mazek's attention. Surely he must be aware of it.

On several occasions this week I've experienced a slight blur-
ring of vision, as though a mist were before my eyes. I'm concerned about the cost involved, but prices and labels have to be
read accurately, so it seems essential that I have my eyes tested.

May 26: What an odd thing! The little cloud has moved from
under the eaves in my bedroom to the kitchen window. Yesterday
when I awoke it wasn't there, and as I was having breakfast,
suddenly there it was outside the window, soft and friendly,
rolling gently against the pane. Perhaps it's my imagination, but it
seems larger. It was there again today, a most welcome sight.

Yesterday was an enjoyable day—the usual cleaning and shopping.

Today was not so enjoyable. Just as I was finishing lunch, I
heard voices under my steps where Sarah parks her car. The
ladies were getting ready for another Sunday drive and when I
looked out, they were concerned over an ominous sound in the
engine. Before I stopped to think, I heard myself offering to look
at it. All the way down the steps I told myself it would be all right,
but as soon as I raised the hood, the blackness and nausea came. I
couldn't see and somewhere far away I heard a voice calling,
"Allie! Allie, where are you?"

Somehow I managed to find the trouble and get back upstairs.
Everything was shadows, threatening. I couldn't catch my breath
and my hands wouldn't stop shaking. Suddenly I was at the
kitchen window, straining to see down into the fishpond. I'm
afraid I don't know what happened next.

But the worst is over. I'm all right now. I have drawn the shade
over the kitchen window so I will never see the fishpond again. It's
going to be all right.

I wish it were tomorrow and time to be with Mr. Mazek again.

May 30: Gloria takes advantage of him. I have watched her
carefully this week and she is useless in that store. Mr. Mazek is so
warm and gentle he tends to overlook her inadequacy, but it is
wrong of her. I see now she's also a shameless flirt, teasing almost
every man who comes in. Today she and a pharmaceutical salesman were in the back stockroom for over an hour, laughing and
smoking. I could see that Mr. Mazek didn't like it, but he did
nothing to stop it. I've been there long enough to see that he and I
could manage that store quite nicely. We really don't need Gloria.

I have an appointment for my eyes. The mist occurs frequently now.

June 2: The cloud *is* getting bigger. Yesterday morning the sun shone brightly in my bedroom, but the kitchen was dim and there was a shadow on the shade. When I raised it a fraction, there were silky fringes resting on the sill. I stepped out on the landing and saw it pressed securely over the pane. It is warm, not damp to the touch—warm, soft, and soothing. I have raised the kitchen shade again—the cloud blots out the fishpond completely.

Yesterday I started down the steps to do my marketing, my eyes lowered to avoid sight of the fishpond, and through the steps I saw the top of Sarah's car. Something stirred across it like currents of water, and suddenly I was so weak and dizzy I had to grip the railing to keep from falling as I crept back up the stairs.

I have stayed in all day.

June 7: I have been in since Wednesday with the flu. I began feeling badly Tuesday, but I worked until Wednesday noon when Mr. Mazek insisted I go home. I'm sorry to leave him with no one but Gloria, but I am certainly not well enough to work.

I came home to bed, but the sun shining through my window made disturbing movements in the room. Everything is so green, and the pulsing shadows across the ceiling made it seem that I was underwater. Suddenly I was trapped, suffocating, my lungs bursting for air.

I've moved my bedding and fashioned a bed for myself on the living-room couch. Here I can see and draw comfort from the cloud. I will sleep now.

June 10: I have been very ill. Sarah has come to my door twice, but I was too tired and weak to call out, so she went away. I am feverish; sometimes I am not sure I'm awake or asleep and dreaming. I just realized today is special—the first month's anniversary of my new life. Somehow it seems longer. I'd hoped

June 11: I've just awakened and am watching the cloud. Little wisps are peeping playfully under my door. I think it wants to come inside.

June 12: I am better today. Mrs. Wright used her passkey to come in and was horrified to find I'd been so sick and no one knew. She and Sarah wanted to take me to a doctor, but I cannot get inside that car, so I convinced them I'm recovering. She brought hot soup and I managed to get some down.

The cloud pressed close behind her when she came in, but

didn't enter. Perhaps it's waiting for an invitation. Poor Mrs. Wright was so concerned with me she didn't notice the cloud.

June 13: Today I felt well enough to go downstairs to Mrs. Wright's and call Mr. Mazek. I couldn't go until after noon— Sarah's car was down there. I became quite anxious, sure that he needed me in the store. He sounded glad to hear my voice and pleased that I am better, but insisted I not come in until Monday when I am stronger.

I am so ashamed. Suddenly wanting to be with him today, I heard myself pleading. Before I could stop, I told him my entire plan for letting Gloria go and having the store just to ourselves. He was silent so long that I came to my senses and realized my mistake, so I laughed and said something about the fever talking. After a moment he laughed too, and I said I would see him on Monday.

I have let the cloud come in. It sifts about me gently and seems to fill the room.

June 21: Didn't go to the bank today. Crowds and lines begin to annoy me. I will manage with the money and food I have on hand.

Mr. Mazek, bless him, is concerned about my health. I see him watching me with a grave expression, so I work harder to show him I am strong and fine.

I've started taking the cloud to work with me. It stays discreetly out of the way, piling gently in the dim corners, but it comforts me to know it's there, and I find myself smiling at it when no one's looking.

Yesterday afternoon I went to the back stockroom for something, and I'd forgotten Gloria and another one of her salesmen were in there. I stopped when I heard their voices, but not before I heard Gloria say my name and something about "stupid hick"; then they laughed together. Tears came to my eyes, but suddenly a mist was all around me and the cloud was there, smoothing, enfolding, shutting everything away.

A note from Mrs. Wright on my door tonight said that the eye doctor had called to remind me of my appointment. No need to keep it now.

June 23: Sarah's car was here all day yesterday, so I did not go out.

I don't even go into the bedroom now. I am still sleeping on the couch. Because it's old and lumpy, perhaps that's what's causing the dreams. Today I awoke suddenly, my heart pounding and my face wet with tears. I thought I was back there again and all the white coats stood leaning over me. "You can go home," they chorused in a nasty singsong. "You can go home at last to live with your mother." I lay there shaking, remembering. They really believed I would stay with *her!*

Marketed, but did not clean. I am so tired

June 27: You see? I function normally. I reason, so I am all right. It's that lumpy old couch. Last night the dream was about Daddy choking out his life at the bottom of Jordan's pond. I was out of control when I awoke, but the cloud came and took it all away. Today I fixed my blankets on the floor.

June 28: Dear Mr. Mazek continues to be solicitous of my health. Today he suggested I take a week off—get some rest or take a little vacation. He looked so troubled, but of course I couldn't leave him like that.

Sometimes I feel afraid, feel that everything is slipping away. I am trying so hard.

Maybe I should be more tolerant of Gloria.

July 5: After several hours inside my blessed cloud, I believe I am calm enough to think things through. I have been hurt and betrayed. I cannot conceive such betrayal!

Today I discovered that Gloria is—how shall I say it?—"carrying on" with Mr. Mazek and has evidently been doing so for years. Apparently they were supposed to spend the holiday yesterday together, but Gloria went off with someone else. I heard them through the closed door of Mr. Mazek's little office—their voices were very loud—and Gloria was laughing at him! The cloud came to me instantly and I don't remember the rest of the day.

Now I begin to understand. It explains so many things. At first I was terribly angry with Mr. Mazek. Now I realize Gloria tempted him and he was too weak to resist. The evil of that woman. Something must be done. This cannot be allowed to continue.

July 8: I found my opportunity today when we were working together in the stockroom. I began by telling her my finding out was an accident, but that now she must stop it at once. She just played with her fingernails, smiled, and said nothing until I reminded her he was a respected married man with grandchildren and she was ruining all their lives. Then she laughed out loud, said Mr. Mazek was a big boy, and why didn't I mind my own business.

July 11: I'm afraid it's hopeless. For three days I've pursued and pleaded with her to stop her heartless action. This afternoon she suddenly turned on me, screaming harsh cruel things I can't bring myself to repeat. I couldn't listen, so I took refuge in the cloud. Later I saw her speaking forcefully to Mr. Mazek; it looked almost as though she were threatening him. What shall I do now?

I am not sleeping well at all.

July 12: I have been let out of my job. There is no less painful way to say it. This afternoon Mr. Mazek called me into his office and let me go as of today, but he will pay me for an extra week. I could say nothing, I was so stunned. He said something about his part-time student needing more money in the summer, but of course I know that's not the reason. He said he was sorry, and he looked so unhappy that I felt sorry for him. I know it isn't his fault. I know he would rather have me with him than Gloria. Even the cloud has not been able to save me today.

July 16: I have not left here for four days. I know, because I have marked them on the wall the way I did when I was there. Tomorrow I will draw a crossbar over the four little straight sticks.

I think I have eaten. There are empty cans on the floor and bits of food in my blankets.

The cloud sustains me—whispering, shutting out the pain.

July 19: It is all arranged. Gloria was alone when I went in this morning for my last paycheck. She seemed nervous and a bit ashamed. We were both polite and she went back to Mr. Mazek's office for my pay.

I felt a great sadness. I love that little store. And I have memorized it so well in the time I was allowed to be a part of it. It is fortunate that I know precisely were everything is kept.

At first she refused my invitation to have lunch with me today. She said she begins her vacation tomorrow. But I was persistent, pleading how vital it is to me that we part with no hard feelings between us. Finally she agreed, and I am calm inside the cloud, and strong and confident again.

She came here to my apartment and it went well. Lunch was pleasant and Mr. Mazek's name was never mentioned. I even told her all about myself, and she seemed no more upset than could be expected. . . .

Tonight I put a note on Mrs. Wright's door saying I'd been called away for a few weeks. I've moved my heavy furniture in front of the door. I must be very still and remember not to turn on lights. There is enough light from the street to write by and the cloud is here to protect and keep me. I have come a long way. This time it is right.

July   : All goes back, goes back. The white coats were wrong. I can't do it.

I saw Daddy again. We stood under the lantern in the big old barn. He showed me all the parts of his old car and how each one of them worked. It felt so safe and good to be with him, and he told me again that I was his good right hand. I wanted

Bad. Oh, bad. Everyone said you were crazy. Mean. Your Bible and your praying and church, over and over, your church every night, shouting and praying, never doing anything to help Daddy and me on the farm. Sitting at the kitchen table with your Bible, singing and praying, everything dirty and undone, then into the old car and off to church to shout and pray some more while Daddy and I did all the work.

Never soothed him, never loved him, just prayed at him and counted his sins. Couldn't go to school, made me stay home and work on the farm, no books, books are the devil's tools, had to hide my books in the barn high up under the eaves. Ugly, you're a big ugly child, girl, and you prayed for my soul, prayed for mine and Daddy's souls. Poor sad Daddy's soul.

Took it too hard they said, oh yes, took it too hard, so they sent me away for the white coats to fix and then they made me go back to you, your Bible, and your praying, and everyone said it was an accident, a tragic accident they said, but you knew, you never said but you knew, and you prayed and sang and quoted the Bible and you broke my Daddy's life. In the clouds, girl's always got her head in the clouds, I loved my Daddy and you prayed for souls and went to church every night and every night   It is hot in here. It must be summer outside. All the windows are closed up tight and it is very hot here under the eaves. In the clouds

Today: I do not know what day it is. How many days I have been here. Markings on my walls, words and drawings I do not understand. I lie here on the floor and watch my cloud. It sighs and swirls and keeps me safe. I can't see outside it anymore. It is warm and soft and I will stay inside forever. No one can find me now.

Gloria is beginning to smell. Puffy Gloria and her long red claws. Silly foolish Gloria who didn't even complain when the coffee tasted strange. I have set my Daddy free.

I am in the barn. Night. I am supposed to be milking the cow. I

am peaceful, serene. I have done it well and now life will be rich
and good. The old car coughs and soon I hear it rattling toward
the steep hill over Jordan's pond. It starts down. I listen. Content.
The sound fades, a voice, the wrong voice, calling my name:
"Allie! Allie, where are you?" The light goes out of the world.

Odaddydaddydaddy, where were you going in the car that
night? Wasn't supposed to be you   supposed to be her her her

Thomas Walsh, winner of last year's Mystery Writers of America Edgar award for the best short story of 1977, was at the top of his form in 1978, producing a number of truly fine stories for Ellery Queen's Mystery Magazine. *This one, which exemplifies Walsh's skill with the compassionate police story, was an MWA Edgar nominee.*

THOMAS WALSH
The Closed Door

That night Detective Shanahan splurged on their fifth anniversary—their fifth monthly anniversary. But on his way home from the precinct he passed the ice-skating rink in Rockefeller Plaza where they had met only last winter, on a blind date with Lou Anderson and his girl, and it came to him how very little they had known each other in those days. What a chance they had taken! What two entirely different people they might have turned out to be from what each had imagined! Whereas in place of that, and although Detective Shanahan had only courted her for three weeks . . . But now, perhaps, it was required of him to be properly thankful, and to show that he was.

So at home he had Christina dress to the nines—she always had great style—after which they had dinner at the best French restaurant in midtown and went on to one of the hit Broadway musicals.

"But my golly," Christina said on the way home. She was always the saving one too. "You must have spent more than a hundred dollars tonight. Know what? I think you're kind of glad you got me, old boy."

"I wouldn't count on that," Detective Shanahan told her, in the way they had. "You're just living in a fool's world, Chris. One of these days I'm liable to turn you in on a new model."

"As if you could," Christina said, contentedly, resting against his right shoulder. "Or me, either. I think if I had ninety million dollars in the bank and was queen of all Hollywood, there's only one man I'd want in the whole world, or ever would want."

"And who's that?" Shanahan demanded. "Confessing, eh? What have you been keeping from me?"

"You just guess," Christina murmured. "Guess twice, even. I'm not going to spoil you any more than I do now. But you better let me out in front of the apartment, Dick. It's beginning to rain."

So Shanahan went on to a parking space down the street and trotted back from it quickly and happily. They only had a three-room apartment as yet, very cramped quarters, and often, when squeezing past one another in the bedroom passage or out in the kitchen, it seemed that Christina had to hug Shanahan for no reason, or Shanahan had to hug Christina. Then they would stand there, arms tight around each other, and laugh at themselves. They were very happy, absurdly happy. Often it seemed to Shanahan that they had discovered a secret, a marvelous and extraordinary secret, that no one else had ever even suspected.

But when Shanahan bounced up the steps into his apartment entryway that night, Christina was not alone. Two men were with her. One crouched over her where she lay, trying to yank the purse out of her hands, and the other spun around instantly when he heard Shanahan. "Now watch it," he ordered in a high shaky voice, eyes darting around, and showing the gun in his hand. "I'm telling you something. Keep the hell out of our way, man."

But of course Shanahan didn't. He went ahead in one blind, maddened lunge, everything exploding in him, aware of Christina's face with all the blood on one side, and of the half-conscious low moan she had uttered. Then the man on his knees smashed her again, as if with the frightened yet frenzied desperation of a drug addict, while the other one fired the gun in his hand.

Shanahan went down sprawling. His right leg felt all smashed. But he was not really conscious of that, and although the doctors said afterward that it was impossible to have done such a thing with his ruined knee, he got up again and ran after the two men down the dark cellarway at the back of the hall. With his first bullet he dropped the first man at the bottom of the steps. He dropped the second one in the yard. Then he ran back up the stairs, again an altogether impossible feat as the doctors saw it, and got Christina in his two arms. She was able to say only one thing.

"Help me," Shanahan heard. "Please help me, Dick. It's the whole side of my head. It hurts so—"

"Well, how it was," Lieutenant Francis McConnell explained uncomfortably the next morning, "she cried out for help when they jumped at her from the cellarway, and we found that two families on the first floor heard her, and one on the second. But they didn't so much as open their doors to see what it was. They were afraid, they said. They didn't think it was their business. But if they had even shouted down to ask what it was, they'd probably have stopped the second smash she got. And then, maybe—what the hell kind of a world are we living in, anyway? What have we come to?"

"I don't know," Shanahan said, one arm over his face, his voice dull and empty. "But I guess I never even knew it before. She didn't come through the operation, did she? That's why you're here."

Francis McConnell said nothing. He only reached forward, took hold of Shanahan's forearm, squeezed it powerfully, and kept his hand there. Shanahan closed his eyes and shivered slightly. Then he pressed his arm over his eyes so that Francis McConnell should not see what he was doing, and turned his head.

He never went back to the apartment. He knew he could not trust himself near the two families on the first floor, and the one on the second. His sister Mary disposed of the living-room set and the curtains Christina had made with her own hands. Always very clever that way, Shanahan recalled, always ironing his shirts or sewing his buttons on or cooking his dinner. "And that nice laugh she had," his brother-in-law Al Kennedy mourned. "What they call infectious, I guess. Every time you heard it you had to laugh right out loud with her. She just made you, somehow. Remember, Dick?"

"Yes," Shanahan said, limping over to look out of the window so that Al Kennedy would not see any more than Francis McConnell had. "Yes, I do. I remember, Al."

But he could stay only two weeks with the Kennedys. Then, still on sick leave, he limped downstairs one morning, got his suitcase out of the hall closet, and began packing. "I don't know," he said, when Mary asked him where he was going. "Just want to be alone for a while, Mary. That's all I can tell you."

He drove north simply because the parkway led in that direction. Late in the afternoon he was up into Adirondack country, mountains and trees, lakes and rivers, and about half-past four he pulled into one of the rest stops. There was great quiet around him when he had shut off the motor, a deep, faintly humming quiet. Most of the foliage was long gone, but now and again a few leaves drifted down lazily in the golden October sunlight. The lake in the valley under him shone very blue, and there were a few tranquil white clouds high up over the mountains. "Help me," he remembered then. "Please help me, Dick. It hurts so—"

What a fool he had been, Shanahan thought then. What a stupid child's world he had believed in, where there were decent human beings to help one another in time of need. Yet the truth, actually, was much different. There had been no one to help Christina. There had been no one to even open a door for her. Trouble? Then keep yourself safely out of it. That had been the help she got. See no evil. Hear no evil. React to no evil. It was not their problem. Then why should they get involved in it?

So now he knew. There had been a time when he had been stupid enough to believe that it was a very fine thing to do whatever he could, when the chance offered, to prevent crime and injustice and violence. But what could he believe now, when the doors had not been opened to Chris, and the human response not made? He had known that such things frequently happened in any city, and in his own working life had known them to happen time after time.

Not until now, however, had he faced up to the brute fact. The human condition was unspeakable beyond words. Decency did not exist and had never existed, just as a girl named Christina Shanahan did not exist now. Aware of the sparrow, one had been taught—and so, obviously, aware of the two men. But like the families on the first floor and the one on the second, no majestic hand had been raised, no desperately needed help had been given.

After a while, after a long while, Shanahan got out of the car. He limped down to the lake, his teeth clenched painfully, tore the detective shield out of his wallet, and threw it as far as he could into deep water. Then he limped back, his teeth still clenched, and about dusk stopped in a small town just off the Northway. His decision was made. From now on Detective Shanahan's door would also be closed.

Before unpacking, he decided to have a drink in the motel bar—he always had to have four or five drinks a night now, in order to sleep—and in the bar had the first adult test of his life.

It was a small motel, not too busy at this time of year, and there

were only a couple of other customers in the bar. One was a big
burly man with flaming red hair, a red face, and a loudly arrogant
voice, and the other was all in gray—gray suit, gray shirt, gray tie,
gray and narrow, tight-lipped young face. They were not, Shanahan could see, mountain people. They had different manners
and different voices, and a city-wise toughness that showed in
everything that they said and did.

They had just been served drinks, but after glancing around at
Shanahan the redhead deliberately emptied his on the floor.

"You mixed it," he told the bartender. "And I wanted it on the
side, Baldy. Try again."

"Then why didn't you say so?" the bartender muttered. "All I
heard you say was a rye and a scotch. Who's paying for that
drink?"

"Couldn't tell you," the redhead drawled, obviously enjoying
himself. "Only I ain't. You get what you ordered, Charley?"

The gray one tried his drink, made a face, and shoved it back.

"What the hell is that?" he demanded. "I asked you for rye,
Baldy. What did you give me?"

A slow flush came to the bartender's cheeks.

"I gave you the bar whiskey," he said. "You didn't ask for any
particular brand, mister. So I—"

"Some bar whiskey," Charley said. "Think maybe you better try
again with me too. You know something? I think he's trying to clip
us, Leo."

"Always did before," Leo said, dropping some coins in the
jukebox. "Every time we come up to this dump. Last time we had
about eight drinks apiece and all he rang up on the register was
for two beers. Clipping the boss too. Think we didn't notice,
Baldy?"

The bartender poured again, his hands shaking either with
anger or fear, but he did not say anything. Returning from the
jukebox, Leo glanced out the window, then at Shanahan.

"How's the weather outside?" he wanted to know. "Getting any
colder, Gimpy?"

Shanahan, the new Shanahan, did not answer. He was nothing
more than an uninterested onlooker now—the way of the world.

"I'll have a very dry martini," he told the bartender. "On the
rocks."

"Well, well, well," Leo drawled. "Very dry martini, Baldy. We
got some class in here now."

Shanahan sat down on the bar stool farthest from them, got his cane into position, and rested the bad leg on it. For a while the jukebox blared away, and Leo and Charley murmured, as the bartender, still flushed and upset, polished and repolished the same highball glass. The gray man drank quickly and edgily, glancing up at the clock often, then drumming his fingers on the bar. At last, after a few more drinks, he got up and touched Leo's arm.

"Okay," Leo said. "Time, huh? What's the tab, Baldy?"

The bartender put down the glass. It was obvious he did not like that name and just as obvious he would not challenge it. But it was not Shanahan's affair—the closed door now.

"Five ryes and three scotches," he said. "Let's see. Dollar ten for the ryes, five fifty, and dollar and a half for the scotches, four fifty. An even ten, mister."

"You think so?" Leo grinned. "How many ryes you have, Charley?"

"Two," Charley said, with a cold grin on his lips, also enjoying himself now. "I decided to keep count, Leo—with this fellow."

"Just like I had only two scotches," Leo said. "Which makes it, the way I figure, two twenty and three dollars. That's all we're giving."

The bartender, glancing at Shanahan, moistened his lips nervously.

"Wait a minute," he said. "I served you eight drinks."

"No, you didn't," Leo said, also glancing at Shanahan with calm and icy blue eyes. "Ask Gimpy there. How many drinks he give us, Gimpy?"

"I'd say eight," Shanahan replied quietly. With the bartender, it had been Leo against something or other; with Shanahan, Shanahan discovered suddenly, it was necessary to be man against man. "You owe him ten bucks, Loudmouth."

"Loudmouth?" Leo repeated softly, moving forward two steps.

"Like in Baldy," Shanahan said, but not because of the bartender. He felt a sudden thick violence in him—to hurt someone or other, to hurt coldly and cruelly. As a young man he had boxed in the Golden Gloves for two years and was not worried at all, even with his bad leg. Leo had quite a potbelly on him. "Like in Gimpy. See what I mean, Loudmouth?"

"Now that ain't good manners," Leo said, even more softly, moving forward another two steps. "Might decide to teach you a few, Gimpy."

"Yes, I know," Shanahan said, getting up from the stool. "One difficulty, though. The way you act, I don't think you could, Loudmouth."

"I don't want any roughhouse in here," the bartender said anxiously. "Just cut it out now or I'll call the troopers."

"Wow," Leo said, shifting to him. "Think of that. Sends kind of a cold shudder all through me, Charley. Hear what he said?"

"Come on, come on," the gray one put in impatiently. "Give him the ten, Leo. We got things to do."

"Yeah, guess we have," Leo said. "I'm coming. Your lucky night, Gimpy. Ain't got the time."

When the door had closed on them, the bartender let out a long shaky breath, wiped his face with the bottom of his apron, and moved down to Shanahan.

"Come up here about two or three times a month," Shanahan was told. "Both of them—and they're always like that. Hellbent for trouble, or at least the redhead. But they're good customers this time of year. Pay me twenty-five dollars a night for the room. Always trying to chisel me on the drinks, though. Think it's funny, I guess. But what can I do?"

"I suppose nothing much," Shanahan said—Shanahan the on-looker. "What do you think they come up here for?"

The bartender used his cloth around Shanahan's glass, and looking over toward the front door lowered his voice cautiously.

"I couldn't tell you that," he said. "But they're always here only for the one night. And you know"—polishing needlessly still— "from what I hear they're running a lot of stuff into the states from Montreal these days. Sneak it over the border first, then somebody picks it up along the line and pays them off for it. But I don't know, mister, and I ain't opening my mouth about it. If I did, I'd wake up some morning and find this whole place burned down to the ground. That's what they do, I hear, fellows like them. Better not take a chance."

"Stuff?" Shanahan said. He felt a small nerve jump in one side of his face, then tighten. There were two other men he could remember and they had turned out to be a couple of drug addicts desperate for a fix. "What's that mean?"

"Have to guess," the bartender said, a feeble kind of hatred showing itself in his words for Leo and Charley. "And I don't want to. But they're even getting the high-school kids onto it up here. Had a case in town only last week. High-school girl named Christina Cawley. Only sixteen years old."

Shanahan felt the nerves in his chest tighten. Who or what had killed another Christina that night? The men or the stuff?

"What's the matter?" the bartender said. "You look funny."

"No, I'm all right," Shanahan heard himself say. "Just the leg, I guess. Gives me a twinge every so often. But you've figured out all this for yourself and you don't do a damned thing, even after that high-school kid?"

"Don't look for trouble," the bartender admitted. "Can't afford to. And what do I know, anyway? What can I prove? Look out for yourself, mister, and keep your mouth shut. That's the only answer there is."

And it was the same answer, Shanahan realized later after unpacking his things in the motel room, that he himself had decided on back there at the rest stop. The stuff then was run in here from Canada, paid for in cold cash somewhere, and brought downstate the next day by people like Leo and Charley. There it was put out on the street at high prices, and to afford those prices two men on a certain night in New York had slipped out of a dark cellarway and gone after a girl's purse when she came in with no escort.

Not sane; not normal; like rabid animals. A Christina Shanahan down there and a Christina Cawley up here—but two victims, in different ways, of the same thing. And what was Detective Shanahan going to do about it? Nothing at all. He had closed his door and had vowed never to open it again, not for anyone. Only Number One from now on.

Yet a bit later, on his way to the only restaurant in town, he could not seem to get Leo and Charley out of his mind. Mountain cold and loneliness all around; more bright stars in the sky than he had ever seen, but distant and unreachable stars; and far off somewhere, or so one was told, a Being who let things happen in whatever way they might. Unless someone or other took a hand in the business; unless that was maybe the whole point. Not me to do it. You to do it. One Christina dead and buried now, gone forever—but another Christina, only sixteen years old, alive and victimized.

And too there were cold and loneliness, grief and squalor and misery everywhere in the world. So Detective Shanahan discovered that he had been a little mistaken. He had not just found out. He had known it the whole time. But a few weeks ago he had been able to close his door to it, to shelter himself. No matter the wretched and inescapable loneliness then, no matter the misery without end, Detective Shanahan had found a way of moving aside from it, of dismissing it.

Before, always and always, there had been a lamp on for him in a certain apartment, and always and always Christina waiting. A Protestant girl too, and Detective Shanahan a Roman, although the difference in religion had never mattered to them, and they had never so much as discussed it. But she had believed in something much more than Detective Shanahan had. She had always kept the Book of Common Prayer on her bedside table and had not liked it at all when Detective Shanahan would thoughtlessly joke about it. She had never hated anyone, but instead had loved every small, gentle, innocent, helpless thing—a stray kitten, a mangy cur, and the two goldfish he had bought her last April when she had a cold—the first present he had ever bought her.

"And don't worry about them at all," Detective Shanahan had told her. "If we have to go away for a few days we'll just stick them into the freezer, Chris. Then all we have to do is take them out again and in half an hour they'll be swimming around lively as ever. Guarantee it to you. The clerk told me."

And after that? After that, Detective Shanahan remembered, a high and irrepressible happy laugh was his reward, and for Detective Shanahan there had never been another laugh like that one and never would be. Would he hear it now, however, this new Detective Shanahan? He had turned his face away from the world.

"Oh, Dick," he could remember now. "I declare I don't know what's the matter with you, talking like an atheist the way you do. Because you have to believe in the Lord, and if you don't—"

He did not know what he ate, or if he ate anything at all, and was lighting a cigarette over his coffee when Leo and Charley came in. Charley, even paler and jerkier now in his gray ensemble, was carrying a blue and white overnight bag. He put it down under the coatrack near the door. Then he and Leo went into one of the booths, out of sight, and not long after, two other men came in. One was also carrying a blue and white bag, and he put in down under the coatrack next to Charley's.

"More coffee?" the waitress asked.

"What?" Shanahan said, watching the two bags. "Oh. Yes, I guess I will. Thanks." So the exchange would be made right here, where two men in one booth and two in a corner would not appear even to know each other. Not a bad way at all. Who would notice or suspect anything in a public restaurant? The two parties would not trust each other so much as an inch, if the bartender knew what he was talking about. The ones from downstate would want to make sure first they were getting the stuff, and the ones from Canada would want to make just as sure they were getting the money. Wait and see then; nice and easy now. Just watch how they handled it.

And they handled it very well, Detective Shanahan saw. In a few minutes Charley reappeared from the booth and went into the men's room, the door of which was visible to Shanahan. Then, seconds later, one of the other men got up, took his bag from under the coatrack, and followed.

Detective Shanahan could not see through the door, but he did not have to by now. In the men's room, he knew, business was being transacted—and private as the grave in there, with the door locked, while Leo and the other man from Canada, probably the bodyguards, remained alertly on watch outside to make sure that neither party pulled anything.

In the men's room it would be Charley's duty to see first, to look, taste, smell, and make sure. Then he would come out with the bag that the other party had brought down from Canada and then it would be Leo's turn to go into the men's room with the money that had been brought up from New York. All the details of the switch had been very carefully thought out. Not until each side was positive it had got what it was bargaining for would they separate, still complete strangers, and go off in different directions.

And so it proved out. Soon Leo went into the men's room carrying his overnight bag and the other man from Canada went in right after him. At that point Detective Shanahan got up from the table, paid his bill, and posted himself just outside the front door in the shadow of an old pickup truck. Presently the second pair of men emerged and drove off in a green Buick with Quebec license plates: point one for the bartender.

Still watching the door, Detective Shanahan edged back into a phone booth beside the road.

"Trooper's barracks," a voice said when his call had got through. "Sergeant Moore speaking. Yeah, what's the problem?"

"A little trouble down here at your town diner," Detective Shanahan told him. "I'd send a car, Sergeant. And there's a green

Buick that just headed north for Canada about two minutes ago. I'd have it stopped somewhere along the line or else at the Canadian border. Two people in it. Male Caucasians, medium height, dark overcoats, thirty or thirty-two. They're carrying a blue and white overnight bag that probably has fifty or a hundred thousand dollars in it, maybe more. The way I see it, they just made a drug deal with two other fellows right here in the diner. Don't waste any time, eh?"

He added the Quebec license number and slipped back to the pickup truck. But now, with everything satisfactorily concluded and nothing more to worry about, Charley and Leo stayed inside for some time, relaxing over their after-dinner coffee. It did not matter very much. Detective Shanahan waited.

A clear cold night still; all those bright mountain stars in the sky; but no lamp on anymore, nowhere in the whole world. Yet what really had changed for him, if he refused to let it change? It was only necessary to love now in a different way, and without the silly human failings of meanness and touchiness and self-pride; the thing reduced and clarified for him to its true essence.

That was how his father must have felt when Shanahan's mother had died, because in going through some papers one day, after his father's death, Shanahan had found a picture of his mother as a young girl, with a few lines of poetry attached.

> Go slowly, love, since you have gone before me,
> God's creature now, bright spirit swift as flame,
> But slowly, love, to sooner hear behind thee,
> When I have come, the whisper of your name.

A faith there, certainly. But a foolish and cowardly faith, trying to pretend to itself, trying to avoid the brutal and inescapable human fact? Detective Shanahan decided not for him, anyway. And yet he was still waiting, everything decided for him now in a new way, when Leo and Charley came out. Leo was carrying the blue and white overnight bag. Charley led the way to their car. He had bent down to unlock the door when Detective Shanahan moved toward him out of the shadow.

"Right there," Detective Shanahan said, his service revolver steady as a rock in his right hand. "Both of you. And put that bag down real slow and real easy, Leo. I want to see what you're carrying around in it."

Yet he made one mistake. He had assumed Leo was the bodyguard. He had not considered it might be Charley, and Charley, at the critical moment, reacted quick as a flash.

But not quick enough. Shanahan had his gun out, Charley did not. So Shanahan placed his first bullet exactly where he wanted to place it, shattering Charley's right arm, but in doing so Leo was able to take the only chance he had left.

"Because you ask me?" Leo said, still holding the bag. "Like hell. Real bright boy, eh?"

"Maybe brighter than you," Shanahan said. "Do what I say."

"Okay," Leo said. "Whatever you say. All we got in here—"

Then he threw the bag at Shanahan's face and came after it, his lips snarling and both arms curved wide to grab Shanahan's legs. But then the choked-off violence finally released itself in Detective Shanahan, and now, very calm in all this, he knocked the bag to one side and decided thankfully that he did not have to use the gun on Leo.

Instead he moved in at Leo just as fast as Leo moved at him. He did not go for the legs, however. He threw just one left hook, always his best punch in those long-ago amateur days, and no other was necessary.

Leo met it head on, stupid Leo; twice the force, consequently. He went down. Charley, clutching his right arm with his left hand, scrambled out from behind the car fender to regain his revolver, but Detective Shanahan kicked it away from him and looked down at them. Leo lay sprawled on his face, arms still curved. He did not move. The overnight bag had come to a stop on Shanahan's left and lay there.

There was not much to do after that. Leo still did not move. Charley had begun to whimper brokenly. Detective Shanahan moved back, at the same time imagining he felt a breath on his face that he would have known among twenty million others. *All right now*, Detective Shanahan thought; *but go slow, Chris, and don't worry about the old boy anymore. I think he'll do fine.*

A frightened head stuck itself out of the diner. More heads followed. But not long afterward, at the nearest Northway exit, they could all hear the siren coming.

In this tale of remembered murder, the people are as important as the puzzle, and the final surprise is everything you'd expect from a writer as skilled as Ruth Rendell. One of England's best and most prolific mystery writers, she published two excellent novels during 1978 and still found time for a number of fine short stories. This is one.

RUTH RENDELL
Truth Will Out

Along the sea front, between the pier and the old town, was a row of wooden seats. There were six of them, regularly spaced on the grass, and they faced the dunes, the sea wall, and the sea. To some people, including Mrs. Jones, they were known by name as Fisher, Jackson, Teague, Prendergast, Lubbock, and Rupert Moore. It was on this last seat, the one that was curiously known by the Christian as well as the family name of the man it commemorated, that Mrs. Jones invariably chose to sit.

She sat there every day, enjoying the peace and quiet, looking at the sea and thinking about the past. It was most pleasant on mild winter days or on those days of summer when the sky was overcast, for then the holiday visitors stayed in their cars or went off to buy prawns and crabs and expensive knickknacks.

Mrs. Jones thought how glad she was that last year, when Mr. Jones had been taken from her, she had bought the house in the old town, even though this had meant separating herself from her daughter. She thought about her son in London and her daughter in Ipswich, good loving children that they were, and about her grandchildren, and sometimes about her good fortune in having a comfortable annuity as well as her pension.

But mostly, sitting on Rupert Moore, between Fisher and Teague, she thought about the first man in her life to whom even now, after so long, she referred always as her darling. She had so accustomed herself to calling him this that to her the endearment had become his name. My darling, thought Mrs. Jones, as some other old woman might have thought of John or Charlie or Tom.

She felt closer to him here than anywhere, which was why she chose to rest on this seat and not on one of the others.

On July 15th, St. Swithin's Day, Hugh and Cecily Branksome sat in their car, which was parked on the promenade, and looked at the gray choppy sea. Or, rather, Hugh looked at the sea while Cecily looked at Mrs. Jones. The temperature was around 10 degrees, according to Cecily, who moved with the times, or 50, according to Hugh, who did not. It was not yet raining, though the indications were that it soon would be.

Hugh was wishing they had gone to the Costa Brava where there would have been high-rise buildings and fish and chips and bullfights, but at least the sun would have shone. Cecily had got it into her head that it was bourgeois and unpatriotic to go abroad for one's holiday.

"I wonder why she always sits there," said Cecily.

"Who sits where?"

"That old woman. She always sits on that particular seat. She was there yesterday and the day before."

"Didn't notice," said Hugh.

"You never notice anything. While you were in the pub yesterday," said Cecily with emphasis. "I waited until she'd gone and then I read the inscription on that seat. On the metal plate on the back. D'you know what it says?"

"Of course I don't," said Hugh, opening the window to let out the cigarette smoke. An icy breeze hit him in the face.

"Do close the window. It says, 'Rupert Moore gave this seat to Northwold in thanks for his deliverance. I was in prison and ye came unto me, Matthew, chapter twenty-five, verse thirty-five.' How about that?"

"Remarkable." Hugh thought he knew all about being in prison. He looked at his watch. "Opening time," he said. "We can go and get a drink, thank God."

On the following morning he went out fishing without her. They met in their room before dinner, Hugh bracing himself to face certain sarcastic questions, not without precedent, as to whether he had had a nice day. He forestalled them by telling her they had caught only one small mackerel, for her censure would be greater if he had enjoyed himself. But he was soon interrupted.

"I've got the whole story about the seat out of that nice man with the beard."

Hugh's memory was poor and for a moment he didn't know which seat she was talking about, but he recognized the nice man from her description. A busybody know-it-all who lived in Northwold and hung about the hotel bar.

"He insisted on buying me a drink. Well, two, as a matter of fact." She smiled archly and patted her hair as if the bearded know-it-all had, at the very least, invited her to Aldeburgh for the weekend. "His name is Arnold Cottle and he said this Rupert Moore put that seat there because he'd murdered his wife. He was put on trial and acquitted and that's what it means about 'deliverance' and being in prison."

"You can't say he murdered his wife if he was acquitted."

"You know what I mean," said Cecily. "It was ages ago, in 1930. I mean, I was only a baby." Hugh thought it was wiser not to point out that at ten one is hardly a baby. "They acquitted him, or he got off on Appeal, something like that, and he came back here to live and had that seat put there. Only the local people didn't want a murderer and they broke his windows and called after him in the street and he had to go."

"Poor devil," said Hugh.

"Well, I don't know about that, Hugh. From what Arnold said, the case was very unsavory. Moore was quite young and very good-looking and he was a painter, though he had a private income. His poor wife was much older and an invalid. He gave her cyanide they'd got for killing wasps. He gave it to her in a cup of coffee."

"I thought you said he didn't do it."

"Everyone *knew* he'd done it. He only got off because the judge misdirected the jury. You can't imagine how anyone would have the nerve to put up a sort of monument, can you, after a thing like that?"

Hugh started to run his bath. Resignedly he accepted the fact, from past experience, that part of the evening would be spent in the company of Arnold Cottle. Cecily was not, and never had been, particularly flirtatious except in her own imagination. It was not that. Rather it was that she liked to get hold of causes or what she called examples of injustice or outrage and worry at them, roping in to assist her any helper who might be on hand.

There had been the banning of the proposed motorway, the petition against the children's playground, the eviction of the squatters down the road. She was not always reactionary, for she worshipped free speech and racial equality and health foods and clean air. She was a woman of principle who threw herself whole-heartedly into upheaval and change and battles that right might be done, and sometimes into cults for the improvement of her soul.

The unfortunate part of all this, or one of the unfortunate parts, was that it brought her so often into the company of bores or rogues. Hugh wondered what she was up to now, and why, and hoped it might be, though it seldom was, a flash in the pan.

Two hours later he found himself with his wife and Arnold Cottle, standing on the wet grass and examining the inscription on the Rupert Moore seat. It wasn't yet dark and wouldn't be for an hour. The sky was heavily overcast and the sea the color of a recently scoured aluminum pot. No one would have supposed, thought Hugh, that somewhere up there in the west was the sun which, contrary to all present evidence, science told him was throwing off light at the rate of 250,000,000 tons a minute.

The others were too rapt to be distracted. He had a look at Fisher (In memory of Colonel Marius Fisher, V.C., D.S.O., 1874-1951) and at Teague (William James Teague, of this Town, lost at the Battle of Jutland) and then he prodded Rupert Moore and announced, for something to say, "That's oak."

"It is indeed, my dear old chap." Arnold Cottle spoke to Hugh very warmly and kindly, as if he had decided *a priori* that he was a harmless lunatic. "You could get oak in those days. This seat was made by a chap called Sarafin, Arthur Sarafin. Curious name, eh? Corruption of seraphim, I daresay. Fine craftsman, lived up the coast at Lowestoft, but he died quite young, more's the pity. My father knew him, and had some of the furniture he made. You can see his initials up there where the crossbar at the top joins the post. A.S. in a little circle, see?"

Hugh thought this quite interesting. He had done a bit of carpentry himself until Cecily had stopped it on the ground that she needed his workshop for her groups. That had been in the days when she was into Gestalt. Hugh preferred not to think about them. He had a look at Prendergast (This seat was placed here by the Hon. Mrs. Clara Prendergast that the weary might find rest) and was about to ask Cottle if this one was oak or teak, when Cecily said, "Where did he get the cyanide?"

"Moore?" said Cottle. "It was never actually proved that he did get it. He said they kept some in their garden shed for killing wasps and that his wife had taken it herself. In point of fact, Mrs.

Moore had written to her sister, saying her life wasn't worth living and she wanted to put an end to it. But this gardener chappie said he'd thrown the wasp-killing stuff away a year before."

"It must have come from somewhere," said Cecily in such a hectoring tone and looking so belligerent that Hugh felt even more sympathy for Rupert Moore.

Cottle didn't seem to mind the tone or the look. "Moore had been to several chemist's shops in the area, though not actually in Northwold, and tried to buy cyanide, ostensibly for killing wasps. No chemist admitted to having let him have it. There was one in Tarrington, up the coast here, who sold him another kind of vespicide that contained no cyanide, and got him to sign the Poison Book. Dear Cecily, since you're so interested, why don't you read up the case in the library? Perhaps I might have the pleasure of taking you there tomorrow?"

The offer was accepted with enthusiasm. They all went into the Cross Keys where Hugh bought three rounds of drinks and Arnold Cottle bought none, having failed to bring his wallet with him. Cecily fastened on to the barman and elicited from him that the old woman who always sat on the Rupert Moore seat was named Mrs. Jones, that she had come to Northwold the year before from Ipswich, and was of Suffolk, though not Northwold, origin.

"Why does she always sit there?"

"Ask me another," said the barman, presumably meaning this rejoinder rhetorically, which was not the way Cecily took it.

"What's so fascinating about that seat?"

"It seems to fascinate you," said Hugh. "Can't you give it a rest? The whole thing's been over and done with for going on fifty years."

Cecily said, "There's nothing else to do in this damned place," which displeased the barman so much that he moved off in a huff. "I've got a very active brain, Hugh. You ought to know that by now. I'm afraid I'm not content to fuddle it with drink or spend ten hours pulling one poor little fish out of the sea."

The library visit, from which Hugh was excused, took place. But books having been secured, a journey had to be made to the house in which Rupert Moore had lived with his wife and painted his pictures and where the crime had been committed. Arnold Cottle seemed delighted at the prospect, especially as the excursion, at Cecily's suggestion, was to include lunch. Hugh had to go because

Cecily couldn't drive and he wasn't going to lend his car to Cottle.

The house was a dull and ugly mansion, now used as a children's home. The superintendant (quite reasonably, Hugh thought) refused to let them tour the interior, but he had no objection to their walking about the grounds. It was bitterly cold for the time of year, but not cold enough to keep the children indoors. They tagged around behind Arnold Cottle and the Branksomes, making unfriendly or impertinent remarks. One of them, a boy with red curly hair and a cast in his eye, threw an apple core at Cecily, and when he was reproved he used a word which, though familiar, is still unexpected on the lips of a five year old.

They had lunch, and throughout the meal Cecily read aloud extracts from the trial of Rupert Moore. The medical evidence was so unpleasant that Hugh was unable to finish his steak *au poivre*. Cottle drank heartily a whole bottle of Nuits St. Georges and had a double brandy with his coffee. Hugh thought about men who had murdered their wives, and how much easier it must have been when you could get wasp killer made of cyanide and weed killer made of arsenic. But even if he could have got those things, or have pushed Cecily downstairs, or fixed it for the electric wall heater to fall into the bath while she also was in it, he knew he never would. Even if he got away with it, as poor Rupert Moore had, he would have the shame and the fear and the guilt for the rest of his life, again as had been the case with Rupert Moore.

Not that Moore had lived for long. "He died of some kidney disease just twelve months after they let him out," said Cecily, "and by then he'd been hounded out of this place. He had Sarafin make that seat and that was about the last thing Moore ever did in Northwold." She scanned the last chapter of her book. "There doesn't seem to have been any real motive for the murder, Arnold."

"I suppose he wanted to marry someone else," said Cottle, swigging brandy. "I remember my father saying there were rumors he'd had a girl friend, but nobody seemed to know her name and she wasn't mentioned at the trial."

"She certainly wasn't," said Cecily, flicking back in her book so rapidly that she nearly knocked Hugh's coffee cup over. "You mean, there was no clue as to who she was? How did the rumors start, then?"

"Dear Cecily, how do rumors ever start? In point of fact, Moore was known often to have been absent from home in the evenings. There was gossip he'd been seen in Clacton with a girl."

"Fascinating," said Cecily. "I shall spend the rest of the day thoroughly studying all this literature. You and Hugh must amuse yourselves on your own."

After a dreadful afternoon listening to Cottle's troubles, how enemies had prevented his making a success at any career, how his two attempts at getting married had been scotched by his mother, and how his neighbors had a vendetta against him, Hugh finally escaped. Though not before he had lent Cottle ten pounds, this being the lowest of the sums his guest had suggested as tenable. Cecily had had a wonderful time, making herself conversant with the Moore case, and now she was in the bath. Hugh wondered if a mighty thump on the bedroom side of the bathroom wall would dislodge the heater and make it fall into the water, but this was merely academic speculation.

After dinner he went for a walk on his own in the rain while Cecily made notes—for what purpose Hugh neither knew nor cared. He poked about in the ruins of the castle; he bought two tickets for the repertory theater on the following night, hoping that the play, though it was called "Murder-on-Sea," might distract Cecily; he wandered about the streets of the old town and he had a drink in the Oyster Catcher's Arms. On the whole he didn't have a bad time.

The morning being better—a pale sickly sun was shining and making quite attractive tints on the undersides of black clouds— he thought they might go on the beach. But Cecily had other plans. She got him to take her to Tarrington, and in the little shopping center she left him to his own devices which included buying two pairs of thicker socks. After that, because it was raining again, there was nothing to do but sit in the car park. She kept him waiting two hours.

"What d'you think?" she said. "I found that chemist, the one that sold Rupert Moore the wasp killer that hadn't got cyanide in it. And, would you believe it, it's still the same firm. The original pharmacist's grandson is now the manager."

"I suppose," said Hugh, "that he told you his grandfather had made a deathbed confession that he did give Moore the cyanide after all."

"Do try not to be so silly. I already knew they had cyanide wasp killer in the shop. It said so in the library book. This young man, the grandson, couldn't tell me much, but he did say his grandfather had had a very pretty young girl assistant. How about that?"

"I've noticed that very pretty young girls often do work in chemist's shops."

"I'm glad you notice something, at any rate. However, she is not the one. The grandson knows her present whereabouts, and she is a Mrs. Lewis. So I shall have to look elsewhere."

"What d'you mean, the one?" said Hugh dismally.

"My next task," said Cecily, taking no notice, "will be to hunt for persons in this case of the name of Jones. Young women, that is. I know where to begin now. Sooner or later I shall root out a girl who was an assistant in a chemist's shop at the time and who married a Jones."

"What for?"

"That right may be done," said Cecily solemnly. "That the truth may at last come out. I see it as my mission. You know I always have a mission, Hugh. It was the merest chance we happened to come to Northwold because Diana Richards recommended it. You wanted to go to Lloret de Mar. I feel it was meant we should come here because there was work for me to do. I am convinced Moore was guilty of this crime, but not alone in his guilt. He had a helper who, I believe, is alive at this moment. I'd like you to drive me to Clacton now. I shall begin by interviewing some of the oldest inhabitants."

So Hugh drove to Clacton where he lost a pound on the slot machines. Indefatigably Cecily pursued her investigations.

Mrs. Jones came back from morning service at St. Mary's, and although she was a good walker and not at all tired, for she had slept well ever since she came to Northwold, she sat down for half an hour on her favorite seat. Two other elderly people who had also been in church were sitting on Jackson (In memory of Bertrand Jackson, 1859–1924, Philanthropist and Lover of the Arts). Mrs. Jones nodded pleasantly to them, but she didn't speak. It wasn't her way to waste in chat time that was more satisfactorily spent in reminiscence.

A pale gray mackerel sky, a fitful sun. Perhaps it would brighten up later. She thought about her daughter who was coming to lunch. Brenda would be tired after the drive, for the children, dears though they were, would no doubt be troublesome in the car. They would all enjoy that nice piece of sirloin and the Yorkshire pudding and the fresh peas and the chocolate ice cream. She had got in a bottle of sherry so that she and Brenda and Brenda's husband could each have a glass before the meal.

Her son and daughter had been very good to her. They knew she had been a devoted wife to their father, and they didn't resent the place in her love she kept for her darling. Not that she had ever spoken of him in front of their father or of them when they were small. That would have been unkind and in bad taste. But later she had told them about him and told Brenda, in expansive moments, about that long-past happiness and the tragedy of her darling's death, he so young and handsome and gifted.

Perhaps, this afternoon when the rest of them were on the beach, she might allow herself the luxury of mentioning him again. Discreetly, of course, because she had always respected Mr. Jones and loved him after a fashion, even though he had taken her away to Ipswich and never attained those heights of talent and success her darling would have enjoyed had he lived. Tranquilly, not unhappily, she recalled to her mind his face, his voice, and some of their conversations.

Mrs. Jones was disturbed in her reverie by the presence of that tiresome woman. She had seen her before, hanging about on the promenade and once examining the seat that Mrs. Jones thought of as her own. An ugly thin neurotic-looking woman who was sometimes in the company of a sensible elderly man and sometimes with that shameless scrounger, old Cottle's boy, whom Mrs. Jones, in her old-fashioned way, called a barfly. Today, however, she was alone, and to Mrs. Jones's dismay, was approaching her with intent to speak.

"Do excuse me for speaking to you, but I've seen you here so often."

"Oh, yes?" said Mrs. Jones. "I've seen you too. I'm afraid I have to go now. I've guests for lunch."

"Please don't go. I won't keep you more than a moment. But I must tell you I'm terribly interested in the Moore case. I can't help wondering if you knew him, you're here so much."

"I knew him," said Mrs. Jones distantly.

"That's terribly exciting." And the woman did look very excited. "I suppose you first met him when he came into the shop?"

"That's right," said Mrs. Jones, and she got up. "But I don't care to talk about it. It's a very long time ago and it's best forgotten. Good morning."

"Oh, but please . . . !"

Mrs. Jones ignored her. She walked far more rapidly than usual, breathing heavily, along the path toward the old town. She was flustered and upset and very put out. To rake up all that now just when she was thinking of the lovely events of that time! For that day, though not, she hoped, for the future, the encounter had spoiled the seat for her.

"Had a good day with Cottle?" said Hugh.

"Don't speak to me about that man. Can you imagine it, I phoned him and a woman answered! She turned out to be some creature on holiday like us who was taking him to Lowestoft in her car. I could come too if I liked. No, thank you very much, I said. What about my finding the girl called Jones? I said. And he was pleased to tell me I was getting *obsessional*. So I gave him a piece of my mind, and that's the last of Arnold Cottle."

And the last of his ten pounds, thought Hugh. "So you went on the beach instead?"

"I did not. While you were out in that boat I researched on my own. And most successfully, I may add. You remember that old man in Clacton, the one in the old folks' home? Well, he was quite fit enough to see me today, and I questioned him exhaustively."

Hugh said nothing. He guessed who had been exhausted.

"Ultimately," said Cecily, "I was able to prod him into remembering. I asked him to try and recall everyone he had ever known called Jones. And at last he remembered a local policeman, a Constable Jones, who got married in or around 1930. And the girl he married worked in *a local chemist's shop*. How about that?"

"You mean she was Moore's girl friend?"

"Isn't it obvious? Her name was Gladys Palmer. She is now Mrs. Jones. Moore was seen about with a girl in Clacton. This girl lived in Clacton and worked in a Clacton chemist's shop. Now it's quite evident that Moore was having a love affair with Gladys Palmer and that he persuaded her to give him the cyanide from the shop where she worked. The *real* evidence is that, according to all the books, that was one of the few chemist's shops from which Moore *never tried to obtain cyanide!*"

"That's the real evidence?" said Hugh.

"Of course it is, to anyone with any deductive powers. Gladys Palmer took fright when Moore was found guilty, so she married a policeman for protection, and the policeman's name was Jones. Isn't that proof?"

"Proof of what?"

"Don't you ever remember anything? The barman in that Cross Keys place told us the old woman who sits on the Rupert Moore seat was a Mrs. Jones." Cecily smiled triumphantly. "They are one and the same."

"But it's a very common name."

"Maybe. But Mrs. Jones has admitted it. I spoke to her this morning before I went to Clacton. She has admitted knowing Moore and that she first met him when he came into the shop. How about that? And she was very nervous and upset, I can tell you, as well she might be."

Hugh stared at his wife. He didn't at all like the turn things were taking. "Cecily, it may be so. It looks like it, but it's no business of ours. I wish you'd leave it."

"Leave it! For nearly fifty years this woman has got off scot-free when she was as much guilty of the murder of Mrs. Moore as Moore was, and you say leave it! It's her guilt brings her to that seat day after day, isn't it? Any psychologist would tell you that."

"She must be at least seventy. Surely she can be left in peace now?"

"I'm afraid it's much too late for that, Hugh. There must be an inquiry, all the facts must come out. I have written three letters, one to the Home Secretary, one to the Chief Commissioner at Scotland Yard, and a third to the author of this very incomplete book. There they are on the dressing table. Perhaps you'd like to look at them while I have my bath."

Hugh looked at them. If he were to tear them up she would only write them again. If he walked into that bathroom now and dislodged the heater from the wall and it fell into the water, and she died and it was called an accident . . . The letters would never be sent, he could have his workshop back, he could chat with pretty girls who worked in chemist's shops, and go on holiday to the Costa Brava and be free. He sighed heavily and went down to the bar to get a drink.

Thank goodness, thought Mrs. Jones, that woman wasn't anywhere to be seen this morning. The intrusion of yesterday had upset her for hours, even after Brenda arrived, but she was getting over it now. Unfortunately, in a way, the weather had taken a turn for the better, and several of the seats were occupied. But not Rupert Moore. Mrs. Jones sat down on it and put her shopping bag on the ground at her feet.

She was aware of the proximity of the barfly who was sitting on

Lubbock (Elizabeth Anne Lubbock, for many years Headmistress of Northwold Girls High School) and with him was a different woman, much younger than the other and very well dressed. With an effort Mrs. Jones expelled them from her mind. She looked at the calm blue sea and felt the warm and firm pressure of the oak against her back and thought about her darling.

How sweet their love and companionship had been! It had endured for such a short time, and then separation and the unbearable loneliness. But she had been right to marry Mr. Jones, for he had been a good husband and she the wife he wanted, and without him there would have been no Brian and no Brenda and no money to buy the house and come here every day to remember. If her darling had lived, though, and the children had been his, and if she had had him to sit beside her on his seat and be the joy of her old age . . .

"Do forgive me," said a voice, "but I'm a local man myself, and I happened to be in Lowestoft yesterday and someone told me they'd heard you'd come back to this part of the world to live."

Mrs. Jones looked at the barfly. Was there to be no end to it?

"I've seen you on this seat and I did wonder, and when this friend in Lowestoft told me your present name, all was clear."

"I see," said Mrs. Jones, gathering up her shopping bag.

"I want you to know how greatly I admire his work. My father had some charming examples of it—all sold now, alas—and anyone can see this seat was made by a craftsman compared with the others." Her stony face, her hostility, made him hesitate. "You are," he said, "who I think you are, aren't you?"

"Of course I am," said Mrs. Jones crossly, another morning spoiled. "Arthur Sarafin was my first husband. And now I really must be on my way."

Among several promising series characters who debuted during 1978, one of my favorites is fat, aging Charlie Dark, a conceited counterespionage agent whose adventures take him to all parts of the world. Brian Garfield is the only writer I know who writes about international intrigue just as convincingly as he writes about the American West. He brings to both his worlds a sense of authentic adventure that's hard to beat.

BRIAN GARFIELD
Checkpoint Charlie

I always mistrust Rice but never more so than on those occasions when he pulls me off a job that's only half-done and drags me back all the way from Beirut or Helsinki or Sydney to hand me a new assignment. Usually it means he's at his wits' end and needs me to bail him out.

This time it was a short trip back to Langley. I'd been in Montreal and consequently managed to arrive at Rice's lair without the usual jet lag; my only complaint was hunger—there'd been nothing but a light snack on the plane.

It was two in the morning but Rice keeps odd hours and I knew he'd still be in his fourth-floor office. I trampled the U.S. Government Seal into the tiles and the security guard ran my card through the scanner and admitted me to the elevator. The fourth-floor hall rang with my footsteps—eerie, hollow like my innards: I was short-tempered with hunger.

"You're even fatter," Rice greeted me. "I didn't believe it was possible. Where do you buy those suits, Charlie, a tent shop?"

I hate him too.

I sat down. "It's late, you're rude, and I'm hungry. Can we get down to it without half an hour of the usual sparring?"

"I guess we'd better."

I was astonished. "It's serious, then."

"Desperate, actually. You've been following the Quito hijack?"

"Just the headlines."

"We're in a bind."

I smiled and he scowled at my smile. "Stop leering at me. One of these days—"

"One of these days you'll ask me to do one of your impossible jobs and I'll refuse. And you'll get fired," I said. "Until then you need me, so I'll leer if I feel like it."

"I need you no more than you need me, Charlie. How long can you survive without my protection? If I stop making excuses for you upstairs it'll take the computer lads about seventeen seconds to program you into inglorious retirement. You're eight years and a hundred and umpteen pounds past retirement standards for field-duty executives. Now let's have no more let-me-do-you-a-favor nonsense, all right?"

The one thing he never admits is the key to the whole matter— the reason why he needs me. It's simple. I'm the best he's got, the best there is, and I'm the only capable executive in the company who'll work for Rice.

Old, fat, and conceited—he hates me for all three reasons. But above all I'm the best.

The kids with computer printouts and space-age gadgets and martial-arts black belts can't keep up with fat old Charlie Dark when the job calls for guts and wits. The blood line has thinned; they don't make them like me anymore. Rice never admits this to my face but he knows it.

I, on the other hand, am candid enough to admit my side of the bargain. I loathe Rice but I'd rather work for him than go into an old folks' home and those are the alternatives.

I said, "What about the hijacking?"

Rice's smile displays a keyboard of teeth reminiscent of an alligator. He rarely employs it to indicate amusement; he uses it mainly when he is anticipating the acute discomfort of someone other than himself.

For a while he smiled without speaking. Then, after he felt he'd struck terror deep into my heart, he spoke.

"The hijackers have nearly one hundred hostages, a Boeing Seven-twenty-seven, and a variety of explosives and small arms. They have a number of ransom demands as well. They've communicated the demands to the world via the plane's radio equipment."

"Does anybody know where they are yet?"

"Sure. We've known their location from the beginning. Radio triangulation, radar, so forth. It's a field the Ecuadorians built a few years ago to give their air force a base against Tuparamos guerrillas. It's been in disuse since March of last year but the runway was sufficient for the Seven-twenty-seven, which is a relatively short-roll aircraft. They couldn't have done it with a jumbo. But they seem to know what they're doing; undoubtedly they took all these factors into account. We're not dealing with idiots."

"Access by road?"

"Forget it, Charlie. It's not an Entebbe situation. We can't go in after them. Our hands are tied."

"Why?"

"International politics. Organization of American States et cetera. Just take my word for it."

"Then what's the scam?"

"The hijackers have demanded the release of seventeen so-called political prisoners who are incarcerated in various countries on charges of terrorism, murder, espionage, so forth. What the liberation people think of as victims of political persecution. Actually most of them are vermin, guilty of the vilest crimes."

"Plus they're doubtless asking for a few million dollars and a free ride to Libya or Uganda."

"Yes, of course. Disregard all that, Charlie. The problem is something altogether different."

"Then why bore me with inessentials?"

"Bear with me. Twelve of the seventeen so-called political prisoners are Ché guerrillas who're incarcerated in various South American jails. Four in Ecuador, seven in Bolivia, one in Venezuela. Four more are in prison in Mexico."

"That adds up to sixteen. Where's the seventeenth?"

"Here. Leavenworth."

"Who is he?"

"Emil Stossel." And he grinned at me. Because I was the one who'd put Stossel in prison.

I didn't give him the satisfaction of rising to the bait; I merely said, "So?"

"So the Latin Americans have elected to accede to the terrorists' demands temporarily, figuring to nail them after the hostages have been freed. The plane has several high-ranking Latin American dignitaries on board. The OAS doesn't want to risk their lives any more than it has to."

I snorted. "They're already at risk."

"It's not for us to decide. The various governments have agreed to turn the sixteen guerrillas loose and give them safe passage to Havana. They're asking us to cooperate by handing Stossel over to the East Germans in Berlin."

"Why not Havana? It's closer."

"He's not Cuban. The Cubans would have little reason to grant him asylum—he'd be an embarrassment to them. He's German. Anyhow that's the demand and we've got to live with it." Rice glanced at the clock above the official photograph of the President. "In two hours we're putting him on a plane in Kansas. It will connect with an international flight at Dulles. He'll be in Berlin tomorrow night."

Then Rice made a face. "It's asinine, I agree—you don't make deals with terrorists. These governments are fools. But we've got no choice. If we held out—refused to release Stossel—you can imagine the black eye we'd get if the hijackers started murdering hostages one at a time."

"All right," I said. "We've got our national tail in a crack. We have to turn him over to the DDR. I don't like turning mass murderers loose any more than you do but I still don't see what it's got to do with me."

Rice smiled again. I fought the impulse to flinch. "How's your broken-field running these days, fat man?"

I saw it coming. His smugness made me gag. He said, "You're going to intercept the pass, Charlie."

"Before or after he crosses the Wall?"

"After."

"Lovely."

"We can't recapture him until after the hijack has been dealt with, can we. The hostages have to be turned loose before we can lay a finger on Stossel."

"In other words you want to deliver him to the East Germans and wait for the hijack to end and then afterward you expect me to get him back and put him back in Leavenworth to finish out his sentence."

"Right. After all, we can't have the world think we've gone soft, can we. We've got to prove they can't get away with it. Carry a big stick and all that."

"We could kill him," I said. "It's a lot easier to assassinate him in East Germany than it is to bring him out alive. No, never mind, don't say it. I know. We won't be stampeded into committing public murder, especially on hostile soil. We have to bring him back alive because that's the best way to rub their noses in it."

"You have the picture, I'm happy to see."

I said, "It's impossible."

"Of course it is. They'll be expecting it. They'll leave no openings at all."

He smiled slowly, deliciously. "Charlie, it's the kind of job you do best. You get bored with anything less."

"Ever since that caper with von Schnee I've been persona non grata in the Eastern sector. If they catch me on their side of the Wall they'll lock me up for a hundred and fifty years. In thumbscrews. On German peasant food."

"Yes. I know. Adds a bit of spice to the challenge, doesn't it." And he smiled more broadly than ever.

Emil Stossel had cut his eyeteeth on Abwehr duplicity and he'd run a string of successful agents in the United States for the Eastern bloc intelligence services. The FBI hadn't been able to crack him and I'd been assigned to him about twelve years ago before we all got dumped into a fishbowl where we were no longer permitted to do that sort of thing domestically. It took time and patience but in the end we were ready to go in after him. His HQ was in Arlington not far from the Pentagon—Stossel had nerve and a sense of humor.

The actual bust was an FBI caper and as usual they muffed it. Stossel got away long enough to barricade himself in the nearby high school and before it was finished he'd killed several of his teenage hostages. It had led to five life sentences, to be served consecutively, and even the Red diplomats had been wise enough not to put up more than token objection.

But Stossel remained one of the cleverest operatives the DDR had ever fielded. He was an embarrassment to them but they wouldn't mind having him back; he could be of use to them: they'd use his skills. He'd soon be directing clandestine operations again for them, I had no doubt of it; they'd keep him out of sight but they'd use him and we'd feel the results before long. It was another excellent reason to get him back.

Stossel's callous annihilation of the teenage innocents in the high school naturally had endeared him to the verminous terrorists who infested the world of "liberation" movements. He was a hero to them; it didn't matter whether he was a professional or an asinine leftist incompetent—it was his brutality that made him a hero to the Quito hijackers. At the same time the East Germans, to whom Stossel was undoubtedly a public embarrassment, could not disown him now without offending their Marxist disciples in Latin America. They would have no choice but to grant him asylum; and once having done so, as I say, they would use him.

Of course that wouldn't do.

I managed to arrive at Templehof ahead of him by arranging for his plane to undergo a refueling delay at Gatwick. It gave me time for a brief meeting at Templehof with an American Air Force colonel (Intelligence) who was dubious about cooperating until I put him on a scrambler line to Washington. The colonel grunted into the phone, stiffened to attention, said, "Yes, sir," and cradled the receiver with awe. Then he gave me the item I'd requested.

I'd had time on the plane, between meals and extra meals, to work out something approximating a plan. It is what distinguishes me from the computer lads: flexibility, preparedness, the ability to improvise quickly and precisely—ingenuity guided by experience. It's why I am the best.

The plan had to account for a number of factors such as, for example, the undesirability of my having to set foot physically on their side of the Wall. Much better if I could pull off the caper with long strings, manipulating my puppets from afar. Also there was the fact that Stossel undoubtedly would have several days' grace inside East Germany before the hijackers released their hostages and the Quito caper came to its conclusion; it would give Stossel time to bury himself far beyond my reach and I had to counter that effect with preparations designed to bring him to the surface at the end of the going-to-ground period.

The scheme was, I must admit, one of the cleverest of my long, devious, and successful career. . . .

I waited for Stossel in a private cubicle at the airport—somebody's office; it was well furnished, the appointments complete right down to a thoroughly stocked bar and an adjoining full bath. Through the double-paned windows I had a soundproofed view of the busy runways.

Two armed plainclothes guards brought him into the room and examined my credentials carefully before they retreated to the far side of the room and left me to talk with him. We spoke in German.

I said, "You remember me."

"Yes. I remember you." He'd had twelve years in prison to think about me and there was a great deal of hate in his voice.

"I was doing my job," I said, "just as you were doing yours." I wanted to soften him up a bit and Stossel's German soul would understand the common concept of duty: he was, above all else, a co-professional. I was leaning on that.

I said, "I've got another job now. My orders are to make sure you get across to your own country in safety. You've still got enemies here."

It made him smile a bit at the irony of it and I was pleased because it was the reaction I needed from him. I went around behind the bar. "A drink? It'll be a little while before our transportation arrives. We want the streets empty when we drive you through West Berlin."

He looked dubious. I poured myself a bourbon and stepped away from the bar. "Help yourself," I said offhandedly, and wandered toward the windows.

A Viscount was landing, with puffs of smoke as the wheels touched. In the reflection of the glass I saw him make his choice. He poured himself two fingers of Polish vodka from a bottle that had a stalk of grass in it; he brought the drink around toward me and I turned to face him. "Prosit." I elevated my glass in toast, and drank. "What's it feel like to be going home?"

"It feels good. Doubly good because it must annoy you so much to watch me walk away." He made an elegant and ironic gesture with the glass and tossed it back Russian style, one gulp, and I watched his eyes close with the pleasure of it—it was the first drink of first-class home-style booze he'd had in a dozen years.

I said, "Did you ever find out what led me to you in Arlington in the first place?"

"Does it matter?"

"It was a trivial error."

"Humans make them."

"Yes. But I have the feeling you'll make the same mistake again—the same weakness will trip you up next time." I smiled. "In fact, I'm sure of it."

"Would you care to bet on it, Dark?"

"Sure."

"How much, then?"

"Your freedom," I said.

He was amused. "We'll never meet again, unless it's in an East German prison—you inside, me outside."

"I'll take the bet, Stossel." I turned to watch the Viscount taxi toward the terminal. "I'd like you to memorize a telephone number. It's here in the Western sector."

"What for?"

"You may want to get in touch with me." I gave him the number: I repeated it three times and knew he wouldn't forget it—he had an excellent memory for numbers.

He laughed. "I can't conceive of —"

The phone rang, interrupting him. I went to the bar to answer it. Listened, spoke, then turned to Stossel. "The car's here."

"I'm ready."

"Then let's go."

I stood on the safe side of Checkpoint Charlie with my hatbrim down and my collar up against the fine night drizzle and watched the big Opel slide through the barriers. The Wall loomed grotesquely. Stossel emerged from the car at the DDR booth and I saw him shake hands with the raincoated delegation of East German officials. They were minor functionaries, police types, Vopos in the background in their uniforms; near me stood an American TV crew with a portable camera, filming the scene for tomorrow's news.

It was all bleak and foreign-intriguish; I hoped they were using black-and-white. The East Germans bundled Stossel into a dark Zis limousine and when it disappeared I walked back to Davidson's Volkswagen and squeezed into the passenger seat.

Davidson put it in gear. "Where to?"

"Bristol Kempinski."

On the way to the hotel he tried to pump me about my plans. Davidson is chief of the Berlin station; Rice hadn't had any choice but to brief him on my mission because there'd have been a flap otherwise—jurisdictional jealousies are rampant in the company and never more ferocious than on the ultra-active stations like Berlin. Rice had been forced to reveal my mission to Davidson, if only to reassure him that I wasn't horning in on any of his own works-in-progress. But he knew none of the tactical details and he was seething to find out.

I had to fend him off without putting his nose too far out of joint. I didn't enjoy it; I'm no good at it—I'm an accomplished liar but that sort of diplomatic deceit is not quite lying and I lack the patience for it. In any case I was tired from the long flight and from the adrenalin that had shot through me during the crucial stage of the setup. If it had gone wrong at that moment . . . But it hadn't and I was still on course and running.

In the hotel room I ordered a huge dinner sent up. Davidson had eaten earlier but he stubbornly hovered, still prying for information, watching with amazement and ill-concealed disgust while I demolished the enormous meal. He shared the wine with me; it was a fair Moselle.

"What did you want from that Air Force colonel who met you at the airport?"

"Look, Arthur, I don't mean to be obstructionist, I know it's your bailiwick, but the details on this operation are classified on a need-to-know basis and if you can get authorization from Langley, then I'll be happy to fill you in on the tedious details. Right now my hands are tied. I ask you to understand and sympathize."

Finally he went away after making it clear he intended to file a complaint. I was relieved to see his back. I tumbled into the luxurious bed and was instantly asleep.

There wasn't much I could do but wait for the phone call. I had to spend the time in the hotel room: some discreet machinations had taken place, through Davidson's offices, to get the private phone line installed on short notice. I might have been in prison for all the freedom of movement I had; it made me think of Stossel with irony. At least I had a comfortable cell; it was why I'd picked the Bristol Kempinski—Old World elegance, hot and cold running everything.

I caught up on reading, watching some soporifically slow German television programs, enticed Davidson and some others into a sixteen-hour poker game that cost them, collectively, some $400, and growled at the phone frequently in an effort to will it to ring.

The television brought me news of the hijack story in South America. All their other demands having been met, the hijackers forced the aircrew to fly them to Buenos Aires on the first leg of a journey to North Africa. While the plane was refueling at Buenos Aires a gang of Argentinian commandos got aboard in mainte-nance coveralls, isolated the hijackers neatly, and brought the caper to its end; passengers and crew were released unharmed; two hijackers dead, three wounded and captured. Case closed.

About that time I had a blistering phone call from Rice. "Are you still sitting on your four-acre duff? You're free to go in and get him now."

"I've still got jet lag. Maybe tomorrow."

"Damn you—"

"You want it done properly, don't you?"

"The pressure's on me."

"Live with it." I rang off, amused and pleased. I hadn't revealed my plan to him. Let him stew. I summoned a whopping great lunch from room service.

Between me and Rice lies the unspoken understanding that he has half his hopes pinned on my accomplishing the objective and the other half pinned on my falling flat on my big face. I'm uncertain which of the prospects gives him the greater anticipatory thrill.

By the fourth day Rice's phone calls were nearly apoplectic and I was rested, replete, and recumbent. Today would be the most likely day for things to break according to the science of the situation.

Rice was issuing ultimata. "I know you're scared of going over into the Eastern zone. Well, it's just too bad, Charlie. If you're still in that hotel at midnight, I'm throwing you to the wolves."

I rang off without replying. I was able to contain my anxiety—if he threw me to the wolves prematurely and then my plan came off successfully, it would make him doubly the fool and he wasn't going to risk that. The threat was empty for the moment. But he might go around the bend at some point, throw self-preservation to the winds in his rage against me. I couldn't do much about that except hope it held off long enough to let things sort themselves out.

The real anxiety had to do with Stossel. Suppose he couldn't get to a phone? If they were still holding him in Debriefing he might not have access to an outside phone. But they'd had him nearly a week now; surely they'd have administered pentathol by now and learned he was still loyal to them.

I knew one thing. Rice or no Rice, I wasn't going over that Wall. No one-way trips for old Charlie Dark. However it topped out, this was going to remain a remote-control job. I'd already pulled the strings and there was nothing left now except to wait and hope the puppet danced.

Davidson kept dropping in when he had nothing better to do. He came to me from oblique angles and doubtless thought himself clever. That afternoon he was pumping me slyly about Stossel. "How did you nail him in the first place?"

"The job was to find him—we didn't know where he was holed up. He ran his network through a Byzantine series of cutouts and blind drops. Nobody had ever been able to trace him back to his lair. We knew he was in the Arlington-Alexandria area but that was the sum of our knowledge. I had to ask myself how somebody might find Charlie Dark if *he* were hiding out, and I answered myself that all you'd have to do would be to find the best Italian food in town and wait for Charlie Dark to show up there.

"It worked the same way with Stossel. Everybody has preferences, colas or a brand of cigarettes or whatever. It takes a lot of manpower to work that kind of lead but we had no choice. We had the dossier on him, we knew his quirks. He's half-Polish, you know. Always had a taste for the best Polish vodka—the kind that's sold with a stalk of buffalo grass in the bottle."

"I've tried that stuff. Once. Tasted foul."

"Not to Stossel," I said. "Or a lot of other people. Most fair-sized liquor stores in the States carry the stuff. It took manpower and legwork—that was FBI work, of course. They staked out dozens of stores and in the end it led us to Stossel. He was tripped up by his preference for Polish vodka. I told him it was a weakness that would betray him again."

"Has it?"

I was about to answer him when the phone rang. It galvanized me.

"Herr Dark?"

"Speaking."

"My people—the doctors—they tell me there is no antidote."

"They're wrong," I told him. "We've developed one."

"I see." There was no emotion in Stossel's voice.

"West side, Checkpoint Charlie," I said, "any time you're ready. We'll be waiting. Come alone, of course." I smiled when I cradled the phone.

The smile wasn't for Stossel; it was for Rice.

Stossel came out at 11:40 that night. It was twenty minutes short of the deadline Rice had given me. There was a satisfying symmetry in that.

Davidson put the handcuffs on him. Stossel was stoic. "How long do I have?"

"You'll be all right now." We rode toward the airport with Stossel squeezed between us in the Opel's back seat. It was safe to tell him now. I said, "It's a benign poison. It has all the attributes and early symptoms of Luminous Poisoning but actually it's the reverse."

"Our doctors told me it was incurable. I had terrible cramps."

"I didn't give you the poison, Stossel. I gave you the antidote. Like a serum. It contains similar properties."

"You bluffed me." He brooded on his handcuffs. "Of course it was in the vodka."

"Where else? I told you the weakness would trip you up."

When I boarded the plane with Stossel I was savagely happy anticipating Rice's rage. On the ten-hour flight I ate five dinners.

I must admit to a weakness for stories set at boys' prep schools, and Louis Auchincloss's The Rector of Justin *and John Knowles's* A Separate Peace *are among my favorite modern novels outside the mystery field. When a prep school setting is combined with murder, as in Jerry Jacobson's fine novelette, the result can be a tantalizing puzzle that sheds light on some darker aspects of the human condition. The setting here is a school in western Canada, and the story marks Jacobson's third appearance in this annual series.*

JERRY JACOBSON
Rite of Spring

Very likely there was an earthly good reason why someone should be pounding on the door to Shaffer's cottage in Cloisters at six in the morning. And even though Shaffer was still half-drugged with sleep, there was no mistaking it for a knock. Boys at St. Andrews University School tended to pound on doors, never quite grasping the distinction that a light rapping was customary and very sufficient for all but the direst emergency. Nevertheless, pounding had been the prevailing form of entreatment ever since Shaffer came to St. Andrews eight years before and it would in all probability become a tradition that would go unbroken for centuries into the future. A dire emergency to a St. Andrews boy included everything from a lost scarf or sock to a stolen pair of nailclippers to a friendly jostling in a campus hallway. Ever it would be.

The pounding persisted as Shaffer hunted on the floor for a stray slipper. He opened the door on Thomas Ames, a boarding boy in the Senior School who was a standout on the track team. He was dressed in his maroon warm-up suit and Nike track shoes. Rain, shine, or holocaust, Ames ran an hour every morning. He was dubbed "The Running Fool" by his fellows, a nickname more of endearment than of malice. He was well liked. His route each day took him down into Chesterton Village and back and then five times around the school's quarter-mile running track. It was a nine-mile jaunt.

"Ames, I warn you," said Shaffer. "This is Saturday morning and we are between terms and I rarely recognize Saturday mornings during Spring Break as part of the day. So suffice it to say this had better be damned good."

Ames looked visibly shaken. His eyes were dancing in their sockets.

"Out the front gate, Mr. Shaffer! About maybe a couple hundred yards down St. Andrews Road! It's a man's body, sir—in the culvert there! Half of him is in the culvert and half in the brush!"

"Is he dead, Ames?"

"I—don't know, sir. I saw him and got scared and just came on back up the hill to the campus. I didn't check."

"Did you recognize him?"

"N–no, sir. His body was face down. I couldn't see his face."

"Well, let's get down there and see what we've got," said Shaffer, turning back to his room to jam on a pair of jeans and some sneakers.

"Do you need *me*, sir?" stammered Ames.

"Ames, somebody's got to show me the spot and you've got all the qualifications. I'm not about to go hiking around the hillside in the dark on a morning I don't recognize as part of the day."

He led Thomas Ames to the rear of Cloisters and the masters' parking lot. It was nearly empty, just four other cars besides his own nine-year-old Volvo. The school had twenty-six men and four women on the full-time faculty, but only ten of the men lived at Cloisters and most of them had gone home during Spring Break. Chambers was still there and so were Carl Hammerick and Gary Forrester. Shaffer had glimpsed them moving about the campus grounds, or coming and going at Cloisters, or down in the village shopping or chugging beers. Benson Hunt had driven down to Victoria for a couple of days but Shaffer thought he'd come back for the weekend for some tutorial sessions with a couple of the boarding boys whose grades were faltering.

The road running behind Cloisters passed behind Greer Chapel, the two residence dorms, Science Hall, and President Thaddius's home. Shaffer saw no one about. If the man Thomas Ames had found was dead, his killer wouldn't likely be lurking on the campus grounds. If one of the students was involved there were a hundred circuitous routes back to the campus and from there back to the dorms.

From the front gate of St. Andrews, the narrow roadway set a corkscrew course as it made its ever-widening circle down to Chesterton Village some 1,000 feet below. Shaffer never liked driving it.

Out of the darkness, Shaffer heard the boy say, "Better slow up, sir. It's just around this curve. On the right."

Shaffer applied the brakes of the old Volvo and saw the body, just a shadowy lump, half in and half out of the concrete culvert that had been built to control the runoff of rainwater during storms, which at times in this part of British Columbia could be fierce. Shaffer came to a halt, leaving his lights on, and got out. Thomas Ames wasn't budging an inch.

When Shaffer got to the crumpled form, he saw there was no need to roll the man over for identification. Shaffer knew that brown tweed sportscoat and bulky gray turtleneck sweater from a mile away. Benson Hunt seemed to wear them constantly. Shaffer stooped and felt the side of his neck for a sign of a pulse. There was none. He was dead. The side of his skull had been caved in.

When Shaffer climbed back into the Volvo, Thomas Ames said, "Who is it, sir?"

"Master Hunt."

"*Master Hunt*, sir?" Ames's voice was quivering.

"None other than."

"Did he get hit by a car or something?"

"Or something," said Shaffer.

"What do we do now, sir?"

"We go down to the village and wake up Constable McElroy at the RCMP and tell him what we've found and where."

The RCMP headquarters in Chesterton Village was a three-man post, which consisted of McElroy and his two deputy constables. Shaffer, when they arrived, told Thomas Ames to stay in the car.

Constable McElroy was making coffee. His day shift began at 6:00 A.M. He gave Shaffer a look of astonishment. "Hal? What are you doing up this early on a Saturday? And between terms, as well. Are you sleepwalking?"

"I was rudely awakened by a student, Mac, who is now off my Christmas list."

"What's the problem?"

"We have a dead body," Shaffer told him. "A fellow master,

Benson Hunt. His body is in a culvert about halfway up St. Andrews Road."

"Did you discover him, Hal?"

"No, the student did. His name is Thomas Ames. He was out running. He's out in my car."

"Did either of you disturb the scene?"

"I felt Hunt's neck to see if he was still alive."

"But nothing else?"

"Not so much as a twig."

McElroy grunted, perhaps at the ungodliness of the hour or perhaps at the awesome prospect of investigating his first killing. "I suppose I better roust Webster and Ackerman out of their beds," he said as he reached for the telephone.

Shaffer led Constable McElroy back through the dawning village and up St. Andrews Road to the spot where Benson Hunt lay dead. McElroy told Shaffer to take Thomas Ames back to the campus. As soon as it was possible, he would take their statements.

Shortly after noon, he met Shaffer at Cloisters and Shaffer escorted him to Todd Hall, a short walk down the rear drive, where he left Ames and Constable McElroy alone and returned to his cottage.

As he walked he gazed out between the buildings. A knot of boys were playing a skeleton-crew game of soccer and a few others could be seen moving back and forth across the campus in a variety of directions. Shaffer wondered if one of them was a murderer.

St. Andrews University School had a total enrollment of 375 boys. Roughly three-quarters of them were day boys, students who lived at home and commuted to the academy daily. The remainder were boarding boys. How many of that one hundred had chosen not to go home for Spring Break was hard to tell. When classes were out of session, none of the masters met in sufficient numbers with them to get an accurate head count. Shaffer tried to count up the faces he'd seen in the past four days, coming or going on the campus and at meals. He guessed there were around forty boys who had not gone home for the ten-day vacation. Constable McElroy, he was sure, would want a complete list of the boarding boys who were still residing on the campus.

Shaffer thought about who would want Benson Hunt dead. Hunt had taught senior courses in French and Contemporary

American Literature. Shaffer knew Hunt had acquired a kind of notoriety for the fact that he allowed only French to be spoken in his foreign-language course and only college-bound senior boys ranking in the top ten percentile were qualified to take his literature course. Hunt had been somewhat of a maniac for pop quizzes, sprung on his students without any warning. The students said Hunt's courses were like quiz shows without prizes. But surely that wasn't a thing over which a master might be murdered.

And Hunt was certainly not hated. He was respected by his students; not well liked, but not hated. Shaffer could think of fully a dozen masters who might rank above Hunt on a students' hate list. Hunt had been strict and academically demanding, but he had also been fair and had played by the academy's rules to the letter.

Then Shaffer remembered the reason Benson Hunt had returned early from Victoria. He had set up Spring Break tutorials with two of his students. During those sessions had something taken place to cause one or both of the boys to become angered with Hunt?

"You cloistered dons are set up pretty cozily," McElroy commented as Shaffer showed him into his quarters. "Living room with a fireplace, study room, bedroom. Do they give you a kitchen besides?"

"A kitchenette," said Shaffer. "One can move about in it very nicely if one doesn't use a large frying pan or pot."

"Nice all the same. I was expecting more monkish austerity— you know: table, chair, naked light bulb hanging down from the ceiling, and a small cabinet for the bread and water."

Shaffer laughed. No water, he told McElroy, but there was some wine if he could stomach it, a little Bordeaux from a lesser known commune in the Medoc, but pleasantly drinkable.

"I don't mind if I do," said the constable. "I've never been one to believe in total abstinence on duty. A little wine can keep the head clear and active and can put a witness or a suspect off his guard as well."

Shaffer ducked into the kitchenette and poured out two glasses. Constable McElroy took a sip, pronounced the wine more pleasant than most he had drunk, and took out a small notebook.

"Mr. Shaffer, how well did you know Benson Hunt?" he began.

"Very well," Shaffer told him. "As well as anyone here at the academy, I would say."

"What sort of man was he? I mean, in terms of his personality?"

"He was a strict academician, but completely fair. He demanded excellence, but he knew the capabilities of his students individually and didn't push them beyond their known potential."

McElroy took a sip of wine. "What we've seen tends to point to a killer here at the school. Hunt wasn't stricken by a motorist. There were no contusions on his body, only the bashed skull. Was Hunt in the habit of walking to the village, or did he have a car?"

"He had a green Vega. It's in the lot out back. But we all walked to the village on occasion. Could he have been robbed?"

"His wallet was found on his body, with eighty-three dollars in it," McElroy said. "And until the time of death is established, we're a bit handcuffed. His body's been taken to the Coroner's Unit in Victoria. We should know more by five or six o'clock this evening. One puzzling aspect has cropped up though."

"What's that?" asked Shaffer.

"There was a residue of dust of some sort on his jacket and trousers—chalk, lime perhaps. But we found nothing of it at the scene."

"The athletic fields," Shaffer said to McElroy.

"What?"

"During the Spring Break, the school's maintenance crew lines the sports field for rugby and soccer. Our Provincial League play begins when the boys return for the Spring Term. The crew was out lining the field yesterday and the day before."

McElroy put aside his wine glass and stood up. "Take me out to the field," he said.

Baker Field was located behind the athletic field house, a new and so far unnamed facility. Shaffer took Constable McElroy south across the wide grassy quadrangle that also doubled as the cricket field, then between the Administration Building and Science Hall, bringing them out onto a stone walk that led to the field house.

"I never realized the campus was this big," McElroy commented.

"Twenty-three acres," said Shaffer.

"Lots of room for a boy to become lost to suit his own purposes."

"It's a thought," Shaffer admitted.

The athletic field was empty, but freshly lined. McElroy and Shaffer searched for lines that had been obliterated, indicating Benson Hunt might have been killed here and his body dragged across the lines, but there were no obliterations.

"Don't they use some sort of cart to draw these lines?" McElroy asked. "You know, a wheeled cart, with a bin on top filled with lime chalk?"

"Yes," said Shaffer. "They keep it in a shop in the basement of the field house." Shaffer turned and gestured back at the field house, where the open garage door showed power mowers, piles of sprinkler hose, and stacks of fertilizer and grass seed in bags. A man in white coveralls moved back and forth inside. He was badly stoop-shouldered: Horst Alm, the eldest of the school's five workmen.

Alm had something very curious to tell Shaffer and Constable McElroy about the liming cart he had used the previous day. "I forgot to put it back in the shop when I finished liming the field yesterday. When I came to work this morning, it was gone. As you know, Constable, we had that light rain last night. I could see where the cart's wheels made their tracks out to the west there. I followed them into that stand of pines out there about a hundred yards off, you see?"

"Take us out there," said McElroy.

They followed Alm west over hilly ground that led into a thick belt of pine trees. The grass was still slightly wet. Shaffer could clearly make out the double track made by the steel wheels of the lime cart, a thing consisting of very little weight itself. Shuddering, Shaffer wondered if it hadn't indeed been used to transport a dead body.

The cart tracks snaked through the trees until they came to an abrupt halt where a hillside ran down to the first serpentine curve of St. Andrews Road. The hill sloped at roughly a forty-degree angle, not so steep that a human couldn't descend it without falling and tumbling out of control the rest of the way down to the roadway.

"There are footprints here at the edge," said McElroy, pointing to the grassy ground where a section was matted and chewed.

"This is where I found the lime cart this morning," said Horst Alm. "Who would want to bring a lime cart to the edge of the hillside and then just leave it here? That's not much of a schoolboy prank, not from what I've seen here over the past twenty years.

One year some boys hiked all of Master Van Dine's cottage furniture up into the chapel belltower on pulleys. And another time, Headmaster Batesford found his Peugeot in the gymnasium, completely dismantled and laid out on the basketball court, labeled part for part."

"I'm afraid this is no prank," said Constable McElroy. "I think the lime cart was used to transport Benson Hunt's body here to the edge and then dumped down the hill. And I think if we take a straight path down we'll come out at the very spot where Hunt's body was found by your track student this morning, Mr. Shaffer. Let's put the acid test to it." He told Horst Alm he could go back to his regular duties and then he and Shaffer started down the hillside.

The footing was not at all treacherous. The earth was hard-packed and layered with pine needles from trees that spiked the hillside in an intermittent stand. Clumps of barberry bushes sprouted on the hill as well, a few of whose leaves and branches looked recently damaged. Perhaps Benson Hunt's body had been stopped by them and his murderer had to pull the body aside to set it to tumbling again.

Both Shaffer and Constable McElroy used the trees and bushes to halt their downward momentum at intervals until they reached the bottom, a descent Shaffer judged to be fully two hundred yards. They hit a brief flat area, perhaps no wider than twenty yards. Neither man said a word about the two slender trails marking the ground where the pine needles had been pushed aside. The needles had made way for the heels of a pair of man's shoes as his body was dragged by the arms. They came to the short slope of bank, stopped at its edge, and looked down into the stretch of cement drainage culvert where Benson Hunt's body had been found.

"I hadn't expected to be this lucky," McElroy said. "It appears we don't have a hit-and-run and no one from the village is involved. Our best suspect seems to be someone directly connected with the school or someone who paid it a visit yesterday."

Shaffer asked about the lime cart.

"The use of that cart inclines me to believe one of your students is involved," McElroy said. "The victim was a big man, over six feet and around two hundred pounds. His killer couldn't carry him and so he had to look around for a means to transport him away from the campus. I'll need an accounting of all the students who have stayed here during Spring Break."

"That won't be difficult. Each dorm has a sign-out register. I think you should know Hunt came back a couple of days ago to tutor two senior boys who needed their marks hiked up for college."

"Do you know which boys?"

"No, but there should be some evidence of that in Hunt's cottage."

"Then you'll need his keys," said McElroy.

"Hunt never locked his rooms," said Shaffer. "Hardly any of us do. The honor system is difficult to perpetuate if students encounter locked doors all over the place."

They climbed back up the hill in silence. On the walk back to Cloisters, McElroy said, "Hal, I've got that autopsy report to get and some other matters to juggle. You'd be helping me out a great deal if you could work up that list of students for me and nose around Hunt's rooms for the names of the two boys he was tutoring."

"You've got it."

"I'll call you tonight. The coroner's report will be in from Victoria and it should give us something more substantial to work with. Do you know anything about Hunt's next-of-kin, a relative I can notify about his death?"

"Hunt was divorced about a year ago," Shaffer told him. "I suppose his ex-wife would be the best person to call. I'll look for a phone number for her."

"Good luck. And keep in mind McElroy's Law."

"What's that?"

Constable McElroy issued a wry smile, "The light at the end of the tunnel nearly always turns out to be the headlight of an onrushing train."

After McElroy left, Shaffer walked over to the two dormitories, Todd Hall and Usatalo Hall. From tables in the lobbies, he picked up both leather-bound sign-out registers and took them back to his cottage, where he crossed out the names on the registers from his master list of boarding boys. When he was finished, his list showed twenty-two boarding boys remaining on the campus during Spring Break.

Benson Hunt's cottage was numbered A-13, two units removed from the laundry room. Its door was unlocked. Shaffer was not a stranger to Hunt's rooms. He had been to meetings here on two

or three occasions and had spent a random evening or two with
Hunt chasing after philosophical notions.

The rooms were still furnished in what Shaffer had come to
call Early Uncertain. There were canvas-backed director's chairs,
a threadbare Moroccan rug, a tapestry-covered couch with eagle-
claw legs made of glass, a brutish dining-room table that
looked Spanish in some places and Queen Anne in others. Hunt
had never been bashful about the hoarding of miscellaneous
junk.

Three of the director's chairs were still arranged in a close
triangle, suggesting Hunt had tutored both senior boys simultaneously the day before. Hunt's study guides and course texts
were in a mound of disarray on the rug next to one of the chairs.
Shaffer looked for textbooks or test papers that would tell him the
names of the boys, but they had been meticulous at picking up
after themselves.

There was a battered secretary across the room, one of the few
items of furniture Hunt had managed to salvage from his defunct
marriage. Shaffer went over to it. It didn't take him long to find
what he was looking for. The day-date desk calendar was still
open on the day before, Friday, the last day of Benson Hunt's life.

The small page contained just the single notation: *Tutorials.
Jeffery Langlois, Mark Spencer, 2–4 p.m. and 6–8 p.m.*

Both Langlois and Spencer lived in Usatalo Hall. Spencer's
roommate told Shaffer he hadn't seen Spencer since lunch, but
he expected him back before two o'clock because he had tutorials
with Benson Hunt. Shaffer didn't mention Hunt's death. The
news would spread fast enough without his help.

Shaffer found Jeffery Langlois alone in his room, hunched
over a copy of Joyce's *Ulysses* at a study table set at a window which
overlooked the quadrangle. "Have you got a minute, Langlois?"

"Sure, Master Shaffer. Do you know anything about Joyce,
sir?"

"A little."

"Well, I'm taking Master Hunt's Contemporary American Literature II, so what is he doing making me read Joyce? Isn't Joyce
an Irish writer?"

"He is."

"O.K. So why not Hemingway or Faulkner or Sherwood Anderson and some of those guys?"

"You take your college boards in a few weeks, don't you, Langlois?"

"Yes, sir."

"Well, what I believe Master Hunt had in mind was to give you a sense of literary association. Didn't he suggest you make comparisons with the characters in Homer's *Odyssey*? Joyce's Leopold Bloom with Homer's Ulysses? Joyce's Mr. Deasy with Homer's Nestor?"

"The library only had two copies of the *Odyssey*," Langlois said. "So how am I supposed to make comparisons when some other jerks are hoarding them and won't turn them back in?"

"Calm down, Langlois. I'll lend you my copy."

"Master Hunt wants us to read *The Dubliners* too."

"I'll lend you both," said Shaffer. "But I'm here to talk to you about your tutorials with Master Hunt."

"We've got one at two o'clock. Me and Spencer."

"Well, I think you'd better forget about the tutorials for today," Shaffer said. "Master Hunt isn't on campus."

"Where is he, sir?"

"He's in Victoria," Shaffer said. "You took tutorials with Hunt yesterday, didn't you? A session in the afternoon and a session in the evening?"

"At two o'clock, yes, sir. Me and Mark Spencer."

"And at six o'clock, after supper?"

"No, sir. I mean, we went over to his cottage in Cloisters, but he wasn't there. We went into his rooms and sat around for about fifteen minutes waiting for him to show up, but he didn't. So we just came back to our rooms."

"Then the last time you saw Master Hunt was at four P.M. when your first tutorial ended?"

"Yes, sir. We left Cloisters a little after four o'clock and Spencer went over to the gym and shot some baskets. Then we went to supper and after supper we came back to the dorms and flaked out until six and then went over to Master Hunt's cottage."

"Did you see Master Hunt in the dining room at supper?"

"No, sir. But he could have come in after we left," said Langlois.

Mark Spencer had, meanwhile, returned to his room. His account of the events of the past twenty-four hours corroborated Jeffery Langlois's. If either boy had been angered at Benson Hunt for some reason, it was being well concealed. But Shaffer knew the deceit of which young schoolboys and all humans are capable.

Had one or both of them killed Hunt? Spencer had gone to shoot baskets in the gymnasium, and it was at the rear of that building that Benson Hunt's body had been dumped into the liming cart and wheeled into the pine grove to be pitched down the hillside.

But what would be their motive? Tutorials? They were dispensed constantly to students who were achieving far below their potential. Shaffer saw the headlight of a train driving directly at him down the tunnel.

At 6:00 P.M. Constable McElroy turned up at Shaffer's door at Cloisters.

"I thought you were going to call me," Shaffer said.

"A couple of things needed my personal attention. You wouldn't still have some of that excellent Bordeaux left, would you?"

Shaffer got them each a glassful.

When they were settled, McElroy said, "The coroner nailed down the time of death at between six and eight P.M. last night. Now that body didn't lie in that culvert for ten hours. Exposed as it was, a pedestrian or a motorist surely would have seen it along the roadway."

"What does that tell us?"

"It tells us," said McElroy, "that Hunt's body remained on the campus grounds for several hours, perhaps until after midnight or early this morning. It was covered or hidden until his killer could decide what to do with it. Panic after an act of murder usually leaves the murderer in a state of confusion. He's created a dead body out of a human and he's faced with the problems of getting rid of it."

"What else?" Shaffer said.

"The blows delivered to Hunt's skull," said the constable. "The killer seems to have used two murder weapons. The skull shows two distinctly different depressions. One type is rather wide, about four inches, the other perhaps only a half inch or so. The latter were probably the blows that were fatal. It's almost as though Hunt's killer delivered blows with a first weapon and when they didn't seem to be doing the job he seized upon a second weapon."

"They'll all have to be questioned," said McElroy when he'd read Shaffer's report.

"Tedious work," commented Shaffer.

"But sometimes very productive. Stories dovetail or don't, they point to the consistent as well as the inconsistent."

At McElroy's request, Shaffer accompanied him back to the soccer field behind the field house. With dusk, the grounds were peppered with schoolboys returning to their rooms, their after-supper games of tennis, soccer, cricket, or frisbee put up finally for an evening of studies.

The soccer field was empty. Neither Horst Alm nor any of his maintenance staff were about. The shop was locked up for the evening.

"I'm almost certain we're standing at the scene of the killing," said McElroy. "No schoolboy could have dragged a man the size of Benson Hunt any great distance to this spot. And if we can place trust in the coroner's estimation of the time of death, some-one would have seen something at that early-evening hour."

"What are we looking for?" asked Shaffer.

Constable McElroy's eyes swept the areas behind the field house and came to a stop on a good-sized pile of tarpaulin stacked about ten feet from the maintenance-shop door. "That, perhaps."

"The tarps?"

"Yes. What are they used for, do you know?"

"They're used to cover the soccer field," he said. "They come in ten-foot sections that are anchored with bricks or whatever is handy to keep the winds from blowing the works into the next province."

"Let's have a look at them," said McElroy. Shaffer followed him over to the four-foot stack of canvas. "Just the top one or two sections should tell us something, if there's anything to tell."

They had to look only as deep as the topmost tarpaulin. Three folds down, splotches of rusty red stained the material, splotches still faintly damp to the touch. "Well," said McElroy, "this isn't a picnic blanket and these stains aren't strawberry jam. This is what wrapped Hunt's corpse to keep it concealed here until his killer could sneak back in the darkness and remove it from the scene."

Something Jeffery Langlois had told Shaffer now struck the master as of possible importance. "If you're going to interview those two boys," he said to McElroy, "I suggest you begin with Mark Spencer."

"Why Spencer?"

"Well, the other boy, Jeffery Langlois, told me that Spencer went to the field house after the tutorials were over to shoot baskets. I'm afraid that places him near the scene of the crime around the time Benson Hunt was murdered."

"That doesn't look good for him," said McElroy. "Let's go see what he has to say for himself."

Both boys were in their rooms. Mark Spencer was sitting on his bed trying to mend a sock with a light bulb jammed into it.

"Mark," Constable McElroy said, "where did you go after your tutorials with Master Hunt at Cloisters yesterday afternoon?"

Spencer ceased his mending.

"I told Jeff I was going over to the gym to shoot some baskets. I asked him if he wanted to come along, but Jeff said he wanted to go back to the dorm and do some studying."

Shaffer excused himself, left Spencer's room, and went across the hall and knocked on Langlois's door. Jeffery Langlois answered, dressed in just his shorts. "I figured it must be a master. Nobody else in this place ever knocks on a guy's door. Come on in, sir."

Shaffer could see a pile of books and papers on Langlois's study table. "Burning a little early-evening oil, Langlois?"

"Well, you can really get a jump on the competition this way, Mr. Shaffer. The other guys waste as much time as they can. I want to make the Headmaster's Honor List."

"Are the books I loaned you of any help?"

"Are you kidding me? If you get all the characters matched up, *Ulysses* is a breeze. Penelope is Mrs. Bloom, right? And we got Cerberus, he's Joyce's Paddy Dignam. And Tiresias is Leopold Bloom's old man. It's a piece of cake, sir."

"I'm glad they helped," said Shaffer. "There's something I want to talk to you about."

"What's that, sir?"

"After your tutorial yesterday afternoon, Spencer went off to shoot some baskets and you came back to the dorms, is that right?"

"Yes, sir. Spencer's on the varsity B-team and he can shoot the eyes out of a basket. I watched him play when we played Royster Academy, so it doesn't do any good when he tries to hustle me into playing Horse with him. He always wants to play for money or snacks or desserts, but I've got his number."

"Did you do your studying at the table here?" Shaffer asked.

"I always do. That way I can look out the window every so often and see what's happening down on the quadrangle."

"How late did you study?"

"A little after five o'clock, I guess. If you've got a room that looks out over the quadrangle, you don't have to keep looking at your watch to see what time supper is. You just keep an eye on the quad and when everybody down there begins to head for the dining hall, you know it's chow time."

"Think back, Langlois. What can you remember seeing down on the quad yesterday afternoon?"

"Well, let's see. Some guys were kicking a soccer ball around. And Thom Greavy picked a fight with Burleigh Anderson, the tackle on the football team."

"What else?"

"Not much more. Guys were lying around on the grass studying, the usual horseplay. Some kid from the Junior School threw his frisbee up into a tree and couldn't get anyone to hike him up onto a limb so he could climb after it. A few senior guys tried to get up a cricket game, but they didn't have enough players."

"Were you at the study table when they began to break up and head for the dining hall?"

"Yes, sir. Friday is steak night. Man, you should have seen them take off! If you find yourself at the rear of the line on Fridays, you get something that looks like it fell off somebody's shoe."

"And you saw nothing else down on the quadrangle?" Shaffer asked.

"No. Except for Master Hunt."

"What?"

"Yeah. I guess he came out from Cloisters to sort of monitor the activities. He broke up the fight between Greavy and Anderson, as a matter of fact."

"What did you observe of Master Hunt?" asked Shaffer.

"Well, for one thing, he was talking with Mouse Lewis about something or other."

"You mean Cameron Lewis," said Shaffer. He didn't think much of disparaging nicknames and tried to squelch them whenever they came up in the boys' conversation. A St. Andrews boy had enough academic and social pressure to deal with without the additional burden of an ego-diminishing nickname. Cameron Lewis had tested in the genius category, but his slight stature and foolishly large eyeglasses made him the perfect butt for small-people jokes.

"Yes, sir, Cameron," Langlois said. "They talked for about ten minutes. Maybe they were talking about Cameron getting into Amherst. Master Hunt is on the College Admissions Recommendations Board. Cameron's dad is an Amherst graduate and Cameron says if he doesn't get into Amherst he might just as well not go home. Amherst is a family tradition."

Shaffer had forgotten that Hunt had been on the Recommendations Board. It was a six-member panel of masters which, along with Headmaster Batesford, made the crucial decision whether a St. Andrews boy would receive the school's recommendation to the college of his choice. A St. Andrews recommendation was tantamount to acceptance, the lack of it a disaster. As far back as Shaffer could remember, no St. Andrews boy with a recommendation had ever been rejected by the college of his choice. It was a rite of spring nearly every boy endured with high expectation and dread.

"So you watched Master Hunt and Cameron Lewis in discussion for several minutes," said Shaffer. "What happened then?"

"Well, sir, the quadrangle was vacant then. I figured they'd head off for the dining hall like the rest."

"You mean they didn't?"

"No, sir. They started walking in the direction of the field house. They were talking and gesturing and just strolling along. Mouse—I mean Cameron, sorry, sir—was carrying a cricket bat."

Shaffer's stomach did a turn. "Was that as much as you saw?"

"Yes, sir. I closed up my books and went downstairs for supper."

"You told me before that you didn't see Master Hunt in the dining room."

"No, sir."

"What about Cameron Lewis?"

"I didn't see him at supper either," Langlois said.

"Does Cameron Lewis live here in Usatalo?"

"No, sir. He's in Todd."

Shaffer found Cameron Lewis alone in his room in the adjacent dormitory.

"May I come in, Lewis?"

The boy was lying on his back on his bed. When Shaffer entered the room, Lewis sat up. His face seemed to drop.

"If you've got a few minutes, Lewis, I'd like you to take a little walk with me," Shaffer said.

"A walk, sir? Where to?"

"Just around the campus."

"Well, I really should be studying, Mr. Shaffer."

"Put on your sneakers, Lewis. And you'd better grab a jacket. It's getting a little chilly."

It was only a little after seven o'clock. By now the quadrangle, a rolling green in daylight, was transforming itself into a black pit. Shaffer and Cameron Lewis stood on its lip, next to a set of bleachers.

"Lewis, were you out here on the quadrangle yesterday afternoon just before supper?"

"Yes, sir."

"I'm told you spoke with Master Hunt," Shaffer said.

"Yes, sir. Master Hunt is on the Recommendations Board. He wanted to talk to me about my plus-factors. I'm shooting for Amherst, sir, and they place heavy emphasis on a student's plus-factors. Amherst gets over 5,000 applicants and accepts only around 600."

"What happened when Meal Bells rang?" asked Shaffer.

"The usual, sir. Everybody took off like a bullet for the dining hall."

"Did you do the same?"

A gap came in Lewis's response.

"I didn't go right along to supper, no, sir."

"Why not?"

"Master Hunt felt we should talk about my application a little more. An admissions application is very tricky, like grant-writing. You have to put your best foot forward and sort of hide the other from view."

"Did you go back to Cloisters?"

"No, sir."

"The library then?"

"No, not there either."

"Perhaps to Baker Field."

There it was, as clear as handwriting, another response lag.

"I'm waiting for an answer, Lewis," said Shaffer.

"Y—yes, sir. Baker Field. We walked over to Baker Field."

"Fine. Let's head in that direction."

They took virtually the same route Shaffer had taken with Constable McElroy when it became all too clear how Benson Hunt

had died. They moved between the Administration Building and
Science Hall and then onto the flagstone walk leading to the field
house.

The darkness raised Shaffer's already acute sense of isolation.
His mind fell on the possibility that Cameron Lewis might be
psychotic, that the refined network St. Andrews used in its testing
contained holes through which a boy like Cameron Lewis could
slip undetected. He was a murderer, of that there was little doubt
left in Shaffer's mind. But what was his capacity for killing a
second time? Was he concealing a knife or some other small
weapon? Shaffer was letting him walk ahead, leading the way. He
wasn't going to show his back to Lewis for a split second.

They reached the field house and skirted it to the rear.

"We'll stop here, Lewis."

The boy turned. In the dim light it was impossible to read his
expression.

"Lewis, is this where it happened?"

"What, sir?"

"Lewis, you were tested at the Speech and Hearing Clinic in
Victoria along with every other junior boy when you entered St.
Andrews. I can't believe you've suddenly gone deaf."

A whimpering sound came up from Lewis's throat. "Please
don't make me, sir," Cameron Lewis said.

"It's going to come out sooner or later, Lewis. You can make it
easy or difficult."

Seconds passed, almost unbearably tense. "Yes, I did it, sir. I
killed him."

"Why, Lewis? Was it over your Amherst application?"

"Yes, sir. But it was worse than that."

"Isn't killing someone the worst thing one human can do to
another?" Shaffer asked.

"But it *was* worse, sir." Cameron Lewis was shaking and sobbing. "It was my plus-factors, sir. I don't have them. I played on
the Junior Bs in soccer, but I didn't follow through with it. And
this year I was the first one cut from the varsity cricket team." He
paused to gain control. "I'm not a class officer and I didn't get on
enough committees. I placed too much emphasis on academics.
Sure, I kept up an accumulated A-minus, which got me onto the
Headmaster's Academic List. But the plus-factors, I entirely ignored them."

"I can't see what you're driving at, Lewis."

"It was Master Hunt, sir. He told me that all those deficiencies in my plus-factors could be corrected. He said there were ways." Shaffer caught a darkness entering the boy's tone. "No, not corrected, he said they could be *altered*.

"We were standing just about where you and I are standing now, sir. Master Hunt started to tell me stuff about his life. You know, about what it was like for him as a kid growing up, things about his father and why his marriage ended. Mostly about that, about the breakup of his marriage. He began to explain to me why some men get divorced, how some men wage war against their natural inclinations because of society's pressures to conform. But they finally reach a point when they can't hide their true feelings any longer . . ."

Shaffer felt a knot start to grow in his stomach. He had thought he knew Benson Hunt so well. *Qui addit scientiam, addit et laborem.* He that increaseth knowledge increaseth sorrow.

"Then," continued Cameron Lewis, his voice coming thinner from its dark corner, "Master Hunt said what he really wanted. He told me we could go back to his cottage at Cloisters and no one would ever see or know anything. He said that was what I would have to do, that it was the only way I could get my plus-factors doctored on my application to Amherst. Then he put his hand on my cheek."

Shaffer closed his eyes.

"I—I guess I went sort of crazy then, sir. I couldn't push him away, he was so much bigger than me. I stepped back and he started coming toward me again. That's when I hit him. And then I hit him again. I was so scared, I didn't count the number of times I hit him. I didn't want him to touch me anymore and I didn't want to do those things he wanted me to do. Finally, he fell down. I knew he was dead. His whole head was caved in and the blood was everywhere."

Shaffer said, "Lewis, the autopsy shows two types of wounds. Wide wounds and thin wounds. You had your cricket bat with you, didn't you?"

"I had it with me when I was out on the quadrangle, sir. It got turned in my hand when I was hitting him, probably. Some blows with the flat side, some with the edge."

"Master Hunt was too heavy to carry off into the woods," Shaffer concluded. "So you covered his body with one of those field tarps piled against the maintenance-shop wall."

Lewis nodded in the darkness.

"You came back here later, last night sometime, got his body into the lime cart, and wheeled it through the pine grove to the top of the cliff, then dumped the body over the side."

"It wouldn't roll all the way down," said Lewis. "The trees would stop it and I had to climb down and free it. When I got it to the bottom I dragged it to the highway and pushed it over the last ridge into the culvert."

"You should have removed Master Hunt's wallet from his pocket," said Shaffer. "It would have looked like a robbery done by someone in the village."

"I wasn't thinking about anything like that, sir," Lewis said. "I just wanted him as far away from me as possible."

"I understand, Lewis," Shaffer told him. When he placed a comforting hand on the small boy's shoulder, Lewis didn't pull away. "We'll go back to the dorm now and you'll tell Constable McElroy exactly what you've told me."

"Y—yes, sir. I just hope I don't have to tell the story too many more times, sir."

Shaffer knew what the boy meant. There is a limit to the number of times a nightmare can be recalled.

This story, only the second one that Patricia L. Schulze has published, is a poetic and imaginative tale of a doomed marriage, as the heat of August gradually gives way to the snows of January.

PATRICIA L. SCHULZE
The Golden Circle

I watch through the bars of the hospital window and wait for the car. The August heat is rising in waves from the asphalt below. Across the parking lot the ugly backs of apartment buildings shimmer and sway in the heat. There is a young woman with golden hair looking out of a third-floor window in the middle building. I wave but she doesn't see me. The sun glares off the window and I can't see into her room.

Down below, a fire hydrant has been opened and the water snakes out in a sweeping arc. The asphalt steams and hisses where the spray hits it. There are children in cut-off jeans dancing in the jet of water from the hydrant, dancing under the rainbow the sun casts on the spray.

There were children in August a year ago, and I watch them from my apartment window after shaking out a rug. Children dancing under the spray of a fire hydrant in cut-off jeans.

I turn, laughing. "Theo, do you remember when the year started in September? Do you remember jeans?"

He is packing the folders from his file cabinet into sturdy cardboard cartons. He shakes his head.

"You know, how the new jeans in September were so stiff, so unyielding. They cut into your stomach when you tried to bend over. Then, by the time winter was over, they had grown softer, and by spring they were too short."

He stares at me. "What are you talking about, Julie?"

"Jeans. In summer mother would get out her giant scissors and those poor jeans, faded and thin in the knees, would be transformed into cut-offs."

He writes something on a slip of paper on his desk. "Jeans. That's a good idea, Julie. We'll pick some up when we leave town."

I watch him as he goes back to his packing, then I fold the rug and put it on top of a box by the chair. I walk across the room and run a finger over the piano keys.

"There's no way we can take the piano, is there?"

Theo slips a folder into the carton. "We've been over that before, Julie."

"It just seems so long."

Theo fixes tape over the carton flaps. "Six months, Julie, only six months. Then you can tinkle away all you want." He smiles at me over the carton. "It won't be so bad, you'll have me."

He picks up the carton and carries it down to the car. He doesn't hear my answer. Was there any?

I stand at this barred window, twisting a golden circle on my finger, watching children dancing in the water. Where will Theo take me when I leave here? I have asked Dr. Jouvet this many times.

"Your husband does not choose to take me into his confidence, Julie. He only says he has a place ready." He sees the fear on my face and reaches over and holds my hand. "Where would you like to go?"

"I don't know. Back to the apartment maybe. Somewhere with people and noise, lots and lots of noise, and my piano."

"You need that. Theo understands that now."

"Only Theo knows what Theo understands, Doctor." I see him to the door of my room and bid him adieu, our little game because he is French.

He replies, as he always has, "Say au revoir, Julie, not adieu."

A gardener, watering the hospital flower beds, joins his spray to the hydrant's and the children squeal and duck. Looking up, he sees me watching and playfully jerks his hose toward me. The spray of water washes over the window.

September rain washes over the window, distorting images, washing summer dust off the kitchen window in the farmhouse. We have taken a six-month lease on this farm in the middle of the plains for Theo's sake. Theo is a poet, a prophet, a visionary, striving to capture and confine his vision within the split-rail fences of words.

A poet cannot live with asphalt and concrete and steel. A prophet cannot see the future in the cities of the present. A visionary cannot reach humanity under the crushing presence of man.

There is an oak tree outside the kitchen window and it drops its brown acorns on the mulch of 75 years of leaves. We are gathering the acorns, stuffing them into our pockets, and then Theo starts toward the house.

"Don't you want to help me gather them up? We can feed them to the squirrels this winter."

He holds up the one in his hand. "That whole oak, all oak trees are here in this one acorn."

He goes into the house, to his paper and pen, to capture oak trees.

I gather a few more, then stop and walk out across the field behind the house toward the horizon where the sky meets the end of the earth. There is no mark of man to break its clean line. I think if I keep walking I can reach it, but after a few miles it is still just as far away. I go back to the house to tell Theo about the horizon that always stays the same distance away, but he is busy writing, so I go out and sit under the oak tree, fingering a keyboard of leaves.

Dr. Jouvet leans back in his swivel chair. "So in the beginning you liked the farm?"

"Like, dislike, I had no feelings either way. It was just a place we had come to so Theo could write. It was only for six months. You can take any place for six months."

"Theo didn't talk much, did he?"

I shrug. "Theo is a poet, he lives more in his mind. I'm used to that."

"Still, sometimes you did feel trapped there?"

I reach for the cigarette box on his desk but it is empty. He has stopped smoking. "That's only because I can't drive. There was a town of sorts, but it was too far to walk and Theo couldn't take time off from his work to take me very often." I pull my own pack out of my bag. "I went for long walks. It was all right."

In October there is a killing frost and the leaves of the oak turn golden yellow and then brown. I walk out toward the clean line of the horizon and discover a small graveyard, the stones half-buried in the earth, the inscriptions erased long ago by the weather. Theo is excited by my discovery—the dead are of more use to poets than the living—and works for days to restore the markings. All he manages to get is one: *Baby Jenny, six days.* He will turn it into a poem.

I spend a lot of time walking—the house is too small to keep me busy, and I have noticed something strange. In the sharp October mornings the horizon is a little nearer. When I tell Theo this he takes me to town and I buy wool and needles for a sweater I have seen in an old magazine I found in the attic, something to occupy my fingers.

I still walk every day. I want to reach the point where the sky meets the end of the earth. I want to look over the edge, but it isn't near enough yet. I can't quite reach it.

"Why didn't you come back to the city?" Dr. Jouvet is standing behind my chair.

"Because Theo wasn't ready yet."

"You could have left without him."

I pick up two paper clips from his desk and slip one into the other so that their loops intertwined.

"That's Theo and me."

"The loops can be slipped apart."

I bend the thin wires until they are two interlocking circles.

"But they can't, not unless you break one of the circles."

November sets in with chilling winds that toss the branches of the oak tree and shake down the shriveled leaves to join their older brothers in the mulch below. Theo comes home with a new cow and brings me a steaming cup, bearing it in both hands like an offering. I sip and turn retching from the too-sweet taste, the dusty smell.

"That milk is fresh from our own cow," he says, disappointed in my reaction.

"It's fine, really, I just have to get used to it." I try to placate him.

I watch him milk the cow, directing the pale stream into his mouth, his lips moving closer and closer to the cow's udder. I back away in disgust.

As I cross the yard to the house I look out at the line of the horizon where the sky meets the end of the earth. I rub my hand across my eyes and look again. There is no mistake, it is nearer. Very soon I will be able to reach it.

Theo writes late into the night, sometimes stopping to walk out under the clear November sky looking for inspiration. He is writing a poem about love.

He no longer shares my bed.

Dr. Jouvet chews on the end of his pencil, a substitute for smoking. "Are you starting to hate Theo?"

This surprises me and I have to think about it for a while. Finally I shake my head. "I never hated Theo."

"But you can see what he's doing to you?"

I nod sadly.

"Don't you think you really should leave him?"

I look at him helplessly and tears run down my face. "But I can't, not now, it's too late."

Dr. Jouvet frowns. "Why do you say it's too late?"

"He's already done it."

"What has he done?"

"He's made me into a poem."

It is December and there are frost flowers on the window. One last defiant brown leaf clings to the oak tree, and snow, damp and sticking, covers the graves of the old dead with its cold blanket.

Theo writes all the time now, hardly stopping to eat or sleep. His study door is always closed and the reams of poetry pile up around the room. The roads are blocked so no one can get in to disturb him. Sometimes the weight of the snow brings down the power lines, and then Theo writes by candlelight.

He is reaching heights he never could before. His eyes glow with the intensity of his vision. Everything he sees, feels, touches, becomes a part of his poetry.

He walks to the old graves and lies down in the snow covering them, absorbing their message through his very bones.

Dr. Jouvet shakes his head. "I can see Theo, but where is Julie?"

"She is there, watching out the kitchen window, tracing the frost flowers with her finger."

"And the horizon?"

"It is much closer."

"What do you expect to see when you look over the edge?"

"I don't know."

"You know you can't look over, Julie. There is no end of the earth."

"You're wrong, Doctor. There is."

The water dries on the window and the August sun reflects off the roof of a car turning into the parking lot below. The sunlight flashes into my eyes and I squint and reach for my dark glasses, but they aren't here.

In January I wear dark glasses in the house to cut out the dazzling whiteness of the snow. The sun glares off the snow and starts the jagged lightning flashes at the corners of my eyes, bringing on the headaches that keep me in bed all day.

The frost flowers on the window have become joined in one solid opaque sheet. I finger a Bach fugue on the silence of the window sill and melt a circle in the ice with my tongue to see if the horizon has come closer.

Theo has promised me a trip to town, now that the roads are open again. We are to leave this morning, but our neighbor-landlord comes to ask for help at a mid-winter calving. I protest, but the poet, the visionary, has never seen the birth of a calf. He needs it for his art.

He shrugs into his heavy fleece-lined parka. "Don't take on so, Julie. I'll be back by noon. You can still have your holiday."

I stand throughout the morning in the kitchen, cutting up the cold bodies of chickens, longing for cellophane-wrapped meat. My sharp knife flashes in the sun as it severs legs and wings from bodies, cleaves the breasts. I soak the pieces in a bucket and polish the knife until it gleams.

By mid-day the wind is rising, blowing ripples in the dry snow dunes around the house. The roads are already drifting shut again. I clear a spot in the ice on the window and see my last brave leaf shaken out of the arms of its mother oak.

Theo stamps his feet on the kitchen mat, glowing with the lingering excitement of the birthing and something more, some secret he must share with me.

"I've bought the farm, Julie. I was only going to renew the lease but he wanted to sell so I bought it. In the spring he is going to sell us a sow and some chickens for you to look after."

He hurries for his paper, pen, and ink, the new homesteader, the pioneer on the plains.

The sun reflecting off the drifting snow glints along the knife blade in my hand, flashes into my eyes, dazzling me with its brightness. The stars of brightness flash into my eyes and the knife blade flashes, and again, and again, and I am screaming in the flashing of the knife blade and the glinting of the snow-reflected sun. I am screaming and the horizon is too near and I am screaming and I can look over and I see.

I am one of the new dead, lost under the glistening of the snow.

The circle moves on. January is August. I have lost the months between. I light a cigarette, then put it down in the ashtray by the window.

I hear voices and turn in silence, watching them approach—Dr. Jouvet, my friend who would break the circle if he could, and Theo.

"You're a fool, Theo! You can't take Julie back there. She can't be left alone."

"She won't be alone, I'll be there."

"You were there before!"

Theo smiles his superior poet's smile. "I appreciate all you've done, Dr. Jouvet, but I know what's best for my wife."

Dr. Jouvet shakes his head in wonder at the visionary with his insights and I turn away and trace frost flowers on the window with my finger.

Theo comes to me and smiles. Can he be so unchanged? Then I see the glistening scar that mars his handsome cheek. He too bears the mark of January.

Dr. Jouvet lifts my hand to his lips. "Then this is adieu, Julie. Please take care."

I smile as I withdraw my hand. "Don't look so sad, Doctor. Say au revoir, not adieu."

His eyes search mine. He starts to speak, then looks helplessly at Theo. He gazes at the smoke rising from the ashtray at my side. Carefully, deliberately, he picks up the cigarette, inhales deeply, and walks away, taking his knowledge and his failure with him.

Theo, oh so gently, helps me out of the hospital and into the car. We drive through the city and I must drink in the buildings, the asphalt, the concrete, the steel. Must drink it in and hold it to me for a little while. Too soon we are out of the city and racing along the country roads.

Theo talks excitedly about the hay he is putting up for winter and the new sow with piglets by her side.

I look into his poet's eyes, his prophet's eyes, his visionary's eyes, and see he doesn't see. A cold wind whispers in my ear, whispers a message, and I nod. My fingers play a silent melody along my leg.

Winter will come again. January with its snow and wind. The last brave leaf will fall from the oak tree and the horizon, where the sky meets the end of the earth, will draw near.

The sun will be glaring off the snow, sending its dazzling needles deep into my eyes, glinting off the knife blade in my hand. I will strike deep in the flashing of the light. I will cut true in the silvery radiance of the snow-reflected sun. And there, in the glistening January brilliance, I will break the circle.

A detective story in reverse—one in which the killer attempts to deduce the identity of the sleuth on his trail—has been tried at least twice in novels. Pat McGerr's Catch Me If You Can *(1948) and Wade Miller's* Devil on Two Sticks *(1949) both worked variations on this idea. In the short story field "A Matter of Taste" by Dorothy L. Sayers presented a situation in which the reader did not know till the end exactly which character was the real Lord Peter Wimsey. I decided to see what I could do with an idea of this sort. . . .*

EDWARD D. HOCH
Captain Leopold Incognito

It was Fletcher's case in the beginning, and oddly enough that was how it became Leopold's case. "He knows me too well," Lieutenant Fletcher said, taking a sip of coffee from his paper cup. "There's no way I could follow him up there undercover."

Connie Trent, full of department spirit after her recent promotion to sergeant, volunteered, "I could go in his place, Captain."

Leopold smiled. "To a men's health spa? I don't believe you'd stay undercover very long, Connie."

"Don't they have women there too?"

Fletcher shook his head. "Not in the spring. At Dr. Rohmer's it's strictly men now. In the summer they have women's sessions and even coed ones, but now it's men only."

Connie thought about it. "What you need is a cop who looks like he could use a week at Dr. Rohmer's Health Spa. Not some young guy with muscles. You need one who's middle-aged and overweight."

Captain Leopold smiled. "You've just described me, Connie."

"You!"

"Why not? I don't have any pending cases here, and best of all, Walter Hazard is new to this city and doesn't know me. Call the spa and see if they'll take me without an advance reservation. I can go up there tomorrow. And contact the sheriff's office up there. I'll need them to make the actual arrest."

Fletcher wasn't happy. "It's my case, Captain. You shouldn't be taking the risk for me."

"It's the department's case, Fletcher."

The object of all this discussion, Walter Hazard, was a 41-year-old man with a long record of dealing in narcotics. He'd come to Leopold's city only recently, apparently intent on taking over the heroin trade from a man named Max Guttner, who controlled the drug traffic throughout southern New England.

Max Guttner had died ten days ago, shot twice in the head by a silenced .22-caliber target pistol. It was a weapon becoming more and more popular in criminal circles because it could be effectively silenced. And at close range it was just as deadly as a .45. Fletcher was convinced Hazard had killed Guttner to get control of the heroin traffic, but knowing it and proving it were two different things. They needed the murder weapon. And they needed proof that Hazard was now in charge of the Guttner operation. Fletcher hoped to find that proof at Dr. Rohmer's Health Spa.

The spa, located in northern Vermont near the Canadian border, had long been rumored as a way station in the narcotics pipeline from Canada. Respectable businessmen, relaxing for a week in the Vermont woods, returned with their suitcases full of heroin. "We could stop Hazard on the way back," Connie suggested, but Fletcher vetoed it.

"He'd be clean. He knows all the tricks. He has to be taken at the moment he gets the stuff in his hands. And the only way to do that is with an undercover man. We can hold him on the drug charge and use it as evidence he'd taken over Guttner's organization. That'll give us our motive for the killing."

"All right," Leopold said. "I can use a week up there. What about this man Rohmer who runs the place?"

"It seems he must be involved, though we've got nothing against him."

"Is Hazard there now?"

Fletcher nodded. "He went up last night."

"Today's Monday. If he's staying a full week, chances are the delivery will be made on Thursday or Friday. But I'd better get up there tomorrow, just in case."

"What name will you use?" Connie asked.

"I'll think of a good one."

Walter Hazard arose early Tuesday morning for a brisk run in the woods before breakfast. He was ready to admit there was something to this health spa business, even after only one full day on the premises. A combination of exercise, diet, and steam room had already shown results. It was almost enough to make him forget the reason for his trip.

Hazard had driven up from Connecticut on Sunday night. Dr. Rohmer told him that most clients came by train, but Hazard would have a special need for his car on the return trip. The plan was for a man named Kellogg to cross the border with fifty pounds of uncut heroin on Thursday night. He was expecting to meet Max Guttner, but the word had been passed to him that he'd be meeting Walter Hazard instead.

Hazard was a man without morals, which he insisted was the only way to get ahead in the modern world. He never thought about what happened to the heroin after it left his hands, and he never thought about the men he'd killed along the way to his present position. It hadn't bothered his conscience a bit when he'd walked up behind Max Guttner and fired two bullets into his head at close range. It was the way of the world these days. Only the strong, the unscrupulous, survived.

Hazard had a woman named Margo who'd been with him for the past two years. She was beautiful and smart, and could have succeeded on her own in the business world. Somehow she preferred the uncertainties of Hazard's existence, and he never questioned that. He'd had to leave her behind on this trip, which depressed her, but he'd promised to phone.

In fact he was thinking of phoning her as he completed his run, coming up to the dining-room entrance at a trot. That was when he saw Dr. Rohmer awaiting him. Rohmer was a slim balding man who rarely smiled. At this moment he was looking especially unsmiling. "Can I see you in my office, Mr. Hazard?"

"Now? Before breakfast?"

"Before breakfast."

Hazard wiped the sweat from his face and neck and followed the man inside. "What's up?" he asked when they were alone in the spa's main office. It was after eight and his stomach was growling with hunger.

"I just had a phone call from a friend at the sheriff's office."

"Oh?"

"Do you know a detective named Leopold? Captain Leopold?"

"I may have heard the name. What about him?"

"He notified the sheriff that he's coming here undercover as part of a murder investigation. He wants their help if an arrest needs to be made, since he's outside his own jurisdiction."

"Was my name mentioned?"

"No—but it's you he's after, isn't it? He knows you killed Max."

Hazard merely stared at Dr. Rohmer. Finally he said, "That sort of talk can get you in big trouble, Doctor. When's this Leopold arriving?"

"Today."

"I'll be watching for him."

"I don't want him here, Hazard. Nor you either!"

"Don't worry. There won't be any trouble. How will he arrive—by car?"

"You're the only one this week who came by car. He'll take the train up from Montpelier like everyone else, to avoid attracting attention."

"How's he get here from the station?"

"Fellow from town named Gus brings up the mail every day. Any strays come along in his station wagon."

"Strays?"

"Those with reservations arrive on Sunday as you did. But there are always a few who turn up later in the week unannounced, and we try to accommodate them if there's room."

"What time does Gus get here?"

"Around eleven if the train's on time."

"All right," Hazard said. "Thanks for the warning."

"Are you clearing out?"

"No. I'm staying."

When Hazard saw the station wagon coming up the hill he left his exercise class and trotted over to the main building. A stocky man in soiled coveralls was unloading suitcases from the back of the vehicle. "Are you Gus?" Hazard asked.

The man straightened up. "That's right, mister."

"Where's the fellow you brought up from the train?"

"Fellow? I brought up three fellows. They're in at the desk, registering."

"Three?" Hazard hurried up the steps and into the lobby. There were indeed three men there—all middle-aged and overweight. Typical clients for Dr. Rohmer. One was taller than the others, with white hair and a boyish face. He put out his hand as Hazard entered the lobby.

"Are you Dr. Rohmer? I'm Ed Murray from Boston. I don't have a reservation but I was told on the phone it didn't matter."

Hazard shook hands and said, "Sorry, I'm not the doctor. Just a patient like yourself."

"Oh."

Gus deposited the luggage in the lobby and accepted tips from the men. Then he turned his station wagon around and headed back down the hill. Presently Dr. Rohmer appeared, casting a glance in Hazard's direction, and welcomed the three men. "Our regular week at the $150 rate starts on Sunday. By the day it's $30. If you'll just sign in I'll have one of the boys show you to your rooms."

One of the two shorter men spoke up. "I'm Frank Gibbons, from Springfield. Could you make sure I get an air-conditioned room? I have a bit of an allergy problem, and—"

Dr. Rohmer came close to smiling but didn't quite make it. "You're here to relax and get over things like that. A few sessions in the steam room and some good healthy food and you'll forget you ever had an allergy."

Hazard stole a glance at the registration cards. The third man, well built and probably still in his late forties, was named Sam Young. He gave his home as Providence, Rhode Island, and stood off to one side without speaking.

When they'd been led away to their rooms, Dr. Rohmer came over to Hazard. "Did you look them over?"

"A little. Which one is Leopold?"

The doctor frowned. "I have no idea. I told you I want you out of here."

"Let's go in your office and talk it over."

"There's nothing to talk over." The doctor turned and stalked away.

Hazard watched him go, wondering just how serious he was. If Rohmer did anything to block the transfer of the heroin, he could ruin Hazard's takeover of the Guttner network. Without a leader they'd be selling the stuff on the streets for whatever the market would bring.

Hazard went up to his room and opened his suitcase. From the zipper pouch of toilet articles he extracted his .22-caliber target pistol, a box of cartridges, and the silencer. He went about his task with loving care, checking the weapon to make certain it was still well oiled. It was American intelligence agents who'd first dis covered that such weapons were just about the only production handguns which could be effectively silenced. The information had taken years to seep through to the underworld, but now the pistol was being used with excellent results.

Hazard loaded the gun and attached the silencer. Then he carefully taped it to the skin of his calf, beneath his baggy sweatpants. He'd lose some hair off his leg when he pulled it free, but that was nothing. A brief bit of pain had never bothered him.

He went back outside, watching some of the early comers already heading for the dining room. It was just about noon, almost lunchtime, but he wasn't the least bit hungry. "Going to eat?" a voice behind him asked. It was the white-haired Ed Murray from Boston.

"Not quite yet," Hazard replied.

"Hurry up and I'll save you a seat at our table." Murray had changed into shorts and a sweatshirt and seemed ready to take on the world.

"Sure," Hazard said. "You do that."

He crossed the exercise field to the administration building and entered Rohmer's office through the side door. The doctor was at his desk, checking over a pile of bills from the morning mail. "What—? Oh, it's you again, Hazard. What now? I thought you'd be gone."

"I'm not going, Rohmer. I can't go till Kellogg gets here Thursday night with the stuff."

Dr. Rohmer sighed and went back to checking the bills. "Kellogg won't be coming. I'm putting through a call to Montreal this afternoon, telling him to cancel the trip."

"I was afraid of that."

"Damn it, Hazard, I'm not going to let this business go down the drain for you! Max Guttner always paid me well, but he respected my position too! I can't have Kellogg coming across the border Thursday night with an undercover detective captain on the premises. Especially when I don't even know which one he is!"

"I'll find out."

"Don't bother—the deal's off. I'm phoning Kellogg."

"I'm sorry to hear that."

Hazard squatted as if to tie his sneaker, pulling the pistol free from under his pants leg. He felt the sudden flash of pain as the tape pulled away some hair. Then he straightened up, and without saying a word fired two bullets into Dr. Rohmer's left temple.

There was almost no sound from the pistol, and very little blood from the two small wounds. Hazard quickly stepped to the door and bolted it. Then he lifted Rohmer's body from the chair and half dragged, half carried it across to a closet. It would have to remain there till after dark. He couldn't risk anyone finding it till after Thursday, when he completed his deal. Any hint of Rohmer's murder and Leopold would have the local police in immediately.

Hazard replaced the gun beneath his baggy sweatpants and jogged over to the dining room to join Ed Murray for lunch. The other two newcomers were at the table with him, and they'd saved a chair for Hazard. He wondered who'd had the idea of inviting him. "Sit right here," Murray said. "You come to this place often?"

"First time. How about you?"

"First time for all of us, I guess."

Gibbons, the man from Springfield, patted his bulging stomach. "I been going to these health spas for years, but they sure don't do much for me. This one's a picnic compared to some I've seen. There's a place in the Catskills that's run like a concentration camp, with enforced fasting. That'll take the pounds off!"

"Really?" Hazard sipped his vegetable juice. He turned to the silent Sam Young. "What about you? First visit here?"

"Yeah."

"You don't talk much."

"Nothing to say."

"Only reason I'm here is my wife," the white-haired Murray said. "She's always beefing about the shape I'm in, wanting me to lose weight."

Hazard glanced at Murray's left hand. There was no wedding ring, but that proved nothing. Many men didn't wear them. But Murray said he was from Boston and he talked more like a New Yorker. That might mean something. He tried to put himself in Leopold's place. Would he be more likely to pose as a devoted husband or a health nut like Gibbons or a silent stranger like Sam Young?

The trouble was, Hazard didn't know Leopold.

But someone must know him.

Someone back in Connecticut.

After lunch Hazard excused himself and went to his little room. He had two phone calls to make.

First he got an outside line and then dialed the number of Dr. Rohmer's Health Spa. When the switchboard answered he asked for the front dest. Then, muffling his voice and trying to imitate Rohmer's monotone, he told the room clerk, "This is Dr. Rohmer. I'm in town and something important has come up. I may have to go down to Burlington for a few days."

"Yes, sir," the clerk answered dutifully.

"Tell the staff to carry on as usual. I'll be back no later than Friday."

"Very good, sir."

Hazard hung up smiling. He knew Rohmer's car was in the garage at his nearby house, but that could be moved after dark, along with the body. Rohmer was separated from his wife, so there'd probably be no one to question his disappearance, at least till Friday. By that time Hazard would have finished his business.

Next he phoned his apartment in Connecticut, hoping Margo would be home. She was.

"How are you doing up there?" she asked. "Losing weight?"

"Some. Look, Margo, I want you to do something for me. I need a photograph of a man named Leopold, a detective captain down there."

"What's up?"

"He may be here. If he is, I need to identify him."

"If he's there, how do I get a picture of him?"

"Go down to the newspaper morgue—right now, this afternoon. If he's a captain he must have had his picture in the paper sometime. When he was promoted, if nothing else. Make a Xerox copy of the clipping. If they won't allow copies, steal the damn thing. Call me back when you've got it. I'll give you the number here."

"All right." She didn't ask any more questions. She knew what he wanted and how to get it. "Take care of yourself, Walter."

"Don't worry."

He hung up and went back outside. It was almost time for the steam room and massage.

The silent Sam Young was on the massage table next to Hazard, and he noticed the scar tissue on Young's side. "What's that from?" he asked. "Looks like a bullet grazed you."

Sam Young eyed him with interest. "That's what happened."

"Where?"

"Vietnam."

Young closed his eyes and said no more. Hazard rolled over on his stomach and studied the scar. There was no way of telling if it had been caused by a .50-caliber machine gun in the jungle or a .32-caliber handgun in an alley.

It was just before dinnertime when Margo called back. He could tell from the edge of excitement in her voice that she had what he needed. "You got it?"

"Sure, Walter. No problem. There were lots of clippings about him, and two pictures. I copied them both."

"What's he look like?"

"Middle-aged, a little overweight."

"I figured that much. Does he have white hair?"

"No, it looks dark in these pictures."

"How recent are they?"

"One's about three years old, but the other ran six months ago."

"Can you tell how tall he is?"

"Not from these pictures. They're head-and-shoulders."

"Anything in the articles that might help? Do they mention a bullet wound?"

"No, I don't remember anything like that."

Hazard was feeling frustrated. "What about his face? Anything unusual? Scars?"

"Nothing like that, Walter. It's just a face."

"What color eyes?"

"These are black-and-white pictures, Walter. How the hell do I know what color eyes? Not real light, though."

"All right," he said finally.

"Do you want me to drive up with these?"

"No, no—a woman up here this week would be too noticeable. Besides, it's a six-hour drive. Put them in the mail to me—but take the letter to the post office so you're sure it goes out tonight."

"You probably won't get it till Thursday morning."

"I know." He hated putting himself at the mercy of the mail, but maybe he'd get lucky in the meantime. He still held an advantage because Leopold couldn't know when the shipment from Canada was due—if he knew about it at all.

"Be careful, Walter."

"Don't worry. I'll see you the end of the week."

He hung up, wondering if the phone might be tapped, and

then decided it wasn't. The line went through the switchboard. They couldn't have put a tap on it without Rohmer's knowledge.

After dinner he strolled and chatted with Ed Murray, inventing a mythical Midwestern business he'd managed to counter Murray's stories about the business world of Boston. As they parted, Hazard reflected that at least Margo's information had cleared the white-haired Murray.

Unless, that is, Leopold had dyed his hair.

After dark Hazard went over to Dr. Rohmer's house and opened the lock on the garage door, using a key from the doctor's pocket. He drove the big green limousine up to the rear entrance of the administration building, hoping no one was looking out a window. He could hear the TV sets blaring, and he knew that Murray and the other two were engaged in a three-handed pinochle game. With luck he'd be safe, but he carried the .22 pistol under his jacket just in case.

He pulled Rohmer's body from the closet, hoisted it over his shoulders, went out to the car, and put it in the trunk. There was a large stain of blood on the closet floor that he covered with a little rug from the office. Then he smoothed out the marks of the dead man's heels on the office carpeting.

Hazard drove the big car slowly down the winding road toward the town. He remembered seeing an abandoned marble quarry on the drive up. It wasn't the perfect place to hide a car and a body, but it should serve for a few days.

He left the car deep in the quarry, placing a few wooden planks and tree branches around it to camouflage its appearance from a distance. Then he walked about a mile into town.

The first person he saw was Gus, standing by his station wagon near the train station. "What'll you charge to run me up the hill to the spa?" he asked.

The stocky man spit out some tobacco juice. "Two bucks."

"Good, let's go."

"You been out walkin'?"

"Exercise. Walked farther than I thought. It's easy downhill, but I guess I need a ride back up."

Gus grunted and opened his door. "Get that dust off your shoes. I try to keep my wagon clean."

"Sure," Hazard said.

In ten minutes he was back at the health spa. He paid Gus for the trip and went inside to watch the card game. No one seemed to have missed him.

In the morning, on his prebreakfast run, Hazard was accompanied by Frank Gibbons. The man seemed to have overcome his worry over allergies, but he was still full of horror stories about the other spas he'd visited.

"One place out West," he told Hazard as they jogged along the wooded path, "they all kneel naked in the sun on a stone terrace overlooking the ocean. Men and women together! I tried it for an hour and was sunburned for two weeks!"

"They go for that stuff in California," Hazard agreed. "A bunch of oddballs, if you ask me."

"It cured my allergy though—I gotta admit that."

"How were the women out West?"

"Beautiful! But they were all into this meditation kick. It wasn't a health spa, it was a religion."

The mail arrived a little before noon and was quickly sorted into a row of slots, one for each letter of the alphabet. There was nothing in the H slot for Hazard, but he'd known it was too soon to receive Margo's letter and the pictures.

After lunch he tried to strike up another conversation with Sam Young, but without much luck. He'd just about ruled Young off his list of suspects—certainly Leopold would try harder to be friendly, if only to keep a close eye on him.

That evening he started to grow nervous. Maybe it was all this exercise that had tired his mind as well as his body. He started thinking of all the things that could go wrong, especially with this Leopold on the premises. He wished he knew the name of the person in the sheriff's office who'd tipped off Rohmer. But then he decided the name wouldn't be of much help. The man was obviously loyal to Rohmer, and the doctor was out of the picture now.

But what if Rohmer had lied to him?

What if he'd already phoned Kellogg before Hazard killed him?

He looked through the little notebook he'd taken from Max Guttner's body and found the phone number in Montreal where Kellogg could be reached. But this time he didn't risk using the phone in his room. He went outside and entered Dr. Rohmer's office through the back door. Sitting at the desk where the doctor himself had last sat, he put in the call to Montreal.

There was some trouble reaching Kellogg, but finally he came on the line. Voices in the background suggested a party was in progress. "This is Hazard, at the spa."

"Oh, yeah."

"Will I see you tomorrow?"

"Sure. Why not?"

"Dr. Rohmer had to go away suddenly. I was afraid there might have been a change in plan."

"Not on this end. I should get there before midnight."

"Fine."

"You have the money?"

"Don't you worry about that. It's right here."

"See you, then. By the big rock on the north path."

Hazard hung up, feeling better. All was going well. He was being nervous without the slightest cause.

At breakfast in the morning Ed Murray was talking about the roads. "Driving in this part of the country is murder. Don't you agree, Walter?"

Hazard was immediately on guard. Had Murray seen him in Rohmer's car on Tuesday night? "Oh, I don't know. I brought my car up."

"Over these roads? I don't know how you did it!"

"You took the train?"

"A bus, actually. The schedule was better."

Hazard studied the face across the table, trying to picture the man as a detective captain. It could be. It could easily be.

"Going to the lecture on mental health?" Murray asked.

"I suppose so," Hazard said. "Hope I don't fall asleep."

They sat together during the late-morning lecture, in which one of Dr. Rohmer's assistants expounded on the importance of a correct attitude toward life. Yes, thought Hazard, that's one thing I've got—a right attitude toward life. And toward death too.

The room was only about half-full, and he couldn't help noticing that both Gibbons and Young were among the missing. "I think Young was going for a run," Murray said in answer to Hazard's question. "And Frank Gibbons wanted a dip in the outside pool. This is the first really warm day we've had."

The lecture ended just before lunchtime, and Hazard hurried to the mail slots. The letter from Margo was there. He recognized her slim slanted handwriting at once.

He held his breath and tore it open.

Her note said simply: *Here it is.* He unfolded the clipping and stared at it.

The story was from a Boston newspaper, about a spring visit to the zoo. The picture accompanying it showed a large male gorilla pounding his chest.

Hazard sat down in the lobby, stunned. He knew Margo would never play a trick like this. Someone had got to the mail, removed the letter from its slot while he sat in that damned lecture!

He examined the gummed flap of the envelope. It had been steamed open and resealed with rubber cement. The picture of Leopold had been taken out and this foolish thing substituted. And only one person could have done it—Captain Leopold himself.

The two of them were circling each other like wildcats in the dark, each at a disadvantage. Hazard still didn't know Leopold's cover identity, and Leopold still didn't know the Canadian heroin was arriving that night.

But maybe, just maybe, Leopold had overextended himself.

Because Hazard had been with Ed Murray all morning, sitting right next to him during the lecture, there was no way the white-haired man from Boston could have taken this letter out of the slot and substituted the clipping.

So Ed Murray wasn't Captain Leopold.

And that left just two of them—Gibbons the health nut and Sam Young the silent, with the bullet scar on his side.

One of them was Leopold.

Hazard bit his lip and thought about the gun back in his room. If necessary he could kill them both.

But it would be better just to kill the right one.

Gibbons or Young?

Gibbons's mail slot, the G, would be right next to Hazard's. Gibbons could have taken the letter and returned it later without much risk. And that damned picture of the gorilla! Wasn't a gibbon an ape of some sort? Leopold could be giving him a hint.

But why would he do that? Wouldn't he be more likely to cast suspicion on someone else, on the wrong man?

And why had he left this foolish clipping in the first place?

Of course he had to remove the real picture once he found it, and doing that much was enough to tip his hand. A clipping from a handy Boston paper could do no further harm—and in Leopold's view it might even force Hazard's hand. Sam Young might even have left the ape picture to point suspicion at the Gibbons name.

Hazard went back to his room after lunch and got out the .22 pistol. He'd carry it taped to his leg from now on, until he met Kellogg just before midnight. If Gibbons or Young tried to stop him, he'd kill either as he had Dr. Rohmer.

Hazard's car was in a small parking area down the hill from the swimming pool. He was in the habit of checking it each afternoon, though it wasn't likely anyone would try to steal it. He checked it now, making certain no one was blocking him from a quick exit that night, and then he returned to the pool.

Sam Young pulled himself out of the water as Hazard approached, and began drying himself with a towel. "Beautiful day," Hazard remarked.

"Yeah."

He found his eyes drawn again to the scar on the man's side. "You come to these places often?"

"First time."

"Where do you work in Providence?"

"I'm with the city."

"Oh?"

Young finished drying himself and walked away, leaving Hazard standing there. He watched the man go, thinking in that moment that he'd like to kill him whether or not he proved to be Captain Leopold.

He sat by the pool for a time, until the start of the afternoon calisthenics. Then as he was getting up, something made him glance down the hill at his car. It seemed to be at an odd angle, with the rear end lower than the front. He strolled down for a closer look.

Both of his rear tires were flat.

He glanced quickly in all directions, but no one was around. Yet he was sure the tires had been perfectly all right thirty minutes earlier.

Leopold again—who else?

He tried to decide whether Young could have got dressed and out the other door in time to deflate his tires. Probably not, and that only left Gibbons.

Gibbons was Leopold. He was almost certain of it now. All that talk of allergies and health spas was part of his cover.

But why deflate his tires? What did Leopold hope to gain?

He wanted to prevent Hazard's escape, obviously. If Hazard called attention to the flat tires, or tried to get them changed or inflated in a hurry, it would be a tipoff that he planned an early departure.

No, better to leave the car as it was and find another way out of there. He could always steal a car if necessary.

As he was passing through the lobby a better idea struck him. That man from town had his card tacked up on the notice board. *Gus's Taxi Service—Day & Night.*

He went to a pay phone and called the number. Gus wasn't in, the woman said. This was the drugstore, and should she have Gus call back? No, Hazard told her. He'd call back.

All through dinner he kept his eyes on Frank Gibbons. The man ate heartily, speaking of the appetite he'd worked up. At one point in the conversation he wondered where Dr. Rohmer was, and Ed Murray said, "I hear he's away for a few days."

After dinner Hazard phoned the taxi driver again. This time the woman put him on and Hazard said, "Gus? This is the man you brought up to the health spa the other night. Remember?"

"Yeah, I remember."

"Could you come get me tonight, around midnight?"

"I guess so."

"Don't honk your horn and disturb people. I'll walk down the road to the signpost and meet you there. At midnight. If I'm a few minutes late, wait for me."

"I'll be there."

Hazard hung up and relaxed. For the first time all day he felt some of the tension draining away. It was going to work. In spite of Leopold and his damned gorilla, it was going to come off.

There was one more thing to do and he'd be reasonably safe. He took Dr. Rohmer's keys—his car keys and house keys—from their hiding place in his room and slipped them into the envelope with the money for Kellogg. If the Canadian was caught, or if he tried to double-cross Hazard, he could be blamed for Rohmer's murder. Perhaps he'd have an alibi for the past few days, but it would take time to prove.

Then Hazard opened his toilet kit and took out a bottle of sleeping capsules. He emptied the powder from three capsules into a little fold of paper and tucked this in his pocket. Just in case.

The evening pinochle game hadn't yet begun, though most of the regulars were assembled in the card room. Hazard sought out Frank Gibbons and suggested they have a little wine. It was the only alcoholic beverage to be found on the premises, so there wasn't a great deal of choice. Hazard poured from the decanter, slipping the sleeping powder into the glass intended for Gibbons. They sat on the terrace, drinking and chatting, and Gibbons passed up his game with the others.

"A fine night," Hazard said.

Gibbons agreed. "Look at that moon! Makes you want to run through the woods!"

After a time Hazard saw the sleeping powder beginning to take effect. "Why did you come here?" he asked Gibbons. "To trap me?"

"W—what?" His head dipped forward onto his chest.

Hazard smiled and stood up. "Sweet dreams, Captain Leopold."

He came off the terrace and strolled toward the woods. He'd have an hour or more to wait, but he liked to be early. He crouched and pulled the tape from his leg again, feeling the cool steel of the gun in his hand. Then he moved deeper into the woods, and presently when he'd found the meeting place he sat down on a rock and lit a cigarette.

Kellogg came up the path a few minutes after eleven, giving the bird call that was his signal. "Are you Hazard?" he asked.

"That's right."

"What happened to old Max?"

"He had an accident."

The Canadian nodded. "Those things happen. You got the money?"

"In this envelope."

Kellogg lit a match to count it. "What are these keys?"

"Do me a favor and throw them away in the woods."

"Huh?"

"Do you have the stuff?"

Kellogg unstrapped a knapsack from his shoulders. "Fifty pounds, uncut."

"Good." Hazard did a quick test with the tip of his tongue. It seemed like the real thing.

"When do you want some more?"

"I'll be in touch. Goodbye for now."

He watched the Canadian hurry back down the trail. They hadn't shaken hands because Hazard was holding the silenced pistol in his right hand. The Canadian must have seen it, but in this business such actions weren't that unusual. Hazard glanced at his watch. He had plenty of time to get his suitcase and meet the station wagon.

He hurried back to the spa, where most of the lights were out now, and entered his room. The knapsack went into his suitcase but the pistol stayed in his hand. He was going out the door, weighted down with the heavy luggage, when someone grabbed him in the dark.

He saw the white hair and knew it was Ed Murray.

"Not so fast, mister. I saw you putting something into Frank's drink and he passed out! What's your game, anyway?"

Hazard growled an obscenity and tried to break free, but Murray held him tight. Hazard's right hand came up, unable to get the long-barreled pistol into firing position. Instead, he brought it up and over in an arc, catching Murray across the back of the head. The man's knees buckled and Hazard hit him again.

Then he pointed the weapon at the fallen figure. It was all coming apart—Gibbons and now Murray! Were they both Captain Leopold? But that was crazy.

He realized the silencer had come off the weapon when it hit Murray's skull. He couldn't find it in the dark and he couldn't risk a shot without it. He left Murray lying there and hurried out.

He was panting when he reached the signpost down the road. Gus's station wagon was already there. "You're out of breath," the stocky man told him. "Let me help you with that suitcase."

Hazard brought up the gun. "Don't touch it. Just get in and drive." He slid the suitcase onto the seat ahead of him.

"Sure, mister."

Then, before Hazard realized what was happening, the car door hit his hand holding the gun. He screamed in pain and dropped the weapon, then looked up at the gun in Gus's hand. "Sure, mister," the man said, "I'm driving us right to jail. I'm Captain Leopold."

It was the following afternoon before Leopold was back in his office with Lieutenant Fletcher and Connie Trent. "I saved you some work and our local taxpayers some money," he told Fletcher. "Hazard will be tried in Vermont for killing Dr. Rohmer and we won't have to extradite him unless he beats that rap. Luckily the man he hit on the head wasn't badly hurt."

Fletcher merely shook his head. "I've got so many questions I don't know where to begin."

"Suppose I just tell you what happened," Leopold said. "I had every intention of going to the spa as a guest until I met this man Gus and saw that he was stocky like me. I paid him to let me take his place for a few days, and he filled me in on the layout of the spa and the daily rounds with the mail and such. The story to the townspeople was that Gus was ill and I was his cousin, filling in for a few days. Hazard took me by surprise on Tuesday and asked if I was Gus, so I said I was, and stuck to that story with him. I told the desk clerk the cousin story. Rohmer, who'd know I wasn't Gus, was killed before he ever saw me."

"How'd you know Hazard killed him?" Connie asked.

"On Tuesday night he came into town on foot, looking for a ride back to the spa. There was marble dust on his shoes, from the quarry outside of town. I got somebody to show me the place the next morning and I found Rohmer's car with his body in the trunk. Rohmer had a stooge in the sheriff's office, but once his body was found that guy just wanted to save his own skin. He admitted tipping off Rohmer that I was coming, so I figured Hazard knew it too. When I saw a letter arrive for him yesterday, I steamed it open and found my picture inside. I substituted a newspaper clipping about the Boston zoo, which properly unnerved Hazard."

Fletcher scowled at Leopold. "Opening mail without a warrant?"

"We won't tell the postal authorities that part. Actually, Hazard was so busy suspecting the other guests of being me that he never thought of the most likely person to tamper with the mail—the person who delivered it every day."

"What about the Canadian?"

"They picked him up trying to recross the border."

"How'd you know Hazard would phone you for a ride last night?" Connie asked.

"Well, I'd given him a ride Tuesday night, and I figured if I let the air out of his tires he might decide to call on me again. If he hadn't I'd have been waiting for him anyway."

"You let the air out of his tires?"

Captain Leopold grinned. "There's something about this undercover work that brings out the worst in a cop. But for people like Walter Hazard, the worst is none too bad."

The line between mystery and fantasy can be a very thin one indeed. This story was accepted for publication in the first issue of a new mystery magazine which, unfortunately, never appeared. It was finally published in the Magazine of Fantasy & Science Fiction, *and I think you'll agree it's one of those rare stories that's equally at home in either field. A brief biography of Frank Sisk leads off our Yearbook section, but first read his story of a small-town doctor's very special problem.*

FRANK SISK
The Leech

Miss Hattie Hopkins didn't advertise. It wasn't really necessary.

In these small Southern towns, whenever something special materializes, word of mouth always does the job of selling it. And three months after Miss Hopkins had acquired the old Conway property, rehabilitated it, and moved in, a coterie of misguided creatures was regularly beseeching her alleged wizardry as a teller of fortunes.

Miss Hopkins appeared to be in her late forties. She wore her gray-flecked auburn hair in a large loose bun which accentuated the pallor of a long face that would have been plain except for glowing green eyes and the avid protrusion of the upper front teeth.

She claimed to have originated in Summerville, South Carolina. Nobody bothered to verify this until, certain suspicions justifiably aroused, I did.

Buried somewhere in our town hall's musty vault is an old ordinance that requires licensing of anyone who wishes to practice necromancy, dowsing, palm reading, crystal gazing, or fortune telling. The penalty for practicing these occult arts without a license is a fine of ten dollars or thirty days on the chain gang. In my long memory this ordinance has been invoked only once, and that was a case less judicial than prejudicial against a company of gypsies who set up a soothsayer tent just outside the grounds during a county fair.

On that score, obviously, Miss Hopkins was in no danger of being prosecuted. Besides, as I soon learned, she performed her services gratuitously—as a social lark, one might say.

So it wasn't her exercises with cards or tea leaves that concerned me. Being a physician and county health officer, I normally paid no attention to human peccadillos unless they caused disease. Miss Hopkins's diversion at first seemed harmless enough, and it was not until she began to trespass upon my province that I took serious note of her.

It was Maybelle Cummings, a well-off widow and incurable hypochondriac, who inadvertently apprised me that our seeress was stepping on my toes. Maybelle was in the office for her quarterly blood-sugar analysis. Since her husband's death she had added a fear of diabetes to a long list of ailments keyed to intensive migraines.

After drawing from her plump right arm a 300-cc component of blood, twice as much as was absolutely needed for the lab test, I laid a doctorly palm across her fretful forehead and said:

"Those mean migraines still with you, Maybelle?"

"They lettin' up some, Doc."

"So you've finally started doing the little workouts I pre-scribed."

"No such thing."

"Well, then—"

"Y'awl pardon my English, Doc, but you medicine men don't have *all* the cures."

"I guess not. What kind of magic remedy have you discovered now, Maybelle?"

"I ain't none too sure I oughten to say."

"The secret's safe with me."

"Oh, I don't know now."

"Come on, Maybelle. Don't try teasing old Dr. Devlin."

She heaved a sigh and then, raising puffy hands to her temples, pushed back several thick strands of pink-dyed hair. "Okay, Doc. Lookit here."

Adjusting the overhead light, I leaned forward. Each temple bore a small Y-shaped mark, still faintly livid.

"What you make of that, you s'all-fired smart?" she said smugly.

I recognized the marks as those left by the three jaws of a blood-sucking leech.

"Well, I make out that you've found yourself a quack," I said.

"I found a person give me relief from them terrible head-aches," she retorted. "Which is more'n I ever found here."

"Thanks for the compliment."

"You're welcome and so's your aspirin."

"Tell me, Maybelle, what's the going rate these days for a session of phlebotomy?"

"A session of *what?*"

"Phlebotomy. In plain English, bloodletting. What do you pay for letting leeches suck your blood?"

"I do declare, Doc, you got a nasty way of puttin' things. Why, them little chiggers don't hurt a mite, and they right off get me shet of them headaches."

"How much a whack, Maybelle?"

"Not a blamed cent."

"Cheap enough."

"A smart cheaper than you and your big needle."

"Who's the quack?"

"Miss Hattie Hopkins, if you must know. And she ain't no quack neither. Just a good friend with a helpin' hand."

It's been years since I kept leeches. During the early days, when I first settled here, I used them occasionally in the treatment of polycythemia, a condition caused by overproduction of red blood cells. To prevent the thickening blood from forming clots, a few good leeches were often effective. There are now drugs on the market that do the trick much better.

Maybelle Cummings was perfectly correct in stating that leeches perform their task painlessly. These small aquatic annelids (some, blood-surfeited, become twenty centimeters long) emit with their saliva an anesthetic which totally desensitizes the area to be penetrated by the needlelike teeth. At the same time the wound is injected with an element called hirudin. This expands the blood vessel and acts as an anticoagulant.

Sleeping mammals, some as large as rabbits, overtaken by leeches, have been sucked fatally dry without ever waking.

But, as I say, I haven't used the things in years because new drugs make them an anachronism. Besides, I'm afraid that this time-honored means of bloodletting, if employed nowadays by a licensed doctor even for a sound reason, would generate much morbid gossip. So it's wiser to abide by the piston syringe, acceptable to most people.

James P. Upson entered the office a few mornings after the Maybelle Cummings visit. Right away I noticed his nose.

James P. had inherited the largest of the town's three banks from a stern psalm-singing father. From another ancestor he'd acquired a taste for bonded bourbon and backroom politics. Now, a well-seasoned sixty, he could look back (somewhat blearily most of the time) to a career of public service which included being mayor, tax collector, town clerk, and assessor, more or less in that order.

Over the years his nose had gradually ripened into a large lavender bulb worthy of an Avignon monk's during the time of the Great Schism. Today, however, its size and color struck me as somehow abated.

But it wasn't his nose that brought James P. regularly to the office. It was his gout. Every six months without fail the big toe on his left foot imitated the aspect of his nose, with the added feature of excruciating pain.

These seizures occurred in spite of the medication which was supposed to allay them, primarily because James P., befogged a good deal of the time (even when sitting at the bank's presidential desk), often forgot to take his daily tablet of allopurinol. For a man who swallowed so much else from dawn to dusk, this omission seemed sinful.

Anyway, my semiannual procedure with James P. varied little.

"Good morning, James. Old gout got you again?"

"Good Godawmighty, Doc. Like Satan hisself got holt of that there toe with a pair of hot pliers."

Although James P. had spent two slothful years at a very expensive prep school and most of a year at the state university, he still talked like a good old boy and not deliberately either.

"You've been skipping your medication again."

"Damn, if I ain't. Keep misplacin' that little bitty bottle, Doc."

"Would it help if I told the druggist to use a large bottle next time, something about the size of a fifth?"

James P. chortled. "Now that ain't sech a bad idee at all, Doc."

"I'll give it further thought. Roll up your sleeve, James, and we'll see what your blood's doing today."

"And they call us bankers bloodsuckers. Hell fire, Doc, you taken more pints out a me than Seagram got in vat storage."

I don't have a nurse. In a small-town office like mine they're more hindrance than help. So except for keeping the books and mailing the monthly statements (which is handled by Miss Effie Gunn at her home), I do everything myself. Whenever I draw blood from James P.—and I usually take enough for several lab tests—the uric-acid content is invariably in the top ten milligrams. I write him a new prescription. Give him a useless lecture. Refuse his invitation for a "quick one" at the Commerce Club. Forget him until the next time. This time, though, James P., rolling down his sleeve, introduced a new note.

"Take a gander at my face, Doc, and tell me what you see different."

"Different?" I never referred to his nose because I knew it was a subject of some mortification. "What do you mean *different*, James?"

"My ugly ol' nose."

"What about it?"

"Cain't you see it ain't half so ugly no more?"

"Now that you mention it."

"They's a good chance it might get near back to normal with a couple more treatments."

"Who's performing this minor miracle, James?"

"A little ol' gal name Hattie Hopkins."

"What are her credentials?"

"She ain't got none but know-how. Come to town some months back and bought the Conway property. My bank holds the paper."

"I see. You meet Miss Hopkins in the course of a business transaction; she looks at your nose and says she has a cure."

"Not a-tall like that, Doc.

"Don't nobody hardly ever mention my nose to my face. You know that, Doc. Most folks act like it ain't in place. Fix they eyes on anythin'—my tie or my fly—instead of watchin' my nose."

"Granted, James. Go on."

"The way it came up with Miz Hopkins, she join the Pine Hill Garden Club and prove, accordin' to the missis, that she got the greenest thumb in town. So they invite her to membership in the Thursday Afternoon Bridge Club, where she also do herself proud. Next thing, the Floral Baptist Sisterhood, they don't—"

"Quite a joiner, but get to the point."

I was actually anxious to glean every detail available about this Hopkins woman, but I didn't want James P. to know it.

"I'm gettin' there in my own good time, Doc, so hold your

horses. Well, seems the ladies just naturally cotton to Miz Hopkins because she so plumb filled with good cheer and talent. The missis says she can bake a cake'll make a snake's mouth water. Whup up a batch of peanut brittle while your back's turned. And she downright uncanny, the missis says, with them special fortune-tellin' cards. Name slips my mind."

"Tarot?"

"Right. To hear the ladies tell it, Miz Hopkins can see anything with them cards—past, present, or future."

"Feminine gullibility, James."

"I'da took the same tack a month ago, Doc. But after what happen to the missis, I figgered to have a second look."

"What happened to Sally Ann?"

"Wouldn't want this to get out, Doc."

"My Hippocratic oath on it."

"T'ain't widely known—leastwise I hope not—that Sally Ann got a dark-brown wart on the inside of her right thigh. Hairy ol' thing. She never mention it to a soul because she always been ashamed of it. A few weeks back, whilst visitin' with Miz Hopkins over a cup of tea and them cards, Sally Ann was real surprised when the cards come up with news of that there wart. Fact is, she begun to turn red as a beet from pure embarrassment. Then Miz Hopkins says, 'Sally Ann, they ain't no reason on earth why a body got to tolerate sech an unsightly defect in an otherwise smooth thigh,' she says, 'and if you so wish, I have a way to rid you of the pesky thing,' she says. And Sally Ann says, 'Then you go right ahead and do just that, Hattie,' she says. And you know what that little lady went and done, Doc?"

"She applied a leech to it."

James P.'s florid face registered astonishment. "How come you know that?"

"Keen eyes, keen ears, keen mind."

"I trust you ain't gone badger that lady with some sort a malpractice charge."

"What makes you say that, James?"

"Well, as county health officer you might think they was a case here. But take my word. Doc, she ain't settin' up in business a-tall. She don't accept a red cent for her help. And, damn it, man, that wart's done gone for good, hair and all."

"So now, as it were, you've placed your nose in Miss Hopkins's fabulous hands."

"Damn right. Twice a week. Now be honest, Doc. Don't I look the better for it?"

"Indeed you do, James."

I finally came face to face with Miss Hopkins outside the A&P. She was accompanied by Mrs. Bayard Stoneman, a big-buttocked patient of mine, who performed the introduction.

"Dr. Devlin not only worries about us individually," gushed Mrs. Stoneman, "but en masse. Besides being our sympathetic physician, he's our county's faithful health officer."

Miss Hopkins appraised me with her bright green eyes in which I detected a glint of trepidation. "What I've seen of the town and the county so far, Doctor," she said in a small brave voice, "is all to the good."

"Thank you, ma'am. And where, may I ask, did you previously reside?"

"Oh, a pleasant-enough place over South Carolina way."

"I have friends in Aiken," I said.

"A charming community, Doctor. But I lived in Summerville."

"I have friends there too," I said.

A nearly palpable flutter of apprehension crossed her pale face.

"Oh, do you now," she said after a moment. "Well, I must confess my residence in Summerville was unhappily brief and I made few acquaintances."

"The Castletons perhaps?" The name was sheer invention.

"I never met them personally."

"Or the Ridgewells?" Another invention.

"I recall seeing the names often in the society notes of the Summerville newspaper, Doctor."

"Aren't we fortunate," burst in Mrs. Stoneman, "that Miss Hopkins has come here to join our own little social circle?"

"Most fortunate," I said with a slight bow of departure.

Mrs. Stoneman suffers from chronic sciatica. Once a month, for the past five years, I've been tapping her gluteal arteries, superior and inferior, for 500 cc's of blood. She swears it affords her instant relief even though she can't sit down for several hours afterward.

I was convinced she'd be canceling her monthly appointments as long as Miss Hopkins was around.

The only acquaintance I have in Summerville is the health officer whose name herein shall remain inviolate.

I phoned him a few hours after the A&P meeting. I had reason to believe, I told him, that a person from his town had recently visited ours and left behind a communicable disease I preferred not to identify until more facts were at hand.

Would he check the municipal records for all the information pertaining to Miss or Mrs. Hattie Hopkins and get back to me at the earliest?

This worthy gentleman phoned collect the next morning and reported as follows:

If any Hattie, Harriet, or Henrietta Hopkins—Miss, Ms., or Mrs.—had ever lived in Summerville, she managed it without leaving a trace. No record of birth, inoculation, marriage, divorce, taxes, or death. No voting record. No record that she'd used a public utility—water, electric, gas, telephone. Not even an extant library card.

"You're damned thorough, Doctor," I said.

"My way of life, Doctor," he said.

Obviously our local phlebotomist, for profound reasons I was beginning to fathom, wished to keep secret her real origins.

Effie Gunn, my part-time bookkeeper, phoned in a week later to cancel her bimonthly appointment. When I offered to fix another date, she demurred, explaining that henceforth she'd control her condition by diet.

Effie has long believed the fat forces of cholesterol are on the verge of dominating her capillaries, and she has insisted on a periodic count of their number. Hence, this volte-face was significant.

Effie was a member of the Thursday Afternoon Bridge Club. Knowing this, I regretfully concluded that she'd found in Miss Hopkins a more compatible ally in her war against cholesterol. But I knew something else. Effie would never submit to treatment by leech. She was deathly afraid of anything that crept on its belly. She once confided to me that she'd broken off an engagement with the only man she'd ever loved after watching him bait a hook with a nightcrawler.

From Effie's particular case I inevitably deduced that Miss Hopkins must be taking blood from the finicky element of her growing clientele with medical needle and syringe. And this called for affirmative action on my part.

Our weekly gazette faithfully reports the meetings of the Thursday Afternoon Bridge Club. So I chose that day to move against Miss Hopkins. The gazette said the ladies were convening this week, between the hours of two and four thirty, at the residence of Mrs. James P. Upson.

To play it safe, I rang Miss Hopkins's home a few minutes after two. No answer. Still playing it safe, I drove slowly past the Upsons' stately home. Among the many cars parked in the sweep of the circular driveway, I quickly spotted the red Super Beetle I'd seen Miss Hopkins around town in. I then headed for the outskirts.

The late Judge Conway's house stands solitary amid five or six acres of flat wooded land in Hambleton Lane. The only other habitation along this quarter mile of narrow blacktop is that which makes it a cul-de-sac—the ramshackle Hambleton Mansion rotting away behind its termite-riddled Doric columns. Minnie Hambleton, at eighty the last of her line, still clings to life there, deaf as a post and half-blind.

Miss Hopkins, I note as I pass, has definitely improved the late judge's property. The lawn that was a field of hay is lawn again. Rusty gutters and drainpipes are renewed. Where once was peeling paint there now is a sheen of gleaming white.

A short distance beyond the house I found a good-sized gap in the wild buckthorn and sourwood scrub that bordered most of the lane. I stopped the car and got out to see if the ground at this gap was firm enough to drive on. It seemed so.

Back in the car, I proceeded cautiously through the gap and on behind the tangled foliage until I was hidden from anyone who might move along the road. I sat in the car for a pensive minute. The absolute silence here was marred only by birdsong.

Finally I footed it back through the gap, darted across the road, took to a dry shallow ditch, and hustled toward the edge of the Hopkins property. Reaching the one-car garage, whose up-sliding door was open on utter emptiness, I went around to the back of it.

This low-profile approach was probably not necessary. After all, how many cars would travel up or down Hambleton Lane in the course of a day? Damned few, if any. Yet I continued to be careful, advancing to the back of the house from tree to bush to trellis, because CAUTION was the inflexible watchword in view of what I was planning to do.

Miss Hopkins had refurbished the small rear porch to the extent of having an aluminum canopy placed over it. But she hadn't gotten to the latticework along the underside yet, and much of this was missing, and what remained was jaggedly broken.

Coming closer, I discerned something under there on the dank earth that called for further examination. It was an old nail keg.

Leaning forward, I grasped its damp sides and dragged it out into the open. It wasn't heavy. There was a sound of sloshing. The top was covered with fine-mesh wire screening secured by a heavy-duty staple at one side and hand-crimped the rest of the way around.

I lifted the screening, and there they were at the bottom of the keg in several inches of brackish water—a sluggish mass of leeches, their brown stripes overlapping each other in a series of linear sinuosities. At a guess, I'd say there were a hundred of them.

Crimping the cover back in place, I shoved the keg back under the porch and then mounted to the screen door. It was hooked shut, but, either in deference to the warm day or out of forgetfulness, the inner door was wide open. Like a veteran burglar, I slid a credit card between jamb and frame and lifted the hook from its eye.

The kitchen was spotlessly clean. I went to the refrigerator and opened it. And I found what I expected to find.

The tall, glass-stoppered flacon, half a liter in size, stood with appertinent intimacy between a bottle of milk and a carton of blueberry yogurt. Its contents glowed through the chilled crystal with a color I call salmon pink. Yes, here was what is known euphemistically in arcane circles as a platelet cocktail.

What, one might ask, is a platelet cocktail?

Recipe:

Combine one part of homogenized milk with two parts of blood from *Homo sapiens*, add cracked ice, and mix at high speed for thirty seconds in electric blender. Pour result into cold cocktail glass and garnish to taste with either nutmeg, cinnamon, or a sprig of crushed mint.

Those esoteric few who are addicted to the platelet cocktail will avow it produces a euphoric high different from anything else on earth. And no hangover.

Why platelet?

It's the name of one of four human-blood components and was chosen for its pleasant sound.

On those rare occasions when I've discussed the platelet cocktail in an academic way, the listener invariably shudders and says,
"ech!"

Most of us don't realize how deeply into the history of mankind
the blood-drinking ritual goes. Savages often supped on the heart
of a dead foe to absorb his courage. Biblical prophets, sacrificing a
bullock on a desert altar, swallowed a handful of the spurting
blood. The incubus of demonology reputedly suckled women in
their sleep, drawing out blood with the milk. The African Watusi
subsisted until recently on an exclusive diet of cow's milk and
blood.

But to return to matters at hand, I removed the flacon from the
refrigerator, took out the stopper, and laced the cocktail with a
yellow powder guaranteed to induce stupefying slumber. I then
replaced the flacon precisely where I'd found it.

Next I began to search for the needles and syringes which were
certain to be in the house. I found them almost immediately. Two
syringes and six needles reposed in an autoclave on a shelf in the
bathroom

I was inordinately pleased that I hadn't misjudged Miss Hopkins. Her *modus operandi* was clear. She lured the credulous with
her fortune-telling skill, enraptured them with her cakes, listened
sympathetically to their plaint of ills, eventually offered to cure
them with a bit of painless bloodletting—leeches at first for the
hardy, needle and syringe for the queasy.

But the needle and syringe were her ultimate tools, for they
gave her the wherewithal for the daily sun-downers, the impec-
cable platelet cocktail.

During the five more minutes I spent in the house I discovered
in a desk drawer, beside a pack of tarot cards, the spare key to the
front door. Pocketing it, I went back to the kitchen and rehooked
the screen door. I let myself out the front, hearing the lock click as
the door closed.

It was 3:14 by the dashboard clock as I slid into the car seat. The
Thursday Afternoon Bridge Club was good for more than another hour.

Leaving Hambleton Lane, I allowed myself the luxury of a
cigarette. Though I strongly warned my patients against smoking, I enjoyed a stolen taste of the weed myself.

"Don't you have no damn vices a-tall, Doc?" James P. Upson
once asked when I'd advised him to lay off cigars.

"I have my minor frailties."

"How come you was never frail enough in the head to get married?"

"A frail will doesn't indicate a feeble mind, James."

That afternoon I made several ostentatious house calls. At 5:25 I headed back out to Hambleton Lane. The red Super Beetle was parked in front of the garage. I drove to my former place of concealment. With black medical bag in hand, I walked rapidly to the shining white house, observed only by a squirrel.

I assumed Miss Hopkins had already treated herself to a cocktail and now should be out like a light. Nonetheless, circumspection was demanded. Again I approached the house stealthily from the back of the garage. I looked through the bedroom window first. Nobody there. Bathroom same. Working my way quietly to the front of the house, I peered into the living room. There she was, sagging half off and half on the davenport.

With the spare key I unlocked the front door and entered. I set the medical bag down on a table in the living room and studied Miss Hopkins clinically for a few moments. She was dead to the world. I picked the empty cocktail glass from the rug and took it to the kitchen where I washed and dried it thoroughly and returned it to a cabinet shelf with similar glasses.

I carried Miss Hopkins, who weighed perhaps a hundred pounds, into the bathroom. Her snoring was soft, quite like a cat's purring. Sitting her on the toilet seat, I laboriously stripped her to the pelt, no mean task when the subject is limply uncooperative.

Next I laid her out face-up in the bathtub. A dreamy smile exposed her buck teeth.

I carried the clothing to her bedroom and folded it neatly across the back of a chair as I imagined she would have done if she were disrobing for a bath. In the closet I found a polka-dot dressing gown, which I took back to the bathroom and hung on a hook behind the door.

Back in the living room I got from my medical bag a pair of rubber gloves—the heavy dishpan rather than the thin surgical kind. Then to the kitchen, where I dug up a large aluminum pot known as a steamer. Outdoors, I transferred to this pot with gloved hands every last leech in the keg under the porch.

Miss Hopkins was still possessed by narcosis as I set the pot on the bathroom floor.

I fetched my medical bag. Opening it wide, I got from it a special pipette with a one-pint bulb capacity, three quart-size plastic bottles, and a lovely scalpel.

To facilitate the operation, I peeled the glove from my right hand and grasped the scalpel. Getting on my knees, I leaned in over the edge of the tub. At the interior bend of Miss Hopkins's right elbow I made a dainty but deep incision across the innominate artery. Reaching quickly for the pipette, I applied its beak to the incision.

When the bulb was full I expressed its contents into one of the plastic bottles, meanwhile pressing a finger hard against the incision to prevent the blood from spurting. I repeated this process until all three plastic bottles were full and Miss Hopkins was about three-quarters empty. Selecting three long leeches from the pot, I applied them to the incision. The others I scattered at random over the body. They began to dig in voraciously.

Half an hour later, entering my office, I was nearly overwhelmed by a dark wave of fatigue. In all my long life I had never done anything like this. I trusted I would never have to do such a thing again.

But the simple fact of the matter is that in a town as small as this, two of us was one too many.

I felt I could use a drink.

The Yearbook of the Detective Story

Abbreviations: *EQMM—Ellery Queen's Mystery Magazine*
AHMM—Alfred Hitchcock's Mystery Magazine
MSMM—Mike Shayne Mystery Magazine
MD—Mystery Digest

BIOGRAPHY
Frank Sisk

Frank Sisk was born in Norwich, Connecticut, on October 6, 1915. His formal education ended with graduation from high school in Bridgeport, where he went to work as a reporter for one of the daily newspapers. His newspaper career, which included a variety of jobs, soon led to the editorship of several resort publications—weekly magazines and a small daily—issued in New Hampshire in the summer and North Carolina in the winter.

During these years Sisk met a Boston girl who became his first wife. They were married when he was twenty-three, on New Year's Eve, and had one son, Robert, before the marriage ended in divorce some years later. Sisk began writing fiction around this time and sold his first story to Whit Burnett's prestigious *Story* magazine on the eve of World War II. "North to Jackson" appeared in the January 1942 issue of *Story*, the same year that magazine published J. D. Salinger's first story.

After the outbreak of war Sisk joined the Office of Price Administration as a public relations specialist. Later he enlisted in the U.S. Marine Corps, where he eventually served as a combat correspondent. This experience led to the publication of Frank Sisk's only book to date, *Your Marine Corps in World War II* (Atlanta: Albert Love Enterprises, 1946), an illustrated history with an introduction by Marine Corps Commandant A. A. Vandergrift. The book sold some 15,000 copies, mainly in post exchanges during the postwar years.

After leaving the Marine Corps Sisk worked for two years in advertising and public relations, first in Hartford and later in Boston. But that sort of writing bored him and in 1948 he went to work as a traveling salesman specializing in government accounts. He remained with it for the next twenty-four years, writing short magazine pieces in hotel rooms to pass the time. Much of Sisk's early writing was nonfiction—humorous pieces, odd factual stories, and personal essays which he sold to magazines as varied as *The Saturday Evening Post, American Mercury, Coronet, Climax, Adam,* and *Dude.*

Around 1958 Frank Sisk's writing turned largely to fiction and gradually concentrated in the mystery-suspense field. His stories have appeared in *Ellery Queen's Mystery Magazine, Alfred Hitchcock's Mystery Magazine, Mike Shayne Mystery Magazine,* and other mystery publications, as well as in *Fantasy & Science Fiction* and *Penthouse.* One of his stories was televised on Rod Serling's *Night Gallery* and others have been translated into Norwegian, French, Italian, and Spanish. About a dozen have been performed as radio plays in South Africa. In all, Sisk has published well over two hundred stories and articles, and this year marks his fifth appearance in *Best Detective Stories of the Year.*

Frank Sisk married his present wife, Barbara, in 1952. They are the parents of five children—March, Brand, Page, Régan, and Vaux—and reside in Lyme, Connecticut. When he isn't writing, Sisk enjoys vegetable gardening and cooking.

BIBLIOGRAPHY

I. Collections

1. Charteris, Leslie. *The Saint in Trouble.* New York: Doubleday & Co. Two short novels about The Saint, adapted by Graham Weaver from teleplays by Terrence Feely and John Kruse.
2. ———. *Send for the Saint.* New York: Doubleday & Co. Two short novels about The Saint, adapted by Peter Bloxsom from teleplays by John Kruse and Donald James.
3. Christie, Agatha. *The Mousetrap and Other Plays.* New York: Dodd, Mead & Company. Eight of the best Christie plays, 1944–1960, with an introduction by Ira Levin.
4. Dahl, Roald. *The Best of Roald Dahl.* New York: Vintage Books. Twenty-four stories from four previous collections, mainly criminous.
5. Gibson, Walter B. *The Shadow: A Quarter of Eight and The Freak Show Murders.* New York: Doubleday & Co. Two short novels from 1944 and 1945 issues of *The Shadow* magazine.
6. Hoch, Edward D. *The Monkey's Clue and The Stolen Sapphire.* New York: Grosset & Dunlap. Two short stories about a boy detective.
7. ———*The Thefts of Nick Velvet.* Yonkers, N.Y. (Box 334, East Station): The Mysterious Press. Thirteen stories, mainly from *EQMM,* with an introduction and bibliography by the author. The limited edition contains a fourteenth story, separately bound.

8. King, Stephen. *Night Shift.* New York: Doubleday & Co. Twenty horror stories, mainly fantasy but some criminous, with an introduction by John D. MacDonald.
9. Simenon, Georges. *Maigret's Pipe.* New York: Harcourt Brace Jovanovich. Seventeen stories (one less than the British edition) in a companion volume to last year's *Maigret's Christmas.*
10. Vickers, Roy. *The Department of Dead Ends.* New York: Dover Publications. Fourteen stories, mainly from *EQMM*, with an introduction by E.F. Bleiler.
11. Woolrich, Cornell. *Angels of Darkness.* Yonkers, N.Y. (Box 334, East Station): The Mysterious Press. Eight stories told from women's viewpoints, with an introduction by Harlan Ellison and an afterword by Francis M. Nevins, Jr.

II. Anthologies

1. Ball, John, editor. *Cop Cade.* New York: Doubleday & Co. Twenty stories, mainly about police, in the annual anthology from Mystery Writers of America.
2. Bleiler, E. F., editor. *Three Victorian Detective Novels.* New York: Dover Publications. Three short novels: "The Unknown Weapon" by Andrew Forrester, "My Lady's Money" by Wilkie Collins, and "The Big Bow Mystery" by Israel Zangwill.
3. Gilbert, Elliot L., editor. *The World of Mystery Fiction.* Del Mar, Ca.: Publisher's Inc. A survey of the mystery field as exemplified by twenty-four classic short stories from Vidocq to Borges. Designed partly for use in a mystery fiction course offered by the University of California, San Diego Extension. See also #6 under Nonfiction.
4. Grant, Charles L., editor. *Shadows.* New York: Doubleday & Co. Thirteen new horror stories, mainly fantasy but some criminous.
5. Hardinge, George, editor. *Winter's Crimes 9.* New York: St. Martin's Press. Twelve new stories by British mystery writers.
6. Hitchcock, Alfred, editor. *Killers at Large.* New York: Dell Publishing Co. Fourteen stories from *AHMM*, 1962–1975.
7. ———. *Murder-Go-Round.* New York: Dell Publishing Co. Fourteen stories from *AHMM*, 1961–1976.
8. ———. *Rogues' Gallery.* New York: Dell Publishing Co. Fourteen stories from *AHMM*, 1965–1976.
9. Hoch, Edward D., editor. *Best Detective Stories of the Year—1978.* New York: E. P. Dutton. Fifteen of the best mystery-crime stories of 1977.
10. Kahn, Joan, editor. *Chilling and Killing.* Boston: Hougton Mifflin Co. Sixteen stories of crime and the supernatural, plus five fact crime stories.

11. King, Diana, editor. *Getting Even*. New York: Bobbs-Merrill Co. Sixteen stories of revenge.
12. Kittredge, William and Stephen Krauser, editors. *The Great American Detectives*. New York: New American Library/Mentor Books. Fifteen stories tracing the changing face of the American fictional sleuth.
13. Malzberg, Barry N. and Bill Pronzini, editors. *Dark Sins, Dark Dreams*. New York: Doubleday & Co. Fifteen stories, three of them new, combining crime and science fiction.
14. Queen, Ellery, editor. *Ellery Queen's Anthology, Spring-Summer 1978*. New York: Davis Publications. Twenty-one stories from *EQMM* in a semiannual anthology series. Hardcover edition, *Ellery Queen's Masks of Mystery*, distributed by Dial Press.
15. ———. *Ellery Queen's Anthology, Fall-Winter 1978*. New York: Davis Publications. Seventeen stories from *EQMM* in a semiannual anthology series. Hardcover edition, *Ellery Queen's Napoleons of Mystery*, distributed by Dial Press.
16. ———. *Ellery Queen's Japanese Golden Dozen*. Rutland, Vt.: Charles E. Tuttle. Twelve Japanese detective stories, published for the first time in America.
17. ———. *Masterpieces of Mystery: Detective Directory. Part II*. Des Moines, Iowa (Box 10202): Masterpieces of Mystery Library. Volume 7 in a mail-order series, containing twenty stories about sleuths with various occupations.
18. ———. *Masterpieces of Mystery: The Forties*. Des Moines, Iowa (Box 10202): Masterpieces of Mystery Library. Volume 8 in a mail-order series, containing nineteen stories from the 1940s.
19. ———. *Masterpieces of Mystery: The Fifties*. Des Moines, Iowa (Box 10202): Masterpieces of Mystery Library. Volume 9 in a mail-order series, containing nineteen stories from the 1950s.
20. ———. *Masterpieces of Mystery: Cherished Classics*. Des Moines, Iowa (Box 10202): Masterpieces of Mystery Library. Volume 10 in a mail-order series, containing seventeen classic mysteries.
21. ———. *Masterpieces of Mystery: The Sixties*. Des Moines, Iowa (Box 10202): Masterpieces of Mystery Library. Volume 11 in a mail-order series, containing twenty-one stories from the 1960s.
22. ———. *Masterpieces of Mystery: Stories Not to Be Missed*. Des Moines, Iowa (Box 10202): Masterpieces of Mystery Library. Volume 12 in a mail-order series, reprinting eighteen memorable stories.
23. ———. *Masterpieces of Mystery: Amateurs and Professionals*. Des Moines, Iowa (Box 10202): Masterpieces of Mystery Library. Volume 13 in a mail-order series, reprinting twenty stories about amateur and professional sleuths.
24. ———. *Masterpieces of Mystery: The Old Masters*. Des Moines, Iowa (Box 10202): Masterpieces of Mystery Library. Volume 14 in a

mail-order series, reprinting nineteen stories from the early days of detective fiction.

25. ———. *A Multitude of Sins.* New York: Dial Press. Annual anthology containing twenty-one of the best stories from 1976 issues of *EQMM.*

26. Russell, Alan K., editor. *Rivals of Sherlock Holmes.* Secaucus, N.J.: Castle Books. Unconnected with the 1970 Hugh Greene anthology of the same title, this one reprints forty stories with their original illustrations, from *The Strand* and other turn-of-the-century British magazines.

27. Sullivan, Eleanor, editor. *Alfred Hitchcock's Anthology, Fall-Winter 1978.* New York: Davis Publications. Thirty-five stories from *AHMM* in a semiannual anthology series. Hardcover edition, *Alfred Hitchcock's Tales to Make Your Blood Run Cold,* distributed by Dial Press.

28. ———. *Alfred Hitchcock's Anthology, Spring-Summer 1979.* New York: Davis Publications. A short novel and twenty-six stories from *AHMM* in a semiannual anthology series. Hardcover edition, *Alfred Hitchcock's Tales to Scare You Stiff,* distributed by Dial Press.

III. Miscellaneous Nonfiction

1. Asimov, Isaac. *Asimov's Sherlockian Limericks.* Yonkers, N.Y. (Box 334, East Station): The Mysterious Press. Limericks about each of the sixty Holmes stories and novels.

2. Dale, Alzina Stone. *Maker and Craftsman: The Story of Dorothy L. Sayers.* Grand Rapids, Mich.: William B. Eerdmans. A biography of Lord Peter Wimsey's creator.

3. Davies, David Stuart. *Holmes of the Movies.* New York: Bramhall House/Clarkson N. Potter. A study of the Sherlock Holmes films, originally published in England in 1976. See also #17 below.

4. Eames, Hugh. *Sleuths, Inc.* New York: Lippincott. A study of five mystery writers: Doyle, Simenon, Hammett, Ambler, and Chandler.

5. Garfield, Brian, editor. *I, Witness.* New York: Times Books. Twenty-four members of Mystery Writers of America tell of their personal encounters with crime.

6. Gilbert, Elliot L. *The World of Mystery Fiction: A Guide.* Del Mar, Ca.: Publisher's Inc. A 153-page paperback study guide designed for use in a course offered by the University of California, San Diego Extension. See also #3 under Anthologies.

7. Gross, Miriam, editor. *The World of Raymond Chandler.* New York: A & W Publishers. Fifteen new essays by writers, critics, and friends of Chandler.

8. Haining, Peter. *The Edgar Allan Poe Scrapbook.* New York: Schocken Books. An illustrated volume about Poe. See #11 and #18 below for more detailed biographies.

9. Hall, Trevor H. and Charles O. Ellison. *Sherlock Holmes and His Creator.* New York: St. Martin's Press. Eight Sherlockian essays.

10. Hughes, Dorothy B. *Erle Stanley Gardner.* New York: William Morrow. A comprehensive biography of Perry Mason's creator.

11. Mankowitz, Wolf. *The Extraordinary Mr. Poe.* New York: Summit Books. An illustrated biography of Poe.

12. Monegal, Emir Rodriguez. *Jorge Luis Borges.* New York: E. P. Dutton. A biography of the famed Argentine author whose tales are often in the mystery field.

13. Penzler, Otto, editor. *The Great Detectives.* Boston: Little, Brown. Twenty-six mystery writers tell how their detectives were conceived.

14. Robyns, Gwen. *The Mystery of Agatha Christie.* New York: Doubleday & Co. The best yet of the Christie biographies, with much new material.

15. Scott-Giles, G. W. *The Wimsey Family.* New York: Harper & Row. Lord Peter Wimsey's "family history," compiled from correspondence between the author, a professional heraldist, and Dorothy L. Sayers.

16. Speir, Jerry. *Ross Macdonald.* New York: Frederick Ungar. The first in a new series of critical examinations of leading mystery writers.

17. Steinbrunner, Chris and Norman Michaels. *The Films of Sherlock Holmes.* Secaucus, N. J.: Citadel Press. An illustrated history.

18. Symons, Julian. *The Tell-Tale Heart.* New York: Harper & Row. A comprehensive study of Edgar Allan Poe's life and work.

19. Tracy, Jack. *Subcutaneously, My Dear Watson.* Bloomington, Ind. (Box 1431): James A. Rock. A detailed study of cocaine use in the Sherlock Holmes stories.

20. Tuska, Jon. *The Detective in Hollywood.* New York: Doubleday & Co. A massive study of the American detective film from 1900 to 1977.

AWARDS

Mystery Writers of America
>Best novel—Ken Follett, *Eye of the Needle* (Arbor House)
>Best American first novel—William L. DeAndrea, *Killed in the Ratings* (Harcourt Brace Jovanovich)
>Best short story—Barbara Owens, *The Cloud Beneath the Eaves* (*EQMM*)
>Best biography and criticism—Gwen Robyns, *The Mystery of Agatha Christie* (Doubleday)

Crime Writers Association (London)
>Gold Dagger—Lionel Davidson, *The Chelsea Murders* (Jonathan Cape/U.S. title *Murder Games*: Coward, McCann & Geoghegan)

Silver Dagger—Peter Lovesey, *Waxwork* (Macmillan/U.S.: Pantheon)

John Creasey Memorial Award (for best first crime novel)—
Paula Gosling, *A Running Duck* (Macmillan)

(Note: After last year's volume had gone to press, the announced winner of the John Creasey Memorial Award was declared ineligible because he had published previous crime novels under a pseudonym. The award was presented instead to Jonathan Gash for *The Judas Pair* (Collins/ U.S.: Harper & Row).

Grand Prix de Litterature Policière (Paris)
Translated novel: Ellery Queen, *And on the Eighth Day* (U.S. edition: Random House, 1964)

NECROLOGY

1. Antonich, George (?–1978). Short story writer, contributor to *MSMM* and the 1974 edition of this anthology.
2. Bentley, Nicholas (1907–1978). British writer and publisher, son of E. C. Bentley, and author of four suspense novels, notably *The Tongue-Tied Canary* (1948).
3. Bentley, Phyllis (1894–1977). British novelist who authored two mysteries among her twenty novels, and created Miss Phipps for a popular *EQMM* series (1952–1971).
4. Bogart, William G. (1903–1977). Pulp writer who authored five hard-boiled mystery novels in the 1940s.
5. Brackett, Leigh (1915–1978). Novelist and screenwriter who authored five mystery novels including one, *Stranger at Home* (1946), ghost-written for actor George Sanders. Well known for her science fiction and for the screenplay of Chandler's *The Big Sleep* (1946), on which she collaborated with William Faulkner.
6. Burack, Abraham S. (1907?–1978). Long-time editor of *The Writer* and compiler of several anthologies, including *Writing Suspense and Mystery Fiction* (1977).
7. Cozzens, James Gould (1903–1978). Pulitzer Prize-winning novelist whose books include *The Just and the Unjust* (1942), about a murder trial.
8. Davis, Frederick C. (1902–1977). Prolific pulp writer and author of more than forty mystery novels under his own name and the pseudonyms "Stephen Ransome" and "Murdo Coombs," notably *A Moment of Need* (1947) under the Coombs name.

9. Denniston, Elinore (1900–1978). Author of more than forty suspense novels under the pseudonym "Rae Foley." She also published children's books under her own name and five mysteries under the pseudonym "Dennis Allan."

10. Flower, Pat (?–1978). Australian author of ten or more mystery novels beginning in 1958, some of which were recently published in America for the first time.

11. Hawkins, John (1910–1978). With his brother Ward, author of a half-dozen suspense novels (1940–1958) and numerous short stories in *The Saturday Evening Post, EQMM,* and elsewhere.

12. Jordan, Robert Furneaux (1905–1978). British architect and writer who published five suspense novels under the pseudonym "Robert Player" (1945–1977).

13. Long, Amelia Reynolds (1904–1978). Author of more than thirty mystery novels under her own name and the pseudonyms "Patrick Laing," "Adrian Reynolds," "Peter Reynolds," and—with Edna McHugh—"Kathleen Buddington Coxe."

14. Mallowan, Sir Max (1904?–1978). Husband of the late Agatha Christie and author of *Mallowan's Memoirs* (1977), about their marriage and his career as an archaeologist.

15. Mason, F. Van Wyck (1901–1978). Well-known historical novelist who also authored nearly thirty spy thrillers abut Colonel Hugh North, as well as two collaborative mysteries (with H. Brawner) under the pseudonym "Geoffrey Coffin."

16. McComas, J. Francis (1910–1978). Science fiction anthologist and co-editor with Anthony Boucher of *Fantasy & Science Fiction.* Edited *Crimes and Misfortunes* (1970), a Boucher memorial anthology of mysteries.

17. Montgomery, Robert Bruce (1921–1978). Under the pseudonym "Edmund Crispin," he created Oxford professor Gervase Fen, who became one of the classic detectives of postwar England and starred in nine novels, including *The Moving Toyshop* (1946), *Love Lies Bleeding (1948), Buried for Pleasure* (1948), and the recent *The Glimpses of the Moon* (1977). Fen also appears in a short story collection, *Beware of the Trains* (1953).

18. Norris, Luther (?–1978). Editor of *The Pontine Dossier,* a periodical about Solar Pons, and publisher of several Sherlockian chapbooks.

19. Packer, Joy (?–1977). Author of a single crime novel, *The Man in the Mews* (1965).

20. Pudney, John (1909–1977). British author whose works included one suspense novel, *Thin Air* (1961).

21. Thompson, Jim (1906–1977). Author of some thirty paperback crime novels, notably *The Killer Inside Me* (1952) and *The Getaway* (1959).

22. Weisinger, Mort (1915?–1978). Editor of several science fiction and mystery pulps for Standard Magazines (1936–1941).
23. Whaley, F.J. (1897–1977). British author of nine mystery novels (1936–1941), unpublished in America.
24. Williams, Jay (1914?–1978). Author of historical novels and children's books, who published several mystery novels under the pseudonym "Michael Delving."
25. Williamson, Hugh Ross (1901–1978). British author whose works include one suspense novel, *A Wicked Pack of Cards* (1961).

HONOR ROLL

(One hundred distinguished short stories of 1978. Starred stories are included in this volume.)

Adams, T. M., "The Iceman Cooleth," *EQMM*, March
Bankier, William, "The Eye of the Beholder," *AHMM, April*
———, *"Lost and Found," AHMM,* November
Bell, D. O., "Trial and Error," *EQMM,* November
Block, Lawrence, "Change of Life," *AHMM,* January
———, "The Ehrengraf Method," *EQMM,* February
———, "The Ehrengraf Presumption," *EQMM,* May
———, "The Ehrengraf Riposte," *EQMM,* December
———, "One Thousand Dollars a Word," *AHMM,* March
Breen, Jon L., "The Number 12 Jinx," *EQMM,* May
Brittain, William, "The Man Who Read Isaac Asimov," *EQMM,* May
Bush, Geoffrey, "The Picnic," *The Atlantic Monthly,* September
Cail, Carol, "May the Worst Man Win," *EQMM,* October
Capron, Jean F., "Stranger in Town," *MSMM,* September
Colby, Robert, "Paint the Town Brown," *AHMM,* September
*Collier, Zena, "Little Paradise," *Buffalo Spree,* Spring
Cooney, Caroline B., "The View of Norwalk Harbor," *AHMM,* November
Darling, Jean, "All You Need Is Luck," *AHMM,* December
Dawson, Jim "The Boy in the Casket," *MSMM,* November
de la Torre, Lillian, "Milady Bigamy," *EQMM,* July
Dexter, Colin, "Evans Tries an O Level," *Winter's Crimes 9*
Eckels, Robert Edward, "Only One Way to Go," *EQMM,* August
Ellin, Stanley, "Reasons Unknown," *EQMM,* December
Ely, David, "Going Backward," *EQMM,* November
Fick, Alvin S., "They Always Look Best Framed," *AHMM,* August
Garfield, Brian, "Charlie's Shell Game," *EQMM,* February

*————, "Checkpoint Charlie," *EQMM*, May
Garner, Judith, "Evidence of Intent," *EQMM*, January
Gottlieb, Kathryn, "Call Michael," *AHMM*, November
————, "Dream House," *EQMM*, February
Goulart, Ron, "Invisible Stripes," *Omni*, October
Hamilton, Nan, "Too Many Pebbles," *EQMM*, September
Henseler, Donna, "The Bright Medal," *EQMM*, December
Highsmith, Patricia, "When in Rome," *EQMM*, October
*Hoch, Edward D., "Captain Leopold Incognito," *EQMM*, May
————, "Home Is the Hunter," *AHMM*, June
————, "The Problem of the Old Oak Tree," *EQMM*, July
————, "The Spy and the Cats of Rome," *EQMM*, June
————, "The Treasure of Jack the Ripper," *EQMM*, October
Holding, James, "The Baby Bit," *EQMM*, June
————, "The Photographer and the B.L.P.," *EQMM*, March
Jacobson, Jerry, "Killer Instinct," *AHMM*, December
*————, "Rite of Spring," *AHMM*, November
King, Stephen, "Nona," *Shadows*
*————, "Quitters, Inc.," *Night Shift*
————, "The Woman in the Room," *Night Shift*
Leavitt, Jack, "Demand Note," *MSMM*, July
Legru, Seiko, "Inspector Saito's Small Satori," *AHMM*, December
Lutz, John, "The Other Runner," *EQMM*, October
————, "Something Like Murder," *EQMM*, January
*Lynn, Elizabeth A., "The Fire Man," *Dark Sins, Dark Dreams*
Mackenzie, Ann, "I Can't Help Saying Goodbye," *EQMM*, May
————, "My Dear Jenny," *EQMM*, February
Malzberg, Barry N., "Inside Out," *AHMM*, May
Masur, Harold Q., "One Thing Leads to Another," *EQMM*, April
McConnor, Vincent, "The Terrible Secret," *MD*, December
McCoy, Elizabeth, "Heart's Desire," *EQMM*, April
McGerr, Patricia, "In the Clear," *EQMM*, April
————, "The Writing on the Wall," *EQMM*, August
Morland, Nigel, "The de Rougemont Case," *EQMM*, September
*Nevins, Francis M., Jr., "Filmflam," *EQMM*, June
*Owens, Barbara, "The Cloud Beneath the Eaves," *EQMM*, January
Partridge, David, "One Man's Fancy," *AHMM*, August
Perowne, Barry, "Raffles and the Unique Bequest," *EQMM*, August
Porter, Joyce, "Dover Goes to School," *EQMM*, February
Poyer, D.C., "Too Much at Stake," *MSMM*, July
Pronzini, Bill, "Bank Job," *EQMM*, August
————, "Caught in the Act," *EQMM*, December
*————, "Strangers in the Fog," *EQMM*, June
Rafferty, S. S., "The House on Thirteenth Street," *AHMM*, January

Reasoner, James M., "Man in the Morgue," *MSMM*, November
Rendell, Ruth, "Born Victim," *EQMM*, September
*————, "Truth Will Out," *EQMM*, December
*Ritchie, Jack, "Delayed Mail," *The Elks Magazine*, December
————, "No Wider Than a Nickel," *EQMM*, October
————, "The Return of Bridget," *AHMM*, December
————, "The Scent of Camellias," *AHMM*, March
————, "The School Bus Caper," *EQMM*, March
Savage, Ernest, "Count Me Out," *EQMM*, June
*————, "The Man in the Lake," *AHMM*, November
————, "The Park Plaza Thefts," *AHMM*, June
————, "The Patio," *AHMM*, April
*Schulze, Patricia L., "The Golden Circle," *EQMM*, April
Simpson, Dorothy, "The Sanctuary," *AHMM*, April
Sisk, Frank, "Funeral in Peachtree," *MSMM*, January
*————, "The Leech," *Fantasy & Science Fiction*, June
Thornburg, Dave, "Nature's Way," *EQMM*, November
Togawa, Masako, "The Vampire," *Ellery Queen's Japanese Golden Dozen*
Treat, Lawrence, "Cop Goes the Weasel," *AHMM*, October
Twohy, Robert, "Installment Past Due," *EQMM*, September
Varley, John, "The Barbie Murders," *Isaac Asimov's Science Fiction Magazine*, January-February
Vickers, Roy, "A Classic Forgery," *The Armchair Detective*, October
*Walsh, Thomas, "The Closed Door," *EQMM*, May
————, "The Sacrificial Goat," *EQMM*, January
————, "Stakeout," *EQMM*, March
Ward, William A., "The Drexel Site," *MSMM*, September
Wasylyk, Stephen, "Fishing Can Be Fatal," *EQMM*, August
————, "The Krowten Corners Crime Wave," *EQMM*, March
*Wellen, Edward, "The Adventure of the Blind Alley," *EQMM*, June
Westlake, Donald E., "This Is Death," *EQMM*, November

About the Editor

Edward D. Hoch, winner of an Edgar award for his short story "The Oblong Room," is a full-time writer, mainly of mystery fiction, and his stories appear regularly in the leading mystery magazines. He is probably best known for his creation of series-detective Nick Velvet, whose exploits have even been dramatized on French television. A collection entitled *The Thefts of Nick Velvet* was published by the Mysterious Press. His first novel, *The Shattered Raven* (1969), has recently been reissued. He is the author of *The Transvection Machine, The Fellowship of the Hand,* and *The Frankenstein Factory;* he recently published his first juvenile mystery. Mr. Hoch is married and lives with his wife in Rochester, New York.